by the same author

AN EXCEPTIONAL CORPSE

A Nasty Dose of Death

A stormy winter night on the seamier side of Sheffield. Freelance journalist Mike McLean receives a mysterious phone call from small-time burglar Andy Peters. They arrange to meet at Peters' flat, but when McLean arrives he finds the burglar dead, his neck broken.

Then next morning, ex-con scrap metal dealer James Silvester escapes death by inches when an unknown gunman puts three bullets through the windscreen of his Mercedes.

Are the two incidents linked? McLean starts to ask questions but is discouraged by Silvester's fifteen-stone wife, Pinky, a professional wrestler with nineteen-inch biceps and a taste for blood and pink lycra leotards.

Undeterred, McLean continues to probe the underside of Silvester's business activities, pausing only to visit a massage parlour, take tea with a gay one-armed hitman and pursue his so-far unrequited passion for his beautiful accountant Maria.

But when a second man dies and McLean himself gets pulled in for questioning, he begins to realize that something more than simple murder is at the heart of the mystery.

PAUL ADAM

A Nasty Dose of
Death

THE CRIME CLUB
An Imprint of HarperCollins *Publishers*

First published in Great Britain in 1994
by The Crime Club, an imprint of
HarperCollins Publishers, 77–85 Fulham Palace Road,
Hammersmith, London W6 8JB

9 8 7 6 5 4 3 2 1

Paul Adam asserts the moral right to be identified
as the author of this work

A catalogue record for this book is
available from the British Library

ISBN 0 00 232495 4

Photoset in Linotron Baskerville by
Rowland Phototypesetting Ltd
Bury St Edmunds, Suffolk
Printed and bound in Great Britain by
HarperCollins Book Manufacturing, Glasgow

CHAPTER 1

I was sitting at my desk, trying to stay awake in front of the typewriter, when the phone call came. The man's voice at the other end was low, but hoarse and brittle at the edges. It might have been laryngitis. To me, it sounded like fear.

'You Mike McLean?'

'Yes,' I said. 'Who's this?'

'Andy Peters. We met once.'

I tried to remember where. The name meant nothing to me.

'Harry Raymond gave me your number,' he said. 'I want to see you.'

'See me about—'

He interrupted: 'Shut up and listen. I want to see you now, you understand? Tonight.'

There was a tension in his voice which came over as aggression. He was frightened all right, containing the fear but letting traces of it slip out. I was intrigued, but wary.

'This a story?'

'Maybe.'

'What about?'

'Just come round, will you?' A note of desperation crept in. 'Please, I need to talk to someone. A reporter. There's no one else.' His voice was almost a whisper now. He was pleading with me.

'Where are you?' I asked.

He gave me an address in Park Hill flats, behind the station. I checked my watch. It was nearly half-past ten. Outside in the darkness the rain was sleeting down. I could hear the rattle on the window pane behind me.

'You coming?' the voice said quietly.

I contemplated the desk in front of me: the half-eaten

Cornish pasty on a plate, the cold cup of coffee, the four paragraphs I'd typed of a feature on the decline of the South Yorkshire coalfield which had already stupefied me with boredom. Thunderstorm or not, the world outside seemed suddenly a more attractive place.

'Please,' he murmured. 'You're all I could think of.'

'Give me fifteen minutes,' I said.

I almost changed my mind when I got outside. The rain was hard as buckshot, peppering the pavement in a fierce, continuous salvo. I threw my windcheater over my head and sprinted for the car. It was drier inside, but only just. There were pools of water on the floor under the dashboard and more seeping in through the holes in the doors. I sighed. The whole thing was being held together by a few screws and a prayer. Much more weather like this and it would dissolve into a puddle of rust.

The engine coughed into life on the eighth attempt and I turned cautiously out on to the main road. Water streamed past me in a torrent down the hill, the flooded drains bubbling up like hot springs. After two hundred yards the windscreen wipers packed in and I reduced my speed to a crawl, leaning forwards to peer through the semi-opaque glass. I began to wish I'd stayed in and made a night of it with the Cornish pasty.

It took me twenty-five minutes to reach Park Hill flats and find a parking space round the back. The rain had eased now and through the windscreen I could see the city centre below me, lit up in a blurred haze of streetlamps and neon signs.

I got out and glanced up at the flats. They were like something you'd find in the suburbs of Moscow, only uglier. Huge concrete mausoleums, built in the early '60s by planners and architects who hailed them as the future in housing with all the smug arrogance of people who knew they would never have to live in them.

I ran for the cover of a passageway and walked through

to the front, brushing the droplets of rain off my shoulders. I emerged opposite a short row of shops built into the flats' complex: fish and chips, tattoo artist, legal aid solicitors and betting shop, all the needs of modern civilization catered for.

The chip shop windows were steamed up and I could see people queuing at the counter, but the paved area outside was deserted, a characterless expanse of concrete slabs gleaming dull orange in the lamplight. I'd been here before in the day. It looked better in the dark.

I walked to the main entrance of the flats and located the lift. It was working, which surprised me. I got in and pressed the button for the third floor. The lift walls were daubed with obscene graffiti and there was a stench of urine and sweat. I held my breath until the doors opened. Then I stepped out on to the landing and looked around.

A long walkway, open to the elements along one side, stretched away to my right. The wind funnelled along it, gusting through the gaps in the concrete parapet with a low, intermittent howl. I checked the number on the first door and kept going. Half the ceiling lights were out of order or smashed and in the gloom it was hard to read the numbers, but I counted them off until I got to Andy Peters' flat.

I lifted a hand to knock, then noticed that the door wasn't quite shut. I pushed it with a toe. The door swung inwards. The hallway inside was in darkness but through an open door at the far end a pale light was flickering. I could hear the sound of a television.

'Hello,' I said. 'Andy?'

There was no reply. I called again, louder. There was still no response. I glanced back down the walkway. It seemed narrower, darker than before. My heartbeat increased and I licked dry lips. There was something wrong here, I knew. And I knew also I should walk away, get back to the safety of my car. Yet the thought of negotiating that exposed walkway and the lift again unnerved me more than staying put. Maybe Peters had just nipped out for a couple of minutes, to the chip shop or for cigarettes. He might be back any moment.

I took a step into the flat and walked towards the open door at the end of the hall. There was another door off to one side and a staircase against the wall, but I ignored them. The television got louder, the flickering brighter. I moved close to the wall and craned my neck forwards until I could see the screen. A film was on. I caught a glimpse of flesh, two naked bodies coupling on a beach. A blue movie. Then I was in the room and looking straight at a man in an armchair. He was staring directly at the television, his eyes fixed on the rhythmic movements of the man and woman on the sand. So absorbed he hadn't noticed me come in.

I started to say something, then saw the expression on his face. The features were set rigid like a gargoyle's, his eyes unblinking. I reached out and snapped on the light. The figure didn't move. He wasn't absorbed in the film at all. He was dead.

For a long moment I just stood there. Looking at him. The silence inside my head was complete, numbing. Then the noise of the television intruded and I turned to the screen. A different woman was stripping off her clothes in a bedroom while a man lay back on pillows, watching her. It was tame stuff, but in the presence of death it seemed grotesquely obscene. I took two paces and switched off the television, then the whirring video machine underneath.

Reluctantly, I looked back at Andy Peters. I recognized him now. We'd met briefly once at Harry Raymond's shop near the market, but that was it. One meeting in life, one in death. On balance he'd looked better alive, but it was a close thing.

He was not a handsome man. His narrow face, sharp nose and yellowing buckteeth gave him the appearance of an overgrown rodent. Lank grey hair hung down over his shirt collar, framing cheeks pock-marked by acne which the two-day growth of stubble did nothing to conceal.

He looked the same as he had that day in Harry's shop, only behind the bloodshot eyes the light had gone out. I shivered. Strange how the passing of the soul leaves so little trace on the body.

I moved closer to him. His head was lolling back slightly over the top of the armchair, his eyes staring out sightlessly at nothing. I knew he was dead, but I somehow felt I had to verify it. Yet I couldn't bring myself to touch him. He was wearing a yellow pullover with holes at the elbows, shiny brown trousers and shoes spattered with white blobs, like fresh paint. There was a faint smell of perfume in the air, aftershave or deodorant.

I wondered how he had died and went suddenly still, the skin on my back prickling with a sensation of warning, of close danger. I spun round, my breath quickening, but there was nothing there. Just a blank television, an empty room, an open door.

Then I noticed the room properly for the first time. There were possessions scattered all over the floor: papers, ornaments, records, a few cheap paperbacks. The drawers in the sideboard had been removed and the contents tipped out on to the carpet. Cushions had been slit open and their stuffing tossed in every direction. It was either wanton vandalism. Or someone had searched the room in a hurry.

I took a deep breath. My neck was clammy, my heart palpitating. Half an hour ago I'd spoken to Andy Peters on the phone. Now he was dead. I saw no signs of violence or wounds to his body, but I knew for certain he hadn't died of natural causes.

In those thirty minutes someone else had been here before me, someone who . . . I froze, listening. Had I imagined that faint noise from the adjoining room? I moved slowly round in a wide arc until I could see out into the hall. The front door was open the way I'd left it, the door to the side still closed.

The noise came again, a low, barely audible rattle. I stepped out into the hall, one part of my brain telling me to get the hell out and phone the police, another urging me to stay put and investigate further. Curiosity triumphed.

I pressed an ear to the door for a moment, then turned the handle quickly and darted through, one hand fumbling for the light switch. The fluorescent tube on the ceiling flickered into life, dazzling me with its bluish glare. I blinked and looked around. I was in the kitchen. A damp, dirty room that smelt of fried fish and had coffee, sugar, rice, Cornflakes, God knows what, strewn all over the floor.

There was no one there. But inside a cage on the worktop in the corner a hamster was scampering round in its metal wheel. I leaned back on the wall and exhaled with relief, my imagination back under control.

The killer was no longer in the flat, I was sure of that now. But he must have moved fast. I'd passed no one outside the main entrance or on the way up. He might have used the stairs, of course, but that didn't change anything. In less than half an hour he'd dealt with Andy Peters, searched the flat and made good his escape. That was some feat.

I went back out into the hall and up the stairs. The bedrooms were littered with debris too. Upturned drawers, ripped mattresses, slashed pillows, mounds of clothing tossed out of wardrobes. In the front room were several bits of electrical equipment and a pile of empty cardboard boxes. A hi-fi system, speakers, CD player and a 26-inch Nicam stereo television. It all looked new. The delivery notices from Cole Brothers, the local John Lewis, were still taped to the boxes.

I left everything the way it was and descended to the hall. There was a telephone on a shelf behind the front door. I picked it up, dialled 999 and asked for the police. Then I went into the kitchen and sat down at the table. The living-room would have been more comfortable, but I couldn't face the body in the armchair again.

I stared at the blank wall, listening to the hamster ratt-
ling its wheel and wondering who had killed Andy Peters.
The flat was like a tomb, cold and full of the stale odour
of death.

A bottle of whisky was circulating round the homicide team.
They seemed to be everywhere in the flat, some in uniform,
most plainclothes. Scenes-of-crime officers, photographers,
fingerprint experts, the whole forensic circus. Sipping
whisky from a bottle and recording with dispassionate,
detailed professionalism the end of a man's life.

Detective-Sergeant Chris Strange came into the kitchen
and pulled out a chair, spinning it round to sit on it the
wrong way. He rested his arms on the back, his legs splayed
beneath his beer gut, and looked at me. In the harsh light
his fleshy face seemed pale, unhealthy, the cleft of his
double chin more pronounced.

'You want a drink?' he said.

I shook my head. My stomach wasn't ready for whisky,
not yet. Strange glanced out of the door and I followed
his eyes. A body bag was being carried out of the flat,
accompanied by a short man in a tan overcoat I knew was
the police pathologist. I waited for them to go, then said:

'How did he die?'

'Someone broke his neck. Snapped it like a matchstick.'

I shuddered. Not so much at the imagery as at the clinical
way Strange said it.

'Poor guy.'

'No one's going to shed too many tears over Andy Peters.'

'You know him?'

'He's got a record as long as my dick.'

'You have such a charming way of putting things.'

Strange shrugged. 'It's one less for us to worry about.'

'What did he do?'

'Burglary, petty theft, a couple of amateurish stick-ups.
Building societies, I think. Small-time stuff, but still a pain
in the arse to us.'

Strange took a notebook out of his sports coat pocket and opened it on the table. 'OK,' he said. 'Let's start from the top.'

I told him everything I knew, the phone call, my journey over, coming upstairs and finding Andy Peters dead. He wrote it all down in laborious longhand, then started to ask me questions.

'You knew him?'

'No.'

'So why you?'

'I met him once, at Harry Raymond's. Harry knew him.'

'Harry Raymond? The one with the locksmith's shop in the market and enough form to fill a book?'

'He's straight, Chris. He's done nothing for years, you know that.'

'Nothing we've managed to pin on him. You have some pretty dodgy friends, McLean. Peters say what he wanted to see you about?'

'No.'

Strange gave me a sceptical look but let it pass. For the time being at least. I knew he didn't believe me, but for once in my life I was telling him the truth.

'You say he phoned at half ten?'

'Thereabouts.'

'And you got here at eleven?'

'Maybe a bit after.'

'How did you get in?'

'The door was already open.'

'So you just walked in?'

'I called first, but there was no answer. I walked through into the living-room and he was there in the armchair.'

'You touch anything?'

'I switched off the TV and video. He'd been watching a film.'

Strange sat back a fraction and stroked his sleek moustache, brushing down the fine black hairs with his pudgy fingertips.

'You come up in the lift?'

'Yes. And no, I didn't see anyone.'

'Downstairs?'

'No.'

'Hear anything?'

I shook my head. 'I can't help you, Chris, I'm sorry.'

'What was it you said he wanted to see you about again?'

He slipped it in casually, hoping I'd fall for it. I sighed.

'Isn't it a bit late for this? I told you, he didn't say.'

'Ah yes, I forgot.' Strange looked down at his notebook, pretending to read it. 'So let me get this straight. A man you hardly know calls you up from Park Hill flats and you come over here in the dark and pissing rain without knowing why.'

'I was curious. It's my job, remember?'

He leant towards me, so close I could smell the sour whisky on his breath.

'I remember all right, McLean. I also remember the number of times you've held out on me. This is a murder inquiry, you understand, not some exclusive for you. Anything you know you'd better spill.'

I waited a few seconds, Strange trying to intimidate me with his frozen scowl.

'Can I go now?' I said.

He pulled away, disappointed, but not too much. He knew me better than that. He nodded briefly. 'I want you to come in tomorrow morning and make a full statement.'

'OK.'

I stood up. My feet crunched on something under the table. Broken cream crackers and digestive biscuits.

'Was this place like this when you arrived?' Strange asked, waving an arm at the debris.

'You think I did it?'

'I wonder what they were looking for?'

He was watching me carefully. I turned away as if I hadn't heard. I'd asked myself that same question already, but it didn't seem a good idea to tell Strange. He might think I could help with the answer.

'I'll see you tomorrow,' I said and walked out.

I went down in the lift, past the uniformed constable on the ground floor and ducked under the striped police tapes across the entrance to the flats. It was still raining outside, a persistent drizzle that gusted in icy showers through the tunnels and pillars of the complex.

I walked round to the parking spaces at the back and looked for my car. It was nowhere to be seen. I checked the whole area in case I'd made a mistake, but it wasn't there. Some bastard had nicked it.

I stood very still, feeling the wind and the rain soaking me through, penetrating deep into my bones. Some nights it pays to stay in.

The Cornish pasty and cold cup of coffee were still sitting on the desk when I got home. The four paragraphs in the typewriter stared up at me accusingly but the last thing I wanted to do now was write about the decline of the South Yorkshire coalfield. I stripped off my sodden clothes and towelled myself dry, then threw on a jumper and tracksuit bottoms and poured myself a brandy in a mug.

I'd walked down to Midland Station and taken a taxi home after reporting the theft of my car to the copper on duty outside the main entrance to the flats. He hadn't been surprised. It was probably joyriding kids who'd burn around for a couple of hours then smash it into a wall somewhere. I could pick up the pieces from the pound in the morning. I'd have to fill in a form for the insurance though. It was only third party, I said, the premiums for comprehensive were more than the car was worth. I'd still have to fill in a form. You always do. I thanked him and walked out into the rain again. That would teach me to leave my car at Park Hill flats.

I sat down in an armchair and sipped my brandy slowly, letting it burn my throat, putting off the call I knew I had to make. I looked at my watch. Moisture had seeped into the casing and the dial was misty with condensation. I peered at the hands, wondering if I could pretend it was too late. But there were no excuses. I picked up the telephone and dialled Harry Raymond's number.

It rang for a long time before he answered.

'Who the 'ell is this?'

I told him. 'Did I get you up?'

''Course you bloody did, it's the middle of the night.' His tone softened. He knew I wouldn't ring for nothing. 'Something up?'

I told him Andy Peters was dead. There was a long silence, then he said quietly: 'Jesus. I were only talking to him this evening. He wanted your phone number.'

'I know. I was the one who found the body.'

I heard the sharp intake of breath, then he said: 'I'm sorry, Mike, shooting off at you like that at the beginning.'

'Forget it, Harry. I didn't want you to hear it on the radio in the morning when I could tell you myself.'

'I appreciate that. 'Ow did it happen?'

'He was murdered.'

'*What?*'

'Listen, can I meet you tomorrow?' I corrected myself: 'Today. Lunch time maybe.'

'I'll be at the Oasis. But 'ow . . . I mean, Christ, who would want to kill Andy?'

'That's what I want you to think about,' I said. 'Then let me know.'

I put down the receiver and cupped my hands around the mug of brandy. The gas fire was on but it still felt cold in the flat. I knew I should be detached and professional about the whole thing, write up the murder and phone it over to the Press Association, the night desks of the Nationals. But I didn't have the stomach for it.

I'd been touched by death. Its chill fingers were still on my spine, my skin, the ice melting through to freeze my guts. I'd seen a man dead. Seen how infinitely fine was the

line between this world and the next. It seemed immoral
to profit from it in any way. Maybe that was why I hadn't
got very far, why I still lived in this grotty flat with mice
under the floors, a permanent overdraft and no future. Sen-
timent has no place in journalism.

I took a gulp of brandy, hoping it would sear the frost
and self-pity from my insides. I gazed at the gas fire. In
the flames I saw Andy Peters in the stillness of death, and
a golden hamster running pointlessly round and round in
its wheel.

CHAPTER 2

I stayed in bed late and caught the bus into town in the
middle of the morning. It was like going on a pensioners'
outing. The whole bus was packed with them, travelling
cheaply on their passes, chatting, calling out to one another,
passing round a paper bag of boiled sweets. I sat next to
an old lady in a red mac and see-through plastic bonnet.
She spent the whole journey telling me, and half the bus,
about her hip replacement operation in such exhaustive
detail I could have done one myself.

I got off on Castle Hill, walked to police headquarters
on Snig Hill and checked in at the front desk, then waited
until a young female detective-constable came out to escort
me to the CID offices.

'Sergeant Strange has told me all about you,' she said
enigmatically. She didn't seem impressed.

Chris Strange was drinking coffee with his feet on his
desk, tie undone, a cigarette hanging from his lip. He was
trying hard to look like a detective but I had a feeling he'd
assumed the pose just before I'd walked through the door,
all for my benefit. There was no mistaking the shadows
under his eyes though.

'You been up all night?' I said.

'Most of it.'

I sat down in the chair opposite him. He raised a hand to the DC who'd brought me through and said: 'Thanks, darling,' then watched her hips as she walked away to the other side of the office.

'Doesn't that count as sexual harassment?' I said.

'Not if I just look. Quite something, isn't she?' Drawing me into his male world. 'You want some coffee?'

'Don't mind.'

Strange yelled across the office: 'Hey, Karen, how 'bout some coffee over here?'

I turned in time to see the DC giving him the finger. Strange grinned and swung his feet off the desk, heading for the coffee machine.

'White, extra sugar,' I said. I felt as if I needed the energy.

I studied Strange's desk while he was gone. Untidy, cardboard files piled up along one side, overflowing ashtray, mound of paperclips and rubber bands, and a framed photograph of his wife and kids. That surprised me, I didn't think he was the type. I picked it up. A nice-looking blonde wife, hair pulled back, laughing at the camera; two teenage boys running to fat, taking after their father. I put it down as Strange came back with a polystyrene cup and handed it to me. He stood the photograph back up in the corner of the desk.

'Last summer,' he said. 'Took it myself, walking in the Manifold Valley. You ever been down there?'

'Not for a while.'

'Incredible how you get that river flowing along, then it just disappears underground. Gone. What is it, limestone or something?'

I nodded. 'I didn't know you were a walker.'

'I'm not. I sit in the pub with the paper then drive round and pick up Joan and the boys when they've finished.'

He was being unusually friendly this morning. There had to be a reason.

'I expected you earlier,' he said.

'I had to catch a bus.' I explained about my car.

'You report it?'

'I told one of your lads outside the flats. He put it on the radio.'

'We had a car pinched up there a couple of months back. Call out to a domestic. The officers came back out and found a bunch of twelve-year-olds had nicked their squad car.'

'I don't remember that.'

'You don't think we told the press, do you? I'll see if yours has been found yet.'

He picked up the phone and spoke to someone. I watched him suspiciously. He was acting way out of character.

I'd known him a long time. Close on fifteen years now. We'd met when I was a junior on the *Evening News*, at a football match between the paper and South Yorkshire Police. I could still remember the game. I'd played up front for the newsroom because I was the only member of the team who could run a hundred yards without serious risk of a coronary. At half-time, instead of oranges, we passed round hip flasks to prevent severe alcohol withdrawal symptoms.

Strange, then a DC at Hammerton Road, had played sweeper for the Filth and made up for his lack of speed by hanging on to my shirt and sticking his studs in my leg every time he came near me.

We lost three-nil after a couple of dubious penalties were given against us and it was years later that Strange told me he'd fixed the match, done a deal with the referee in return for sorting out some unpaid parking fines for him. I'd never trusted Strange completely since.

He put the phone down. 'No news.' He took a final drag on his cigarette and stubbed it out, suddenly businesslike. This is it, I thought. I slipped in a question before he could put me on the spot.

'You made any progress since last night?'

Strange hesitated, then shrugged. 'If you mean who did it, or why, no. But it's early days yet.'

'Did anyone else see or hear anything? What about the neighbours?'

'One side they were out, the other's a couple in their seventies. God knows what they're doing there, three floors up in a piss hole like that. They heard banging, maybe a yell, but they aren't sure. Could have been something on the television, they said.'

'Did they go out to take a look?'

'You kidding? In Park Hill flats? You don't open your door after dark if you've got any sense. Especially if you're that age.'

'Whoever did it must have made a fair bit of noise, the mess he left behind.'

Strange nodded. 'He didn't have much time either. Not if what you told us is correct.'

Now we were getting there.

'You think I'm lying to you?'

'Not lying, McLean. You're too smart to do that. But let's go over one or two things again, shall we? Just to get your statement right.'

I sighed and took a swig of coffee. It wasn't too bad for police headquarters.

'Go on.'

Strange produced his notebook and flipped through the pages. I tried to read what he'd written from my side of the desk. The script was rounded, big letters, lots of loops. It had a childlike appearance, as if he'd learnt it at school and it had never developed since.

'Now,' he said. 'You told me you got the call at half ten and arrived at the flats at eleven.'

'Give or take a few minutes.'

'That's a long time to get to Park Hill from your place.'

'I drove slowly. I had to. My windscreen wipers weren't working and it was throwing it down.'

'You know that's a road traffic offence?' His cop men-
tality, unable to resist saying it.

I held my wrists out. 'You want to cuff me now? I'll
come quietly.'

'So you got there at eleven. But you didn't make the
emergency call until quarter past. They keep a record,' he
added, just in case I felt like disputing it.

'I was in a state of shock. You don't walk in somewhere
and find a corpse and pick up the phone immediately.'

'Don't you? I'd have thought that's exactly what you'd
do.'

'It takes a while. To recover, to think what to do next.'

'You had a snoop around, didn't you?'

I took my time answering. There was no point denying
it. 'I thought the killer might still be there.'

Strange raised an eyebrow. 'And you were going to tackle
him all by your little self, were you?'

'I didn't know what I was going to do.'

'You take anything from the flat?'

'No. Why should I?'

'Whoever killed Peters was looking for something. You
wouldn't have found it yourself, would you?'

I leaned forwards over the desk. 'I'm being straight with
you, Chris. I looked around, that's all.'

'See anything odd, anything that struck you?'

'Not really.' I tried to be helpful. 'Except perhaps the
electrical stuff upstairs. All new. It stood out in the midst
of the cheap furniture, the tatty carpets, the mildewed
wallpaper.'

'Delivered that day. Cost nearly three thousand pounds.
We checked. And he paid cash for it. Now where would a
scumbag like Peters get that kind of money?'

'You said he was a burglar. Maybe he nicked it.'

Strange tapped his teeth with the end of his pen. 'Maybe
he did.'

'You got any likely suspects?'

'Only you.' He smiled humourlessly.

I stared at him. He was joking, but it still unsettled me.

'Nine times out of ten, either the person who last saw the victim alive, or the person who finds the body is the one who did it,' he said. 'The other time it's the butler.'

'What's my motive? Why would I call you afterwards? How would I do it? I've no idea how to break a man's neck.'

'Apparently it's not that difficult. You need to be fairly strong, but you're a big bloke.'

'I'd met the guy once before, for five minutes. And that was a couple of years ago.'

'So how come he calls *you* out of the blue last night?'

I wanted to know that too, but I wasn't going to confide in Strange. 'I told you, he wanted to talk to a reporter. Maybe I was the only one he'd encountered. Maybe he thought he could trust me because Harry Raymond's a mutual friend.'

'You want to be careful who you mix with, you know.'

'It's how I do my job. It's how you do yours too. Are you going to tell me you've never had a pint with a villain before? I know all sorts of people the Archbishop of Canterbury wouldn't invite to tea.'

'And you still maintain he didn't say why he wanted to see you?'

My patience was wearing thin. 'I thought I came here to make a statement. How many times do I have to tell you? It's the truth, Chris.'

He watched me expressionlessly for a long beat. 'OK, just checking.' He waved the DC called Karen over. 'I have to go out. Take his statement, will you.'

Strange stood up and tightened the knot of his tie. One of his shirt buttons had burst open and, through the gap, I could see a line of dark hair on the swollen bulge of his stomach.

When he came round the desk he leaned down close and said: 'You're a devious sod, McLean. On past form I wouldn't believe a word you told me, but this time I'll give you the benefit of the doubt. I might want to see you again though. In the next few days.'

'I can hardly wait,' I said.

The DC took my statement down on a typewriter without comment. I initialled the pages and signed at the bottom. Then she escorted me from the office. I said I wanted to call in at the press office on my way out so she took me there and watched while I knocked and entered. For some reason she didn't seem to trust me. Strange's prejudices rubbing off.

Gordon Crieff, the press officer, was behind his desk reading a car magazine and eating a Mars bar. He motioned me to a chair and finished his mouthful.

'What d'ye think?' he said in his thick Glaswegian patois. 'Mondeo or Cavalier?'

'Pardon?'

'My new car. I'm trying tae make up my mind. Maybe a Cavalier's too square, like a rep's car. All free samples and double-breasted jackets hanging up in the back. Someone tells me the Japanese make a good middle range. Nissan something-or-other. Very reliable the Japanese.'

'They're made by Geordies now.'

'Shit, I'd forgotten.' He pulled a face. 'I'm nae sure I'd buy a Nissan built by a Geordie.'

'I wouldn't buy a Nissan built by God,' I said. 'And anyway, don't talk to me about cars. Mine was nicked last night at Park Hill flats.'

'Eventful time ye had up there. I hope ye made a killing with your scoop.'

'Thousands,' I said, wondering how I'd managed to make precisely nothing from it. My finely honed talent for not making money again. 'Chris Strange has just been questioning me about it.'

Crieff's mouth curled sardonically. 'I thought ye looked a wee bit drained. He tell ye anything I should know?'

I shook my head. 'What's the official line?'

'Man found dead, inquiries continuing, witnesses sought. All the usual bullshit for "we havnae a bloody clue".'

I smiled. I liked Crieff. He didn't resort to PR flannel when he briefed reporters. He finished his Mars bar and tossed a wad of daily press releases over to me.

'Ye fellows are in luck today. A murder at the flats last night, attempted assassination in the East End this morning.' He saw my expression of disbelief. 'Hae a look, second page.'

I turned over the front sheet and read the brief outline that followed. A man called James Silvester, described in the text as a 'businessman', had arrived at his office in the Don Valley just after eight o'clock and, while parking his car, had been shot at. Three bullets through the windscreen, none of them hitting him.

'Is this all?' I said.

'It's about all we've got.'

'Who's James Silvester?'

'I'd nae heard of him either. Owns a foundry apparently.'

'He sounds lucky to be alive. No injuries at all?'

'A few small cuts from broken glass, but nothing more serious.'

'Did he see who did it?'

'No. The shots came from long range, he thinks. He wasnae even sure from which direction. A botched job by the look of it. Ballistics are examining the car.'

'Someone with a grudge against him?'

'Could be. I gather Mr Silvester is not being very forthcoming on the matters of who and why. Maybe ye should ask him. He's recovering at home.'

I read the report again and looked back up to meet Crieff's eyes.

'It doesn't give his home address, or phone number.'

'I know. And he's ex-directory. But his office address is there, Titan Works.'

'No one there is likely to give it to me.'

'He disnae want his home details released to the press.

And as ye know, we're bound to respect his wishes. They're here somewhere, but I'm nae allowed to give them to ye.'

Crieff rummaged around on his desk and produced a sheet of A4 paper with a few words and numbers scribbled on it. He placed it carefully on the blotter in front of him and looked directly at me. Then he stood up and went to throw his Mars bar wrapper into the bin in the corner of the office. He did it very slowly, his eyes turned away.

By the time he returned to the desk I had my notebook back in my pocket, my arms crossed, an expression of saintly innocence on my face.

'Anything else I can do for ye?' he said.

'You could work on your handwriting, Gordon, it's bloody hard to read.'

Harry Raymond was already in the Oasis Café when I got there. I picked up a cup of tea and a cheese sandwich from the counter and joined him at his table by the window. Outside it was a bright, crisp winter day. In the Oasis it was steamy, tropical, swirling with the exotic odours of chips, vinegar and fried black pudding.

'Hello, Harry, how are you?' I said automatically. I knew it was a mistake as soon as I said it. For the next ten minutes he told me.

When he'd finished, I said: 'Well if that's all, you've nothing to worry about.'

He gave me a narrow look, perhaps suspecting a note of irony.

'It's serious, Mike. Me 'eart, me lungs, me joints, they're all beginning to go. It's got me so worried I've gone on a diet, started 'aving the Low-fat Special every day.'

I looked down at what he was eating. Bacon, sausage, an egg, fried bread and chips.

'That's the *Low-fat* Special? What does the high-fat one look like?'

'It's got double chips, of course. A man's got to make

sacrifices for the good of his 'ealth, you know. The doctors won't do owt for me.'

'Harry,' I said, 'if the NHS treated all the ailments you think you have, it would be bankrupt by now.'

He looked hurt, his gaunt, lugubrious features sagging a couple of inches. '*Think* I 'ave?'

'Just shut up for a minute and tell me about Andy Peters. How well did you know him?'

Harry comforted himself with a slice of sausage dipped in egg yolk before he answered.

'Not that well. I used to see 'im around, and now and then he'd come into the shop for summat. But he weren't a friend. I didn't really like 'im in fact.'

'Why not?'

'He were a nasty piece of work. Couldn't be trusted. You know the sort, matey on the surface, mean as a rat underneath.'

'You ever do a job for him?'

'No way. I'd've ended up inside for sure.'

'Has he done a lot of time?'

'More in than out. No one with any sense would've touched him. Not as a partner. He had big ideas but none of the talent needed to pull 'em off.'

'Criminal ideas?'

'He never did owt legit in his life.'

I took a sip of tea and chewed on a mouthful of cheese sandwich, studying the bald patch on the crown of Harry's head as he bent over his plate of cholesterol.

Harry too had been a burglar and done time once, before I met him. Yet I never thought of him as dishonest. He owned a locksmith's shop now and his years of crime seemed little more than youthful aberrations, distant follies that had never tainted the underlying virtues in his character.

'When did you last see him?' I asked.

'Months ago. It's not a good idea for someone in my

business to be seen wi' known criminals. His phone call took me by surprise.'

'What exactly did he say?'

Harry shrugged. 'Not much. He remembered I knew a journalist, I don't know 'ow.'

'I met him once in your shop.'

'Did you? Anyway, he wanted your name and number.'

'He say why?'

'To call you.'

'I mean, about what?'

Harry looked bemused. 'Didn't he tell you on the phone?'

I shook my head. 'And by the time I saw him he was dead.'

I told Harry exactly what had happened the previous night. He gave me his full attention. He even stopped eating for a second.

'Jesus, and he were sitting there in the armchair? No blood, no nothing. That's creepy. I'd've run a bleedin' mile and said nowt to anyone. I 'ate death. Even on the telly I can't watch people dying. All them detective shows, you know. When they find the bodies I 'ave to look away.'

'So did I, Harry, believe me.' I finished my sandwich and scooped up the fragments of escaped cheese from the plate. 'Did you have a think after I rang you? About who might have done it, and why?'

Harry eyed me. 'You're not planning on leaving this to the police then?'

'He had something to tell me, Harry. But someone killed him before I could ask what. I'm not going to leave it at that.'

He pushed away his plate. 'Well, the why's probably easier than the who.'

'You know something?'

'Not that will 'elp much. But as a guess I'd say he pushed someone too far. He were like that. Got up people's noses, riled them. He got in a lot of fights, punch-ups outside pubs on a Saturday night, that kind of thing. He were a cocky little sod who never knew when to stop.'

'Do you know anyone in particular he might have upset?'

'I'm just talking generally, from my experience of 'im like. I 'aven't a clue what he might've been up to recently. You could ask his wife.'

I should have guessed already he was married, or had a live-in girlfriend. The flat at Park Hill, when I thought back over it, had a woman's mark on it. The colour of the walls, the bedroom furniture, the lacy cushions.

'Dawn, I think she's called. She works at a massage parlour off London Road. Or used to. The Sphinx. You know it?'

'I don't go to massage parlours very often.'

'I bet she'll 'ave a few ideas who did it.'

'Why?'

'Wives do, don't they? If I were knocked off, the missus would most likely know who'd done it. Come to think of it, she'd probably be top of the list.'

'Thanks, Harry. If you think of anything else, will you let me know?'

''Course. You're not going, are you?'

'I have to.'

'What about some pudding? What's it say on the board?'

He squinted past my shoulder. I turned and looked at the menu behind the counter. I read off the list for him.

'Treacle tart, plum pudding, chocolate sponge.'

'Bugger it,' Harry said. 'I'll start the diet tomorrow.'

I left Harry to his stodge and walked up the hill into the city. The offices of my accountant, Maria, were in a late-Georgian house near Paradise Square, the only bit of the centre that still had any character. Cobbled streets, narrow alleys, iron railings, even an old gas lamp that burned methane from the sewers.

There were few shops or office blocks round here, just shady mews containing barristers' chambers, discreet solicitors and a few accountants, the professional *mafiosi* with nineteenth-century working practices and twenty-first century prices. Add a couple of hansom cabs and some pea soup fog and it could have been the set for a Jack the Ripper film.

I walked in through the front door and braced myself for the inevitable encounter with Muriel, the formidable Gorgon who acted as Maria's secretary, receptionist and bouncer.

She was sitting behind her desk having a genteel lunch. A small slice of bacon and egg pie, 'quiche' she'd call it, and a variety of salads on a porcelain plate. On the desk top, to one side, were a silver napkin ring, a small antique cruet set and a crystal glass of sparkling mineral water. I looked around in case the Duchess of Devonshire was there too.

Muriel dabbed her lips with a starched linen napkin and glared at me as if I were a particularly nasty species of cockroach.

'Hi,' I said. 'Maria in?'

'Miss Wells is with a client at the moment.'

'It's lunch time.'

'She works very hard.'

'Never mind, I'll wait.'

I sat down in one of the soft chairs facing Muriel. She kept her eyes on me, her expression as hard and fixed as her perm. She was wearing a floral print dress that looked like a settee cover and clip-on earrings the size of golf balls. I was convinced she'd been a ship's stoker in the past, but never plucked up the courage to ask.

'Don't let me stop you eating,' I said.

'I won't,' Muriel said.

She took a tiny glass bottle from the cruet set and shook it, then sprinkled the contents over her salad. French dressing. I wondered what she did for dinner.

'You're looking well, Muriel,' I said, trying to be friendly. She ignored me.

I decided to chance my arm. 'How's your sex life?'

'Don't be impertinent,' she said without looking up.

'What're you into these days, bondage, leather, S&M?'

She raised her head very slowly, but I never did get to hear her reply, for the door to Maria's office opened just then and Maria came out with her client: a dull-looking man in his forties, wedding ring on the third finger of his left hand. That was all right.

Maria saw me and shook her head wearily. 'Come in.'

I stood up and walked towards her. As I passed Muriel's desk I reached out with a hand. She slapped my wrist away, but not before I'd pinched a tiny stick of raw carrot from her plate. I popped it into my mouth.

'Too much olive oil,' I said and followed Maria into her office.

Maria closed the door behind us. 'Have you been annoying Muriel again?'

'I do my best.'

She crossed to the sofa at one end of the room, kicked off her heels and lay down.

'Bad morning?' I said.

She nodded and shut her eyes. I looked at her. She could take my breath away every time. Dark hair curling round high cheekbones, sensual, perhaps too-full lips, a dab of peach in her complexion, the softness under the smart business suit. She was quite oblivious to the effect she had on me, and probably every other man she met. There was no guile there, no artifice or coquetry, just that terrible aching beauty.

'Would you like me to get you a coffee?' I said.

'Mmm, that would be nice.'

I filled a cup from the filter machine on the filing cabinet and took it to her. She sat up and held the saucer in one hand, the cup in the other.

I pulled a chair out and sat down. 'You've been overdoing it,' I said.

'I know.'

'You had any lunch?'

'I'm not hungry.'

'Maybe you should relax more. Spend a few evenings in with some caring, sharing sort of bloke. Someone like me.'

She laughed softly and looked at me with her smoky blue-grey eyes. Eyes I could never see behind.

'What do you want, Michael?'

Very direct. I'd have to play this carefully.

'What makes you think I want anything?'

'You haven't just come here to give me health advice.'

How did she always *know*?

'I wanted to see how you were. Do I need a reason for stopping by?'

'No.' She seemed thoughtful now. 'No, you don't need a reason.' She raised her eyes to look at me over the rim of her cup. 'But you always have one. You never call in for nothing.'

She said it without resentment, but it still made me feel bad. Maybe that's where I went wrong. Always having a reason.

'Well, there is one thing.'

'Ah.'

'A small favour. I have to go out and see someone near Hollow Meadows, off a bus route.' I paused. 'And my car was stolen last night.'

'That clapped-out old Cortina? Boy, they must have been desperate.'

That hurt.

'I was very attached to it.'

'I'm sure it will turn up somewhere. In a stock car race maybe.'

'You're not making this easy, Maria. You see, the thing is . . .'

'You want to borrow my car.'

'Yes.'

She didn't say anything. Just sipped her coffee.

'I'll take care, I promise. I'll be back in a couple of hours.

Please, Maria, it's important. There's no one else I can ask.'

'You could take a taxi.'

I grimaced. 'I'm a bit low on funds at the moment.' And every other moment too, but I didn't need to say that. She was my accountant, after all.

'Who're you going to see?' Maria asked.

'Some businessman called James Silvester. He was shot at this morning in the East End. Had a lucky escape. It could be a big story.'

She sighed and stood up, putting her cup down on the arm of the sofa. She padded over to the desk and took a key out of her bag. She held it out.

'The red Mazda outside.'

'A Mazda? You got a new one?'

'Yes. I want it back by six. And Michael, if there's the slightest mark on it, your life expectancy will plummet to zero.'

'I'll look after it.'

I took the key from her hand, taking a couple of steps towards her. I could smell her perfume. She never usually let me get this close. I took a chance and kissed her lightly on the cheek. It was warm, soft as velvet.

'Thanks, Maria.'

When I looked back from the door she was still in the same place, standing there in her stockinged feet, watching me and rubbing her cheek gently with her fingertips.

CHAPTER 3

James Silvester's house was on a steep hillside overlooking Strines Reservoir on the western fringes of the city, where the urban sprawl had long since given way to the desolate, empty hills of the Pennines. It was set back from the road behind a high stone wall and ornate, wrought iron gates, a solitary outpost of civilization surrounded by heather and yellowing grass, a mile at least from its nearest neighbour.

I parked Maria's car on the verge and got out, wondering how anyone could live out here in such depressing isolation. The wind was gusting across from Derwent Moor, rasping around my ears. Below me, in the valley, the reservoir glinted in the wintry sunlight, its surface stippled with tiny waves like tool marks on an engraving.

I went to the gates and examined them. They were firmly shut with a complex lock that looked as if it could be operated electronically from the house. On one of the gateposts was a bellpush and intercom, and above me a video camera on a pole was monitoring my presence. Silvester was clearly not a man who encouraged casual visitors.

I pressed the bell and waited, half bracing myself for the sudden crackle of a voice from the intercom. Nothing happened. I pressed the bell again and held it in for several seconds. The intercom stayed silent. Either no one was at home or they didn't want to see me. I took out my press card and held it up to the video camera. Then I rattled the gates. They remained shut. Maybe Silvester didn't like reporters. People who barricaded themselves in fortresses like this tended not to. That only made them more of a challenge.

Inserting fingers and toes into the wrought iron curlicues, I clambered over the gate and dropped to the ground on the other side. The video camera watched it all, but I didn't care. If the house was occupied, I wanted them to know I was there.

I walked up the drive to the front door, passing well-kept flowerbeds and a crew-cut lawn before skirting round a dark green Range-Rover parked on the forecourt. The gritstone façade towered over me, three storeys high with narrow windows and a roof made of split sandstone tiles. Even in the pale sunlight it was dark and grim, as unwelcoming as the bleak landscape beyond the garden walls.

I rang the bell for the sake of it and was not surprised

when no one answered. I considered what to do next. I was pretty sure Silvester was inside. Gordon Crieff had said he was recovering at home and the Range-Rover was a fair indication that someone was here. I hadn't driven all this way just to go home without getting some kind of an interview, even if it consisted solely of 'piss off', and a door slammed in my face.

I walked round the side of the house, then across a terrace at the back. The rear of the building had a stone extension attached to it with modern glass sliding doors at one end. I peered in through the doors and caught a glimpse of the room inside through the partially drawn curtains. It appeared to be a small gymnasium containing various exercise machines and weight-training equipment.

I tried the handle. The glass pane slid sideways without a sound. I brushed aside the curtains and stepped over the threshold. As I turned my head to look around the room, I sensed a movement to one side, then a thick arm came up around my neck and squeezed my windpipe.

A voice said softly in my ear: 'You're trespassing, sonny boy.'

I just had time to register it was a woman's voice, before I felt myself being lifted off my feet and propelled through the air. I hit the ground again on a gym mat in the middle of the room. The breath exploded out of me like a burst paper bag and for a moment I thought I was going to black out. I whooped desperately for oxygen, ignoring the pain in my side where I'd landed. My chest was a hoop of steel, constricting my breathing. I forced my lungs to start working again, gulping in huge draughts of air, clearing the dizziness from my head.

After a minute of agony I summoned the strength to roll over on to my back and look up. The woman was standing a few yards away, gazing down at me implacably. She was something over six feet tall, maybe thirteen or fourteen stone of packed muscle. Her blonde hair was tied back in a ponytail and she was wearing nothing but a skin-tight gym outfit. She looked like Godzilla in a pink leotard.

A door opened behind me. I sat up and turned my head to see a short, stocky man walk into the room with a glass in one hand, a cigar in the other. I managed to suck in enough air to speak.

'Mr Silvester?'

'Yes, I'm James Silvester.' He waved his cigar at the woman. 'This is my wife.'

'We've met,' I said.

They frisked me and removed the wallet and press card from my jacket pocket. Then Silvester's wife picked me up by the lapels and stood me on the floor like a skittle waiting to be knocked over. I swayed unsteadily on my feet. The left-hand side of my body throbbed with pain but I didn't think anything was broken.

Silvester examined the press card and handed it back to me with my wallet.

'I don't like journalists, McLean,' he said.

'I gathered that.'

'You hurt?'

'Of course not. I hurl myself across rooms all the time.'

'You'll get much more than that if you bother us again.'

'I could sue you for assault,' I said.

Silvester smiled thinly. 'I don't think so. You came on to my property without permission. I'm quite within my rights to use reasonable force to eject you.'

He inhaled on his cigar. I tried to gauge what kind of man he was. Mid-forties, muscular body which had long since turned to flab, hair cropped short revealing a cauliflower ear and rolls of skin on the back of his neck. Hard piggy eyes, powerful hands with traces of dirt around the fingernails, vestiges of a Sheffield accent, not very pronounced but discernible all the same.

He looked like someone who'd made his money the hard way, working his way up from a manual job. Not very well educated but with the shrewdness and ruthless eye for opportunity you need to succeed in business. Considering he'd nearly been killed by an assassin that morning, he seemed remarkably composed. The only sign that anything untoward had happened to him was a strip of sticking plaster on one side of his forehead and a couple of small cuts on his cheek.

'You get hit by flying glass?' I asked.

'Let me throw him out now,' Mrs Silvester said. 'He's getting on my nerves.'

'I'll go,' I said. 'I just want to ask you a few questions first.' I pulled out my notebook and pen. 'Have you any idea who shot at you? A business enemy, a disgruntled employee?'

'You don't get the message, do you?' Silvester said tersely. 'Maybe we'll have to knock it into your thick skull.'

I didn't let him deter me. He was all talk. 'Has anyone threatened you? Letters, telephone calls?'

Silvester turned away impatiently and nodded at his wife. 'Be gentle with him, Pinky.'

Pinky? My jaw almost dropped. Pinky? It was such an absurdly inappropriate name for someone built like a beer truck on steroids. I backed away out of her reach and fired off another question. I had to make the effort now I was here.

'Do you think whoever it was will try again?'

Pinky Silvester moved towards me with surprising speed for someone her size. I tried to twist sideways but she took hold of my wrist and whipped me round in an arc. My feet left the ground and I suddenly found myself horizontal across the back of her broad shoulders.

She began to rotate, spinning me round with her. Then she let go. I flew off her shoulders and for a brief instant experienced a sensation of complete weightlessness. Then gravity reasserted itself and I crashed head first into a pile of rubber mats in the corner of the gym. I turned over and sat up groggily, my head swimming, the notebook and pen still clutched in my hands.

'Shall I put that down as "no comment"?' I said.

I was aware only vaguely of what happened next. Of being picked up, slung over her shoulder like a sack of potatoes, carried out, down the drive and through the gates to the car. She found the keys in my pocket, opened the door and threw me into the driver's seat. She leaned in, her face close to mine. She was a handsome woman with a fine bone structure and deep hazel eyes. Too big to be classically beautiful, but what the Scots would call a bonny lass.

'We have nothing to say to the press, you understand?' she said softly. 'You bother us again and I'll put you in hospital for a year.'

She straightened up and slammed the door. Then she lifted one of her huge legs and hammered the sole of her bare foot into the offside wing of the car, an act of pure, gratuitous malice. I was too weak to care much. I explored the bruises on my body gingerly, before counting my ribs. I was still alive. Just.

I spent the half-hour drive back into the city recovering from my ordeal at the Silvesters', and pondering how to break the news to Maria about the dent in her Mazda MX5. By the time I reached the centre I'd decided there was only one sensible course of action. I wouldn't tell her. It gave me a few pangs of guilt, but I soon shook them off. My instinct for self-preservation has always been stronger than my conscience.

I parked the car on a meter near the City Hall and walked round the corner into Carver Street. I had someone to see before I went back to Maria's office. I climbed a narrow flight of stairs next to an Italian restaurant and opened a door at the top. A chipped plastic sign in the middle of the door read 'South Yorkshire Industrial Bulletin'. There was a bell to one side but I didn't bother ringing it. I knew it didn't work.

Sam Fielding was sitting at a desk in one corner of the

office inside, hunched over a pile of papers and a large packet of chocolate digestive biscuits. He didn't look up as I entered so I pulled out a chair and sat down opposite him to wait. Sooner or later he'd notice I was there.

I glanced around. It was one of the scruffiest offices I'd ever been in, and each time I visited it seemed to get worse. The floor was covered in stacks of files and old newspapers, interspersed with patches of shredded carpet. The furniture would have been rejected by even the most undiscerning junk shop and the paint on the walls was peeling off in sheets as if the whole place had some kind of architectural psoriasis. It smelt of damp, garlic from the restaurant below and stale tobacco smoke.

Sam was even scruffier than his surroundings. A cadaverous man in his early fifties, unmarried, rumpled, dandruff scattered over his shoulders and arms like the 'before' model in a shampoo ad. He wore thick glasses which distorted his eyes and suits so old they'd already come back into fashion three times since he bought them.

'Hello, Sam,' I said eventually.

He started and looked up. 'Michael! My goodness, I'm sorry. Have you been there long?'

'Just since lunch time.'

'Really? I didn't notice you when I came back in.'

Sometimes I wondered if Sam lived on the same planet as the rest of us.

'I was engrossed in this,' he said apologetically, holding up a few sheets of paper.

'What is it?'

'A breakdown of special steel sales in Eastern Europe and the Baltic States. Fascinating stuff.'

'I'm sure.'

'You want to hear some of it? The figures for high-speed tool steel are particularly interesting.'

'Later, Sam,' I said. 'When I've got a couple of weeks to spare.'

He looked disappointed. Sam was one of those great

eccentrics that add such colour to this drab little island of ours. He had one of those intense passions that he found uniquely absorbing, but which was of almost no conceivable interest to anyone else. Like train spotters or people who collect Victorian commodes. Only Sam's passion was the steel and coal industry, a subject he knew more about than anyone I'd ever encountered. He'd spent half a lifetime studying it and for the past ten years had published a quarterly bulletin about it, a thick periodical packed with arcane facts and lengthy articles so boring I'd never got beyond the first paragraph of any of them. Occasionally I did some work for him, when he wanted a less technical piece to lighten up the bulletin, but only when I was desperate for cash. Which was nearly always.

'I wanted to ask you something, Sam,' I said. 'Do you know anything about a man called Silvester, James Silvester?'

Sam sat back in his chair and peered at me through the jam-jar lenses of his spectacles. He appeared vague in the extreme, but his mind was stiletto sharp.

'James Silvester,' he repeated slowly. 'Used to be known as Jimmy, owns the Titan Works at Attercliffe?'

'That's the one.'

'Off the top of my head, or do you want me to look him up in the files?'

'You'll know more than enough for my purposes without looking him up.'

Sam took a pipe out of the breast pocket of his jacket and stuffed it with tobacco from a pouch on the desktop. Then he went through the complicated business of pressing down the tobacco, lighting matches and puffing which seems to take up most of a pipe smoker's time. Sometimes I think that's the real purpose behind it all, the actual smoking being merely an incidental side effect. After four matches he finally got the thing lit and inhaled.

'Well,' he said, through a cloud of noxious fumes, 'he's someone with fingers in a few pies. Fancies himself as a tycoon, but he's basically a scrap metal dealer who's diversified.'

'He was in scrap metal?'

'Still is. He's got a yard off Brightside Lane.'

'What else does he do?'

'Deals in spare parts for cars, speculates a bit.'

'In what?'

'Mostly property until a few years ago. He got out before the market collapsed. Made a fair bit of money, I'm told. Now he'll buy and sell anything if there's a profit in it.'

'What's his reputation like?'

'Dodgy.'

'He done anything illegal?'

Sam smiled cynically. 'He's a scrap metal dealer, Michael.'

'All right, anything illegal that he's been caught for?'

Sam took his pipe out of his mouth and inspected the bowl closely, another esoteric pipe smoker's ritual. The mouthpiece looked as if it had been gnawed by a starving gerbil.

'You know what happens in that world.' He popped the pipe back in, apparently satisfied that all was well. 'If you have a grievance, you send a few boys round with a sledge-hammer to sort it out. The law doesn't generally come into it much. But a couple of times he's been careless.'

I helped myself to a chocolate digestive. 'Has he got a criminal record?'

'Oh yes. He's been inside too. A long time ago.'

'What for?'

'Assault, I seem to recall. He's a violent man. Or was. Nowadays, I'm sure, he gets someone else to do his dirty work. But he nearly went back a few years ago.'

'To jail?'

Sam nodded. 'A small matter of illegally exporting goods to Iran during the Iran–Iraq war.'

'What sort of goods?'

'Leyland bus engines.'

'Was that illegal?'

'It broke a UN arms embargo.'

I frowned. 'Bus engines aren't arms.'

'That depends what you use them for. The engine in a
Leyland double-decker also happens to be the engine for a
Chieftain tank. The Iranians had a lot of those, sold to the
Shah by us. And they needed plenty of spares during the war
with Iraq.'

'I don't remember reading about any of this.'

'It never came to court. But I found out about it a couple
of years after.'

'What happened to Silvester?'

'Nothing. It was all hushed up. The government wasn't
too keen on publicizing the illegal arms trading that went
on during that war.'

'No, I don't suppose they were. That's their prerogative,
isn't it, selling arms to oppressive regimes.'

Sam shrugged. He wasn't interested in politics. 'Everyone had their snouts in the trough: South Africa, China,
North Korea. Silvester was small fry.'

'But he still made money out of it. Money out of blood
and misery.'

'Someone always makes money out of wars. Isn't that
what they're for?'

I nodded. What did I expect? Since time immemorial
the arms trade has operated on the morality of the cheque
book.

Sam said: 'Why are you interested in him?'

'Someone tried to kill him this morning. Shot at him
three times as he arrived for work.'

Sam's eyes opened a little wider. 'Is he badly hurt?'

'The bullets all missed. You know of anyone who might
have wanted him dead?'

'He's a crook. Probably anyone who had dealings with
him would be glad to see him in a coffin. But most of them
wouldn't miss.'

'It was a long-range, probably a rifle.'

'I can't help you, Michael. I don't know enough about him. I'm mainly concerned with more reputable businessmen.'

'He owns a foundry, doesn't he?'

Sam's lip twisted into a sly smile. 'That doesn't make him reputable. He bought it cheaply from the receivers about two years ago. He probably thought it would give him a certain respectability, but you don't buy integrity. Have you spoken to him?'

'I went to his house. His wife threw me out.'

Sam looked incredulous. 'And you're still in one piece?'

'You've met Pinky then?'

'No, but I've seen a photo of her. Silvester sends me tickets and promotional stuff for her bouts.'

'Bouts?'

'I assumed you knew. She's a professional wrestler.'

That explained a lot: the gymnasium, the pink leotard, the practised violence. I was more relieved than ever that all I'd come away with were a few bruises and a wounded pride.

'Why does Silvester send you tickets?' I said.

Sam delayed his reply while he attempted to relight his pipe.

'He doesn't,' he said in time. 'But he employs a PR agency which does. They've got me on their press list, God knows why. I don't think they have a clue what I do. I suppose it fills the seats.'

'Does she wrestle often?'

'You interested? Here.' He rummaged in a drawer and pulled out a couple of dog-eared tickets. 'They came the other week. The tenth, that's tomorrow, isn't it? Take them.'

He thrust the tickets across the desk.

'You sure, Sam?'

'Wrestling at the City Hall is hardly my line.'

'Thanks. And thanks for your help.'

I stood up and pinched another chocolate biscuit from

the packet. I was halfway to the door when Sam said: 'By the way, how's that colour piece on the coalfield coming along?'

I'd been hoping he wouldn't ask that.

'Nearly done,' I said confidently.

'I want it as soon as possible.'

'It'll be in the post tomorrow.'

He puffed on his pipe and nodded, apparently satisfied. That's one of the things I like about Sam. He always believes me when I'm lying.

It was dark by the time I got to Maria's office. I left the Mazda outside under a broken streetlamp, praying she wouldn't notice the dented wing in the poor light.

She was standing by the desk, packing up her briefcase, when I walked in through the door. The weariness was obvious in her face.

'I haven't kept you waiting, have I?' I said.

Maria shook her head. 'I've only just finished. How was your trip?'

'Well, I found the house all right. But I didn't get much of an interview. His wife roughed me up and threw me out.'

'His *wife*?'

'Yeah, it is a bit humiliating, isn't it? But I didn't like to resist in case I hurt her.'

Maria clicked her briefcase shut and took her overcoat down off a peg on the wall.

'Are you injured?'

'Not fatally.'

'You don't make things easy for yourself, do you? People always seem to be doing this to you.'

'I know. I can't think why, a nice, fully house-trained fellow like me.'

'Why do they let you in if they don't want to talk to you?'

I helped her on with her coat. 'They didn't exactly let me in. I climbed over the gates and invited myself in.'

She turned and looked at me briefly, her expression half

exasperation, half resignation. Then she sighed. 'Come on, I'll give you a lift home.'

Maria locked up the office and we went out.

'Thanks for the car,' I said as we walked down the steps. 'Nice little number. When did you get it?'

'A fortnight ago.'

'You're obviously charging clients like me too much.'

'You haven't paid your last bill yet.'

'Haven't I?'

'And we sent the invoice out at least four months ago.'

Time for a change of subject.

'Why don't I drive?' I said brightly. 'You look tired.'

She glanced at me, not fooled for a second, but too weary to argue.

'Thanks. I don't think I can face the traffic right now.'

I opened the passenger door for her, then went round and got into the driver's seat. First task accomplished: I'd kept her away from the offside wing.

We hardly spoke on the journey to Burngreave. Maria sat with her head back, eyes closed, her briefcase resting on her lap. Occasionally I looked across at her, taking in that quiet beauty, the calm serenity of her face. I wanted to put an arm around her and let her sleep on my shoulder. But even in the confines of the car, just a yard or less apart, she was too far away for me. Maybe she'd always be too far away.

I touched her gently on the arm when we reached my flat. She awoke with a start and looked around.

'Oh, I must have dropped off.'

'You sure you're up to driving home, or do you want to come in for a bit?'

'I'll be all right. Thanks anyway.'

She smiled fleetingly. I nodded, disappointed and re-lieved at the same time. I wanted her to come in, but I didn't want her to see the squalor inside. She would hate the way I lived. I opened the door and got out. Maria slid across behind the wheel. I held the door open, leaning on the top, thinking suddenly, impulsively, of a way to see her again.

'You doing anything tomorrow night?' I said.

She hesitated. 'I don't know. Why?'

'I've got a couple of tickets for a show at the City Hall. Should be an experience. I'd like to say thank you for lending me your car. Will you come with me?'

She considered for a long moment. She'd turned down so many invitations in the past, I thought she was going to say no. But then she nodded. 'All right. Do you want a lift?'

'I'll meet you outside. It starts at eight.'

'I'd like that,' she said. 'I haven't been out for ages.'

I closed the door and watched her drive away, wondering if I'd done the right thing. I hadn't told her what the show was. But then some things are better as surprises.

CHAPTER 4

I had a long soak in the bath, letting the hot water soothe the pain in my bruised body. My left shoulder and ribs had already turned a nasty shade of purple and my elbow was starting to stiffen up where I'd landed on it. The rubber mats had cushioned my fall to an extent, but the impact had still jarred.

I relaxed in the deep, foaming tub and thought back over the previous twenty-four hours. I couldn't recall a more eventful day in my entire career as a journalist. One man dead, another nearly shot in broad daylight. A body in an armchair, eyes fixed on a blue movie they could no longer see, a pile of new electrical goods on a bedroom carpet, a hamster in a cage. A lonely house on the edge of the moors, a businessman with three bullets in his car and maybe another one somewhere with his name on it, a monstrous blonde in a pink leotard and a whole list of unanswered questions.

The events had happened so close to each other it was hard to separate them in my mind, even though the two cases were completely different. Yet it was the similarities which registered most. Two men with criminal records, physically unattractive men with suspect pasts and violent presents. One with an uncertain future, his life perhaps still in danger; the other with no future at all. And in both cases there was any number of people who might have hated them enough to want them dead. All I had to do now was find out which ones had translated their desires into action.

I pulled myself out of the water and got dried, then wandered into the bedroom in search of fresh clothes. I was down to my last two shirts, both creased and unironed, but at least they were clean. I put on one, in faded blue cotton, and consigned my old clothes to the swelling mound of dirty laundry in the corner of the room. I made a mental note to take a couple of days off work and hire a team of porters to accompany me to the launderette.

Now for something to eat. I went into the kitchen and opened all the cupboards. They were empty except for some spaghetti, a jar of sauce and a long cardboard packet so engulfed in a greenish fungus it was impossible to make out what it was. Or had been. Maybe I could make a bit of extra cash by growing mushrooms in here, I thought.

I took out the spaghetti and the sauce. The label on the jar said: 'Bolognese Sauce—just add meat.' That surely had to be an offence under the Trade Descriptions Act. How could it be Bolognese sauce if it didn't have meat in it? You might just as well sell a completely empty jar and label it: 'Bolognese Sauce—just add meat, water, tomatoes, garlic, onions and any other ingredient you feel like.'

I put the whole lot on to cook and settled down in an armchair with a copy of the *Evening News* I'd bought at the corner shop after Maria had dropped me off. The murder of Andy Peters was the splash, and the shooting at the

Titan Works the clumper along the bottom of the front page. My name was mentioned in the Peters story along with a mug shot of me they must have dug out of the files from the days when I worked at the *News*. The caption said: 'Freelance journalist, Mike McLean, who found the body.' It was a blurred photo, at least ten years old and such a poor resemblance it might have come from my passport.

I read both articles thoroughly. They contained nothing I didn't already know, and I was glad to see from the line, 'Mr Silvester was unavailable for comment,' that no one else had got any further with him than I had. I threw the paper on to the table and served up my spaghetti bolognese minus meat. It wasn't at all bad for a trade description offence.

Afterwards, I made a cup of tea and leafed through my notebook for the telephone number of Andy Peters' flat which I'd scribbled down from the dial when I was there last night. I called the number and let it ring. There was no reply, so I looked in the phone book and wrote down the address of the Sphinx Massage Parlour. It was time to follow up Harry Raymond's suggestion and talk to Dawn Peters.

The woman behind the reception desk was blowsy and overblown, hair piled high above a coarse, heavily made-up face, breasts sagging in a loose crimson dress which was cinched tight at the waist with a glitzy silver belt. She looked like the madam of a down-market brothel, which I suppose is what the Sphinx was.

She looked me over carefully as I walked in, sizing me up, then waited for me to speak first. Maybe she thought I was a cop.

'I'm looking for Dawn Peters,' I said.

'Oh yes.' Not a question, nor a statement, just a prompt for more information.

'Does she work here still?'

'Who wants to know?'

I told her my name. Her eyes flicked over my face and down my body. Shrewd, diamond eyes with lifeless centres.

'You come for a massage?'

'No.'

'Then see her some other time, she's working right now.'

I could see this was going to cost me. 'What's the charge for a massage?'

'You pay ten pounds now, that's the registration fee.' She made it sound as if I was signing on for an evening class. 'Anything else you negotiate with the masseuse.'

I didn't ask what she meant. I took a ten-pound note out of my wallet and handed it to her. She put it away in a drawer and gave me a cloakroom ticket.

'You give that to the girl.'

The number on the ticket was sixty-nine. I wondered if that was the tally of clients for the night, or some in-house joke.

'You want Dawn, I take it?'

'Yes.'

'She's engaged at the moment. You'll have to wait.'

She nodded at a couple of plastic chairs against the wall. I sat down and inspected the room. I'd never been in a massage parlour before, straight or illegitimate. Was there such a thing as a straight massage parlour?

I hadn't missed much. It was done out like a dentist's waiting room, only less welcoming. The walls were bare, painted plain white, and the floor was covered in heavy-duty industrial carpet. They probably needed it to cope with the throughput. The only personal touches were a vase of plastic flowers on the reception desk and, on the low table in front of me, a stack of magazines: *Penthouse*, *Mayfair*, *Men Only* and, somewhat incongruously, a well-thumbed copy of *House and Garden*.

The woman behind the desk said: 'You want a drink while you're waiting?'

'Why not, what've you got?'

'Beer, whisky, or you can have a cup of tea if you like.'

A cup of tea? What kind of place was this? Did she not realize she was destroying all my illusions about brothels?

I opted for the beer. She took a can of Tetley bitter and a plastic beaker out of a drawer and brought them over, then charged me three quid. It's an expensive business being a pervert.

After ten minutes or so, a door in the far wall opened and a man in a smart grey suit came out carrying a large salesman's briefcase. He was either another client or the Durex rep. He nodded to the woman at the desk and went out.

'OK,' she said to me. 'She's free now.'

I finished my beer and stood up. 'Where do I find her?'

'Third door along on the left.'

I went through into a narrow corridor lined with doors. I knocked on one and entered. The room inside was about seven feet square, harshly lit and just big enough for a chair and a high padded couch, the sort you find in a doctor's surgery. Sitting on the chair, smoking a cigarette, was a woman in a pink robe. She glanced up without interest as I came in.

I said: 'Are you Dawn Peters?'

She nodded listlessly. 'You got your ticket?'

I gave her the cloakroom ticket. She tucked it away in the pocket of her robe and stubbed out her cigarette.

'Get on the couch. How do you want it?'

Businesslike, utterly detached, not even pretending to look on me as anything other than a paying customer. I couldn't imagine why any man came here.

'Can we talk?' I said.

She pulled a face. 'Jesus, not another one who wants to talk. What is it, your wife, your girlfriend, your kids?'

'Your husband.'

Dawn went very still. Her face was expressionless, nothing registering at all. Then she said: 'He's dead.' Even then there was no emotion.

'I know. I was the one who found his body.'

She looked up at me, surprised. 'You're the journalist?'

I nodded. 'I want to ask you a few questions. I tried phoning, but—'

She didn't let me finish. 'Not now, I'm working. I can't afford to waste time on chat. Does *she* know why you're here?' She inclined her head towards the reception.

'No. She thinks I'm just another punter. I won't keep you long.'

Dawn held out a hand. 'Give us a tenner. For my time. I could be earning while I'm gassing to you.'

'I've already paid ten pounds.'

'That was for her. This is for me.'

I took my wallet out and handed over my last ten-pound note. This really was proving an expensive night. It had better be worth it.

Dawn lit another cigarette and offered the packet to me. I shook my head and sat down on the edge of the couch. She looked about thirty-five but the thick make-up and fluorescent lighting did her no favours. She might have been three years younger, or older. Her hair was loose around her shoulders, dyed blonde but with the original mousy brown coming through at the roots. Underneath it all she might have been passably pretty, but the surface was so off-putting I couldn't see anyone wanting to probe deeper. Maybe she didn't want them to.

'So what do you want to ask me?' Dawn said.

'About Andy. Did he ever mention my name to you? Particularly over the last few days.'

'No. Until the police told me you'd found the body, I'd never heard of you. Why?'

'He rang me up last night. Said he wanted to talk to me. You don't know about what, do you?'

'He never said anything to me. But then we didn't talk much at the best of times.'

'Did he have something on his mind? Something he might have confided in you.'

She laughed sharply. 'If he did, I'd've been the last to know. Or care.'

'You don't seem too upset about his death.'

'I'm not.' She blew smoke out of the side of her mouth. 'Look, we were married for twelve years. For one of them he was in Egypt on a building contract, the only proper job he ever had. For eight more he was inside, on and off. He only came out long enough each time to get caught again, stupid sod. I learnt to live without him, and I'm sorry he went the way he did, but don't expect me to sob my eyes out with grief.'

She appeared callous, but it was difficult to tell if she was really that unfeeling, or whether it was simply a mechanism for protecting herself. Hardening herself against the pain of loss.

'Do you know who murdered him?'

'No. The police asked me that this morning. Some wanker of a sergeant even suggested I might have done it.'

That would have been Chris Strange. He'd enjoy that description. 'And what did you say?'

'I was here all night. And besides, why should I do him in? What would I have gained?'

'Money? Freedom?'

Dawn snorted. 'Freedom? I've got all the freedom I want. And money? Andy didn't have the money. He lived off me. When he was at home.'

'He had enough to buy a new television and hi-fi.' She gave me an enquiring stare. 'I saw them upstairs.'

She shrugged. 'I don't know where the cash for that came from.'

'Did he steal it?'

'He certainly didn't earn it.'

She crossed her legs. The pink robe fell away from her knee, briefly exposing the inside of her thigh. I knew she was naked under the robe. A different woman, a different setting, it might have been erotic. But not here.

'Someone searched your flat,' I said.

'Don't I bleedin' well know it. It took me hours to clean it all up.'

'Do you know why? Was Andy hiding something?'

'He was a secretive man. But there was nothing of value in the place. Nothing anyone would want.' She narrowed her eyes at me. It gave her a sleek, curiously feline look. 'What's your interest in all this?'

'Someone had a reason for killing him,' I said. 'And Andy was frightened when he rang me. I think he knew his life was in danger. Had he been behaving differently recently?'

'Not that I noticed.'

'How did he spend his time? Did he have a job?'

Dawn laughed contemptuously. 'A job? You joking?'

'What about other work? Did he do any break-ins?'

'I don't know.' She looked at her watch. 'Your time's nearly up.'

'It's important, Dawn. Maybe not to you, but it is to me. I feel involved in all this. If I'd got to your flat fifteen minutes earlier Andy might still be alive. If you can't help me, give me the name of someone else who might. Don't you want to know why he died?'

She held my gaze for a while, thinking it over.

'You don't have to get involved,' I said. 'I won't mention your name.'

'All right,' she said finally. 'He did do a job, the week before last. I don't know what it was, but it must have paid because he was throwing money around like confetti a few days later.'

'Did he do it alone?'

Dawn shook her head. 'With a friend. Tony Napier.'

The name was familiar for some reason. I couldn't remember why.

'Where do I find him?'

She half smiled. 'He's away.'

'Away where?'

'Nice little place, over near Hull. The Wolds, it's called.'

I knew suddenly why she'd smiled. 'Wolds Remand Prison?'

'He got caught red-handed last weekend on a different job. Not with Andy.'

I sighed. That complicated things. Made them more difficult, but maybe not impossible.

'Thanks. I hope I haven't taken too much of your time.'

'You paid for it.'

I pushed myself up from the couch and felt a twinge of pain in my side. The battered muscles were starting to stiffen up. What I needed was a good rub.

I said: 'Do you actually know anything about massage?'

Dawn grinned. For the first time her face looked animated, the air of bored weariness dropping away. Maybe this was the real her.

'Depends which bit of you you want massaging,' she said.

She stood up and took a pace towards me. 'You're not bad looking you know. I'll give you one for nothing if you like.'

She was playing games with me now. She let her robe fall open provocatively. I caught a glimpse of the curve of a breast and a dark shadow lower down.

In the best traditions of journalism, I made my excuses and left.

I sensed something was wrong the moment I walked into my flat. It was hard to identify exactly what, but I knew someone had been in during my absence.

The front door lock showed no signs of having been tampered with, but the living-room just didn't look the same. My possessions were strewn all over the place, odd items of clothing dumped on chairs, dirty plates and mugs gathering dust where I'd left them. That was normal. Yet the mess was different. There's a certain order to my untidiness which makes it very personal. To an outsider it might look simply chaotic; to me it has a distinct familiarity which only I can appreciate. That familiarity had gone.

I examined the room carefully. The furniture had been moved, I was sure. The legs of the table and armchair had been put back just fractionally out of line so they no longer nestled in the holes they'd sunk in the carpet. I checked the desk. It all looked in order, but someone had been through the notes I'd made for my article on the decline of the South Yorkshire coalfield. The sheets of paper were stacked too neatly for me.

In the bedroom, the mound of laundry was still where I'd left it, but there was a different shirt on the top. And the wedge of cardboard I used to keep the wardrobe doors shut had been put back in the wrong place.

I was intrigued. Someone had been very thorough, and competent. They knew how to open locks without damaging them, how to search a place with the minimum of disruption. They'd slipped up on one or two minor points but it still looked like a professional job to me. I thought suddenly of Andy Peters' flat. How different that had looked. Yet was it a coincidence that twenty-four hours later my own flat had also been searched?

I got undressed and went to bed. For a long while I lay awake thinking, wondering what the searchers had been looking for. And why they thought I might have it.

CHAPTER 5

The morning was cold, the chill January air penetrating deep into the flat. There was ice on the inside of the bedroom window and when I exhaled, my breath drifted upwards towards the ceiling in a fine cirrus cloud. I got up late again, reluctant to leave the warm embrace of the duvet, and sat huddled in front of the gas fire in the living-room with three jumpers on. Oh for the comforts of central heating.

I made some tea and toast and rang Directory Inquiries

for the number of Wolds Remand Prison. Then I telephoned the prison itself and asked about visiting Tony
Napier the following day. It was easier than I expected.
No appointment necessary, visiting hours eight-thirty to
eleven-thirty, one to five.

Gordon Crieff was next in line for a call.

'Are ye nae coming in this morning then?' he said, after
we'd exchanged a few pleasantries.

'You missing me? Maybe later, Gordon. Now what about
the Andy Peters case? You got anywhere?'

Crieff made a sucking noise between his teeth. It sounded
like interference on the line.

'Progress is slow.'

'What does that mean?'

'It means we've got bloody nowhere, but it's tae embarrassing to admit.'

I chuckled. 'I won't quote you on that. What about
James Silvester?'

'A bit better, but nae much. I've got a ballistics report
if you're interested.'

'What does it say?'

'They found three bullets embedded in various bits of
Silvester's Mercedes. All fired from the same rifle.'

'D'you know from where?'

'From the trajectories, they think the assassin was up the
hill, on a wee patch of wasteland which overlooks the car
park at the back of Silvester's office.'

'How far's that?'

'Two hundred and fifty yards at least.'

'That's some shooting.'

'Nae good enough though. Two of the bullets hit the front
passenger seat, the other shattered the rear-view mirror and
ended up in the boot.'

'Silvester's a lucky man. I don't suppose you've got any
witnesses, have you? Or even a suspect.'

'Nope. The gunman appears to have done his stuff and
disappeared without trace.'

I took a sip of my tea, thinking.

'Ye still there?' Crieff asked.

'Mmmm.' I swallowed, then said: 'It's a curious way to do things, don't you think? If I wanted someone dead I wouldn't have a go from two hundred and fifty yards. I'd have to be a crack marksman even to get near him.'

'Maybe he wasnae as good as he thought.'

'And why only three bullets? If he's going to take that kind of risk, why not empty the magazine and shorten the odds?'

'Ye asking me?'

'No, just mulling things over. What's the unofficial theory about it all?'

'I dinna deal in theories, laddie, only facts.'

'Come on, Gordon, give me an idea. Someone must know something. Silvester's an old friend, isn't he?'

There was a pause on the line. Then Crieff said: 'What d'ye mean?'

'I know he's got a record. There must be something in his file to give you a lead, surely.'

'I told ye, Mike, we've got nothing to go on.'

'Has Silvester been any more forthcoming?'

'No.'

'What if the assassin tries again? Has Silvester asked for police protection?'

'Not to my knowledge.'

That was interesting. If someone had just tried to shoot me, I'd have been screaming my head off for armed guards.

'Maybe he's going to handle it himself,' I ventured. 'He's that type of bloke, isn't he?'

Crieff didn't take the bait. 'Ye think I'm stupid enough to play guessing games with a journalist?'

'OK, Gordon, thanks anyway. Let me know if anything else comes up.'

'It has. Not to do with this. But Chris Strange asked me to tell ye, they've found your car.'

'They have? Where?'

'That's the good news.'

I sagged back in my armchair. I knew what the bad news was.

'Don't tell me. A write-off.'

'I'm afraid so. Burnt out completely.'

'Shit.' I hammered a cushion with my fist. 'That's all I need.'

'I'm sorry, Mike. The remains are in the pound. Give them a call.'

'I'll take care of it. Thanks, Gordon.'

I put the receiver down slowly and stared at the wall. I wished now I'd stayed in bed.

Hughie O'Donnell was Burngreave's resident professional Irishman. A small, ruddy-cheeked man with rampant eyebrows and a white streak in his hair like a badger's stripe.

He ran a second-hand car business from a disused service station behind the cemetery and favoured loud shirts, suits with lapels that reached his armpits and an exhausting line in sales patter. In all, the archetypal used-car dealer, if it hadn't been for one unfortunate character defect that forever sullied his reputation. He was honest.

I found him inside the dilapidated wooden hut which served as his office, warming himself by an electric fan heater. He was a devout, but undogmatic, Catholic and on the walls of the hut were a crucifix, a picture of the Virgin Mary and a framed letter from the Vatican thanking him for his tireless charitable work over the years. It had such a religious atmosphere I felt as if I ought to crawl in on my knees.

'Mike, my boy!' Hughie said, standing up and wringing my hand in his horny palm. 'Where've you been all this time? You must call in more often. Here, take a pew.'

That wasn't just a figure of speech either for he really did have an old church pew in his office, sawn into sections to make individual chairs. I dragged one up nearer the heater and sat down, holding my frozen hands in the flow of warm air. Hughie seemed delighted to see me.

'What can I do for you?' he said.

'I'm looking for a car.'

'Really?' He was even more delighted to see me. He wasn't *that* different from other dealers. He took out a bottle of whisky and filled two glasses. It was early in the day, but too cold to worry about the time.

'Get some of this down you, take the edge off this terrible weather.'

I sipped the spirit gratefully while Hughie launched into a long diatribe about the English winter, comparing it unfavourably to the mild, indeed almost Mediterranean, climate of his native Galway. I let him ramble on for a few minutes and, when he surfaced for air, said: 'About the car, Hughie.'

'Oh yes, the car. I'll be forgetting me own name next. Now what are you looking for? You see anything outside you like? I've got a lovely F-reg Astra, came in last week. Only fifty thousand on the clock, good bodywork, well looked after.'

'One careful lady owner, I suppose?'

'It's funny you should say that. You're right. A nun. Sister Mary-Louise from St Joseph's Convent School. You know her? Wonderful lady. Getting on a bit now though, and her eyesight's fading. Very sensible of her to give up driving. It's a fine car. Been to Lourdes and back four times but it's in beautiful nick. You want to see it?'

The thought of driving around in a nun's car was too much for me. It seemed so, well, inhibiting, for someone with my habits.

'It sounds a bit expensive,' I said.

'How much are you looking to pay?'

'Five hundred at the most.'

Hughie pursed his lips, then assumed the concerned tone of a priest in the confession box. 'Now, Mike, do you really

think that's wise? You want a few years out of it, don't you?
It never pays to make false economies.'

'It's all I can afford.'

'You trading in?'

I shook my head. 'Not unless you'll give me anything for
a box of cinders.'

I told him what had happened to my Cortina. He clicked
his tongue sympathetically.

'I'll see what I can do. Come outside.'

I downed the last of my whisky. It was like acid on my
throat. I followed Hughie out on to the forecourt and we
walked down the rows of cars to the edge of the lot. Hidden
away behind a transit van was an orange and white Lada.
I studied it for a while before I realized it was actually a
white Lada; the orange was rust.

'It's not much,' Hughie said. 'Eight years old. But it goes
all right. It's done only eighty thousand miles, though I
suspect someone's put the clock back. Not me, of course.
For you, I'll make it the Deal of the Week.'

He was perfectly serious. An eight-year-old Lada with
180,000 miles under what was left of the bonnet. The Deal
of the Week? He was beginning to sound like a real second-
hand car dealer.

'Shouldn't you be paying me to take it off your hands?'
I said.

He looked genuinely hurt. 'Please, Mike, this is a fine
car. It's yours for three fifty.'

'Three pounds fifty. That's a bit steep, isn't it?'

He ignored the comment. 'It's all I have for under five
hundred. I'll give you a six-month warranty too. What
d'you say?'

I looked the Lada over. It probably wouldn't last more
than six months, but I needed a car.

'Two fifty,' I said.

Hughie brushed his long hair out of his eyes. 'OK. If
you buy some raffle tickets too. For the church roof fund.'

We went back into the hut and did the deal. Two hundred and fifty pounds cleaned me out almost completely. Hughie took a cheque and let me drive the car away without waiting for the cheque to clear. He was that kind of man.

I headed down Burngreave Road towards town. The car didn't exactly purr like a well-oiled machine, but the asthmatic growl of the exhaust was reassuring for one reason at least. No self-respecting joyrider would dream of stealing a Lada.

'You want a jam doughnut?' Harry Raymond said.

We were in the cluttered back room of his locksmith's shop, drinking coffee amid piles of cardboard boxes and surplus stock.

I said: 'I thought you were on a diet?'

'I can't starve myself, can I? Got to keep me energy levels up.'

He opened the safe on the wall and took out a large paper bag. He held it out and I helped myself to a doughnut.

'Why do you keep them in the safe, Harry?' I asked.

'Where else would I keep 'em?'

It wasn't worth pursuing it. I bit into the doughnut. It was dried out and stale.

'How long've you had these?'

'Only a week. Got a job lot from the bakery. Fifty for two quid. Don't you like it? Dunk it in your coffee, they taste better like that.'

He sat down in the tatty armchair opposite me and picked up the copy of the Yellow Pages he'd been flicking through when I arrived.

'What're you looking for?' I said.

'Somewhere to take the wife. It's our anniversary tomorrow.'

'Wedding? How long?'

'I'm trying to forget.'

'Come on, Harry.'

'Twenty years.' He didn't sound as if he regarded it as a cause for celebration.

'What are you planning to do?'

'I dunno. Last year I just gave 'er some flowers but she weren't best pleased.'

'Why not?'

'I nicked 'em from the graveyard on me way 'ome. How were I to know there were a card tucked in the middle of 'em which said: "To my dear departed Grandad in loving memory"?'

I smiled. 'Yes, I can see she might not have taken that too well. You going out for a meal?'

'That's why I'm looking in 'ere. You know any good restaurants?'

'There's the Frog near the cathedral.'

Harry winced. 'Do me a favour. You seen the prices they charge there?'

'I thought it was a special occasion.'

'Not that special. I think maybe I'll take 'er to the pictures. I 'ate watching films, but at least then we don't 'ave to talk to each other.'

The joys of marriage. I thought back to my own three years of wedlock, mercifully long ended. It had seemed hard when we were breaking up, but at least we'd never got to the stage of going to the pictures to avoid talking to each other. Maybe that was where we went wrong. Perhaps the couples that stay together do just that.

Harry threw the Yellow Pages on to the floor and finished off his doughnut in two enormous bites.

'What brings you down 'ere?' he asked, his mouth bulging.

'I wanted to pick your brains. You heard of someone called Tony Napier, friend of Andy Peters'?'

He nodded, swallowing his doughnut before saying: 'What about 'im?'

'Who is he?'

'Like you said, a crony of Andy's. They used to 'ang about together. Andy was the leader, Tony the follower.

Did whatever he was told. Weak-willed, one of life's mugs, not enough guts to make his own decisions.'

'Why do I know his name?'

'Do you?' Harry thought for a time. 'Could be that court case a few years back. You cover that?'

'Which court case?'

'That obscenity trial. Snow White. Tony was the artist.'

It all came back to me now. 'Of course. Was Andy involved in that?'

'No. Why're you interested in Tony?'

'Dawn Peters mentioned him.'

'You've spoken to 'er then? She doesn't think Tony killed Andy, does she?'

'No. She said they did a job together. I think it might be relevant. I'm going to see Tony tomorrow, at Wolds Remand Prison.'

Harry didn't seem remotely surprised. 'So he's back inside, is he?'

'Will you write a note for me, Harry? Something I can show to Tony so he knows who I am, knows he can trust me.'

'Sure. You got any paper?'

I passed him my notebook and he scribbled a few words on a blank page. He held it out to me.

'That do?'

'Perfect. Thanks.' I took the notebook back and slipped it into my pocket.

The bell on the shop door tinkled. Harry rolled his eyes and levered himself out of his armchair.

'Bloody customers, always bothering me. 'Elp yourself to another doughnut.'

'Thanks, but I'd rather hang on to my teeth, if it's all the same to you.'

He was gone about five minutes. I drank my coffee and wondered how I was going to broach the other topic on my mind.

'Two more deadlocks off the shelf,' Harry said, coming

back in and sitting down. 'Thirty quid apiece, you know. But it's cheaper than patching up after a burglary. You want some more coffee?'

I shook my head. 'There's something else, Harry. Something you might well know. If I wanted to rub someone out, is there anyone round here who could take care of it for me?'

Harry stared at me. There were traces of jam on his lips. 'Don't ask me questions like that, Mike.'

'There's no one else I can ask. I'm serious. Is there anyone in Sheffield?'

It was a moment before he replied. 'I don't know much about that kind of thing. I got out of that world a long time ago.'

'I know,' I said. 'But you're still a lot closer to it than I am.'

This wasn't something he wanted to talk about. His shoulders moved dismissively. 'I suppose if you went to the right pub you'd probably find 'alf a dozen boys who'd do it if the money were right.'

'I don't mean a couple of thugs who'd knock someone over in a dark alley. I mean a pro. Someone who can shoot a rifle from a quarter of a mile and hit the target.'

His eyes came back to my face. 'You'd better give me the rest of it.'

I told him about James Silvester and the shooting at the Titan Works.

'You think that was a pro?' he said, when I'd finished.

'Maybe.'

'But he missed.'

'I know. But there're two ways of looking at it. Either he wasn't very good. Or he was very good indeed.'

Harry squinted at me. 'What you on about?'

'Everyone is assuming the gunman tried to hit Silvester and failed. But there's another possibility. He tried to miss him, and succeeded.'

'Why should 'e do that?'

'I don't know. Maybe to warn him. A few shots across the bows. That's why he only fired three bullets. A pro intending to kill Silvester would have seen he was still alive after three and finished the job with the rest of the magazine. This fellow left it at that. Why? I think this is more complicated than it seems.'

'You're certainly making it that way.'

'Is there anyone round here?' I asked again.

Harry looked down at his hands, rubbing them together anxiously. His heavy jowls seemed to droop under the weight of some undisclosed burden.

'What is it?' I said.

'I don't go in for giving advice much.' He paused. 'And I've never known you take any. But I 'ope you know what you're doing. This isn't something you should mess with.'

'Let me worry about that, Harry. Give me a name.'

He sipped his coffee, but didn't reply. I gave him time to think it over. Then I prompted gently: 'I'll be careful. A name.'

'I'm not sure I want you to know that now. But in the past there were talk about him. No proof, no real evidence, but the word on the street said he were for hire. And good.'

'Who?'

'They call him the Bandit. I've never met him, but he's dangerous, Mike. I mean that.'

'My eyes are wide open. Where do I find him?'

'It could've been someone from out of town. What makes you think he were local?'

'It's a good place to start,' I said. 'Silvester's been here all his life. His business dealings all take place here. He's clearly upset someone. It's more than likely that someone is also local. Maybe someone who knows who to hire from around here.'

Harry hesitated. 'You're making a mistake, Mike. Maybe one you'll regret.'

'Don't be so melodramatic. Where do I find him?'

'His real name's Crispin May. He's got a shop on Ecclesall Road. Interior design.'

I didn't expect that. 'He has a *shop?*'

'Don't believe only what you see on the surface. This bloke's different.' Harry licked the jam off his lips. 'You're going to see him, aren't you?'

'Perhaps.'

'Don't.'

I studied Harry's face. 'You're frightened, why?'

'For you. Don't go, Mike, it's not worth it for some poxy story.'

I felt a prickling sensation down my back, like pins and needles in my spine. Maybe Harry's fear was contagious.

'I'm only thinking about it,' I said reassuringly. 'More likely than not, I won't bother.'

But I knew I would. I was that kind of fool.

I pulled in by the kerb and turned off the ignition. The Lada's engine shuddered violently and took a few seconds finally to cut out. I let my ears recover in the silence while I looked out of the window at the shop across the road.

Crispin May Design had a double frontage in between an antique shop and an up-market boutique. It looked pretty much like every other interior design business I'd ever seen. Some fancy graphics on the sign, a few manufacturers' names stencilled on the glass, window displays of curtain material, soft furnishings and a mock kitchen and bathroom done out in striking primary colours, no doubt the latest fashion in interior décor.

It was the last place I would have thought of looking for a hired killer. But maybe that made it the best place for one to hide.

I lifted up the handle to open the car door, and stopped suddenly. Someone was coming out of the shop. A woman. Jesus! I ducked down quickly, concealing my face. It was Pinky Silvester.

I poked a cautious eye over the dashboard and watched

her. She turned right along the pavement and walked up the street. She had a distinctly feminine gait despite her lumberjack build. Her clothes were pink again, though this time the leotard had been replaced by a long flowing skirt and a smart woollen jacket over a high-necked pullover. She was wearing knee-length black boots which clicked on the paving stones and carrying a leather shoulder bag only slightly smaller than a mail sack.

She got into the green Range-Rover and drove away, banging her horn and pulling out across the oncoming traffic to barge her way in between two cars. She drove with the same unique subtlety that characterized the welcome she gave visitors to her home.

Interesting, though. I wondered what business she'd been transacting in the shop. It might have been entirely innocent, of course—a preliminary call to discuss new cushion covers or the drapes in the bedroom—but I had a suspicious mind, particularly as far as Pinky Silvester was concerned. Was it a coincidence that the day after her husband was nearly killed she was paying a visit on someone I'd been reliably informed was a professional assassin?

Perhaps. But in my mind she was always going to be guilty until proven innocent. I might have been doing her an injustice, but first impressions are often telling. She'd made a powerful impact on my consciousness that one time we'd met. And an even more powerful impact on my ribs.

I crossed the road and entered the shop. The inside was as predictable as the outside. More fake rooms built on plinths with every item carefully matched, everything immaculate and contrived, rooms bearing no resemblance to any that real people actually live in. Lifeless façades, as fake and misleading as Santa's Grotto.

Standing behind a counter at one side was a man in his mid-twenties. Tall, brawny, with the swollen muscles and shrunken brain of the committed body builder. He had a deep suntan, probably from a UV lamp, the pretty but vapid looks of a male model and dead eyes. If this was

Crispin May, the dangerous hitman, I was disappointed. He had all the menace of a stick insect.

He smiled at me automatically, revealing neatly capped teeth which looked as if they glowed in the dark.

'Good afternoon, sir. Can I help you?'

I moved towards him. 'Crispin May?'

He shook his head. 'Did you want Crispin? I handle most things out here. Are you sure I can't be of assistance?'

'I'd like to see Mr May if he's in. Is he?'

The young man examined me. I returned his gaze equably. There was still nothing in his eyes. I got the impression of bulk with no substance behind it. He might have been a cardboard cut-out.

'I'll see if he's free.'

He went to a door at the back of the shop, knocked and entered. A few seconds elapsed, then Crispin May emerged. I don't know exactly what I expected, but it certainly wasn't the man who came out of the office.

He must have been pushing fifty, in good shape but nevertheless showing a few signs of age. A paunchiness around the middle, the beginnings of a double chin, thinning hair and the slightly flushed complexion of someone who likes a drink or two. He was elegantly dressed in a cream suit, cream shoes, black waistcoat and matching bow tie. Glinting on his right wrist was a heavy diamond bracelet. He looked more like a hairdresser than a hitman.

He crossed the shop towards me. It was then that I noticed the left sleeve of his jacket dangling free. The shock stunned me momentarily. He only had one arm.

'What can I do for you?' he said. He had a soft, cultured voice bordering on the effeminate.

I recovered my composure. I'd almost decided to walk out, but I'd come this far. I had to make sure.

'Mr May?' I said, hoping there'd been some mistake.

'Yes. I'm Crispin May. You wished to see me, I gather.'

I thought fast. 'I was interested in discussing a few ideas with you. For a . . .' I glanced around the shop quickly,

'. . . well, a kitchen. I'm thinking of installing a new kitchen.'

'Indeed? Perhaps you'd like to talk things through with Gavin here first. He is most knowledgeable about kitchens. And bathrooms, and bedrooms. Aren't you, Gavin?'

Crispin touched the young man familiarly on the arm and smiled at him. 'I'll leave it in your capable hands, darling.' He started to go back to his office.

'Mr May.' He turned. 'I'd particularly like to discuss things with you. You were recommended to me by Mrs Silvester.'

I threw it in on impulse, to test his reaction. His inscrutable expression didn't change.

'Ah, you know Penelope, do you?'

So that was her real name. I didn't think it likely she'd been christened Pinky.

'She said I should speak to you personally.'

'Did she?' He stroked his jaw thoughtfully, his eyes never leaving my face. Then he made a decision. 'Come into the office.'

I followed him through. He closed the door behind us and went to a table under the window.

'Sit down, please. I was just about to have some tea. Would you join me?'

'Thank you.'

He busied himself at the table, his back towards me. I inspected his desk. It didn't take me long. There was nothing on it except a plain white envelope. No papers, no out- or in-trays, not a thing to indicate he did any work on it. It was the tidiest desk I'd ever seen. There was something pathological there. Never trust tidy people is my motto.

I took a closer look at the envelope. It was addressed to Crispin May, but had no stamp on the front. Hand delivered. Probably very recently. May was not the sort of person to leave things lying around on his pristine desktop for very long.

I glanced at him. He was filling a teapot with boiling

water from a kettle. It was worth the risk. I lifted up the envelope and peeked inside quickly. It contained a thin strip of shiny card. I saw the word Lyceum and the date, January 12th. It was a theatre ticket.

May started to turn. I put the envelope back hurriedly and folded my arms. I was pretty sure the ticket had been delivered by Pinky Silvester. I wondered why.

'I do think afternoon tea is such a civilized tradition, don't you?' May said, putting a tray down on the desk.

'Oh yes,' I agreed. 'I never miss it.'

'Milk?'

'Please.'

He poured milk into a china cup from a matching jug.

'I always put the milk in first. The tea tastes better that way, I believe. I'm told it's something to do with the enzymes in the milk neutralizing the tannin in the tea, taking away some of that bitter edge. It doesn't work if you put the tea in first.'

I nodded, pretending I knew what he was talking about. As far as I was concerned, the only thing milk did to tea was turn it white.

May sat down in his chair and smoothed his silvery hair back with the tips of his fingers.

'Do have a scone,' he said, offering me the plate. 'I baked them myself last night. I find bought scones are so tasteless. I think it's all the preservatives they put in. I'm a firm believer in natural ingredients, aren't you? They're so much healthier.

'I'm afraid that's butter on them. You eat butter, I hope. I do my best to keep down my fat intake but I do draw the line at those dreadful low-fat spreads. There's nothing quite like butter on scones, even if it is bad for the tummy.'

This had to be a wind-up. A gay, one-armed hitman who baked his own scones. What else did he do, work nights for the Samaritans? I made a firm resolution to break Harry Raymond's legs for setting me up like this.

'Now,' Crispin May said. 'What about your kitchen?'

I had to go through with it. 'Well,' I began, 'I want to start from scratch, new sink, new units, the lot. What would you suggest?'

'Let me get you some brochures. That will give you an idea of what's available.'

For the next twenty minutes we talked about kitchens: laminated surfaces, split-level cookers, fan-assisted ovens, waste disposal units, concealed lighting, built-in dish-washers, Scandinavian pine, teak veneer, a mammoth list of subjects I had never discussed before and never wanted to discuss again.

I sat opposite him, sipping tea and nibbling a scone, pretending to be fascinated, thinking: If only my ex-wife could see me now. What am I doing here? This man has never done a hit in his life. What the hell is a marbled Italian draining board?

Yet, as I half listened to him describing his philosophy of kitchen design, I began to wonder if there wasn't more to Crispin May than met the eye. Indeed Harry had told me quite specifically not to believe only what I saw on the surface, and Harry was someone I'd always trusted. Perhaps I was being unjust in doubting him. If he said Crispin May was rumoured to be for hire, then there was probably some substance to it. Harry's contacts were good and he certainly hadn't faked his concern for my safety. He truly believed May was a dangerous person to meddle with. Maybe I'd do well to be wary of him.

I studied the man behind the desk, the cream suit, the manicured fingers, the smooth complexion with no hint of facial hair. He was so different from my idea of an assassin that it was difficult to focus on him properly. Yet what did an assassin look like? I'd never met one. My perception was based entirely on the clichés of the cinema. If he didn't have a trench coat with a pistol in the hip pocket, or spats and an exaggerated Italian accent, did that mean he couldn't be the genuine article?

What better cover could there be for the serious

professional than the soft-spoken, effeminate interior
designer in front of me? He had the face of a choir boy, but
then anyone who's been within a hundred yards of a church
vestry on a Sunday morning knows what choir boys are
really like.

'I do hope I've been of some help to you,' Crispin May
said.

'Pardon? Oh, yes, it's been a revelation,' I replied.

He stood up. 'Do get in touch again when you've studied
the brochures and made up your mind.'

'I will, thank you.'

I hesitated. May looked at me enquiringly. I had to make
an attempt to find out. Why else had I bothered to come?

'There was one other thing,' I said. 'Nothing to do with
kitchens. But I thought you might be able to help.'

He sat down again and fixed me with his pale blue eyes,
eyes which had a hypnotic intensity. I had his full attention
all right. I wondered if he knew what was coming, if this
had happened many times before.

I chose my words carefully. 'There's someone who's caus-
ing me a little bit of trouble. A small indiscretion on my
part, I won't go into it. But they will continue to give me
problems unless I do something about it. Are you with me
so far?'

'I'm not sure I am,' May said. 'But go on.'

'Well, I hope you know what I mean.' I paused. I was
trying to be circumspect. Anything more direct, I sensed,
would frighten him off if he really was for hire. 'What I
need is a solution. A permanent solution.'

I knew I'd blown it the moment I spoke. Why, I didn't
know. For just an instant his eyes flared. I saw cold, steely
fire in the pupils. An anger and ruthlessness that suddenly
seemed his true character. Instinctively, I knew I'd been
right to wonder about him.

Then he was back in control, the mask in place. He
forced a benign smile but it was too late. I'd seen behind
the façade. And what I'd seen frightened me.

He stood up abruptly. 'I'm afraid I don't know what you're talking about.'

'My mistake. I've obviously been misinformed.'

'Obviously,' he said icily.

He came round the desk and opened the office door. If he didn't know what I was talking about, why the sudden change of manner? Why the agitation in place of the relaxed informality?

He seemed to take hold of himself as we crossed the shop and at the door he was all smiles and bonhomie again. We shook hands and I left clutching my pile of brochures.

When I got back to the car, I found my palms were sweating, my heart thumping just a bit faster than normal. Crispin May was watching me impassively from the window of his shop.

I began to pray my instincts were wrong, that he was nothing more than a harmless interior designer. If my instincts were right, I'd probably just walked out with a price on my head.

CHAPTER 6

Maria came up the steps of the City Hall towards me. I watched her, taking in the slim shape under the billowing folds of her open coat, the light accentuating the soft lines of her face, the midnight hair. She had no business looking so lovely. And I had no business standing there waiting for her. Yet once in a while we get lucky, and the things we don't deserve fall right into our hands. If only for an evening.

She was slightly out of breath when she reached me. 'Sorry, am I late? I couldn't find anywhere to park.'

She smiled. I looked at her, not saying anything. Just looking. She turned away shyly. She was wearing a black skirt and a cream sweater with a simple design embroidered on it in silver thread. I felt an ache deep in the pit of my stomach.

'Have you been here long?' she said, the silence embarrassing her.

'Just a couple of minutes.'

'Shall we go in?'

We went through the doors into the warmth of the foyer. It was bustling with people.

'I forgot to ask,' Maria said. 'What is it we're seeing?'

I forced a path through the crowd, pretending not to have heard. I showed our tickets to the usher.

'We're upstairs, in the circle.'

'I'm impressed. I don't usually go up there.'

'For you,' I said. 'The best seats in the house.'

We went up the broad, carpeted steps. In front of us was a large group of men and women, a noisy, raucous group. The women nearly all blonde or tinted, shoe-horned into skimpy dresses; the men looking like over-the-hill boxers: battered faces, squashed noses, a collective IQ only just into double figures. They were passing a bottle of vodka around between them.

Maria said: 'I'm looking forward to this. I haven't heard any live music for months.'

One of the Piltdown Men ahead of us swayed suddenly sideways, his arm swinging round drunkenly as he tried to regain his balance. I caught his wrist just before it hit Maria in the face.

'Now then, watch it.'

He turned his head and eyed me belligerently, his other hand balling automatically into a fist. I pushed him away firmly and guided Maria round the side of the group, hoping he was too drunk to bother coming after me. I didn't want to leave on crutches.

Maria glanced back briefly, her nose wrinkling with distaste.

'There are some strange people here. What a horrible man.'

I was beginning to have doubts about this whole venture.
I'd thought it might be a novelty, an unusual night out for
us, a simple excuse to see Maria again. But now I wasn't
so sure it was such a good idea.

We located our places in the front row and sat down.
Maria took her coat off and folded it on her lap. Her eyes
were fixed on the front of the hall where a roped-in ring
had been erected on the platform. I looked down and concentrated intently on the programme I'd bought.

'Mi-chael,' she said slowly, making it two long syllables.
I knew I was in trouble. 'What exactly have we come to
see?'

I lifted my head. 'Pardon?'

'A show, you said yesterday. I thought it was going to
be a concert, or a musical.'

'You'll love it,' I said confidently. 'Wrestling's supposed
to be a great spectacle.'

She stared at me incredulously. 'You've brought me out
to watch *wrestling?*'

'Beats *Brigadoon* any day,' I said.

The two men in the ring were pounding each other against
the ropes, engaged in a bizarre contest that was part sport,
part showbiz. At times it seemed like a clumsy dance routine, choreographed for hippopotami like the sequence in
Fantasia. One moment they were entwined on the canvas,
twisting and writhing in apparent agony, the next posturing
around the ring making obscene gestures to the crowd.

The moves seemed pre-planned to provide maximum
entertainment, but occasionally one of the contestants
appeared to forget the script and do something genuinely
unexpected. Retribution from his opponent was swift and
violent: an elbow in the face, a boot in the chest, a tear-
wringing half-nelson or vicious stamp to the instep which
set the spectators cheering and booing.

I'd never seen anything like it. People standing on their
seats yelling encouragement and abuse, middle-aged

matrons screaming four-letter words, pensioners hurling their programmes at the referee. It was like the blood feasts in the Colosseum in the heyday of the Caesars. Perhaps a bit more civilized, but only marginally.

Maria sat next to me with her eyes tightly closed.

'This is awful, Michael. How can you watch it?'

'You don't want to take it so seriously. It's not real, you know.'

'It looks real enough to me.'

She opened her eyes and looked towards the platform, just in time to see the wrestler in the black hangman's hood jump on his opponent's stomach as he lay stretched out on the floor. She shuddered.

'It's so violent.'

I touched her hand on the arm of her seat. She pulled it away as if I'd burnt her.

'It's cartoon violence, Maria,' I said. 'Like an overweight version of *Tom and Jerry*.'

A cheer went up as the man in the hood was thrown clean out of the ring. Two little old ladies in the front row of the stalls immediately leapt forward and laid into him with their umbrellas. I gaped at them in disbelief. So it really did happen.

'And the spectators are even worse,' Maria said.

'That's part of the act. Those old dears are brought in and paid to do that. Like the claque in Italian opera houses. It's a game.' I never thought I'd hear myself defending wrestling.

'I want to leave.'

'OK, we'll go at the interval. We'll never get through all these people until then. Besides, the next match on is a women's. That's an experience we don't want to miss.'

Maria turned her head and looked at me with barely concealed horror. 'Speak for yourself, mate.'

I didn't recognize Pinky Silvester when she first came on. It was only the presence of her husband in the entourage accompanying her to the platform that gave me a clue. She was draped in a long silver cloak that touched the floor as she walked, and wearing an elaborate Amazonian head-dress that made her look even more enormous than she already was.

When she stepped into the ring, the crowd cheered loudly, a sharp contrast to the boos that had greeted her opponent. So Pinky was cast as the good gal in all this. I couldn't see it, but then I was prejudiced by the bruises on my ribs.

The master of ceremonies, a bouffant-haired clown in a dinner jacket, introduced the two contestants. Pinky was up against the Greasbrough Strangler, a mountain of a woman who looked like the Incredible Hulk, only not nearly so feminine.

I stood up and gave the Strangler a cheer, punching my fists in the air.

Maria said: 'What on earth are you doing?'

I sat down, shamefaced. 'Just getting into the swing of it.'

'We leave after this, promise?'

'I promise.'

The two women stripped off their fancy dresses to reveal leotards and high wrestling boots. The Strangler was in red and black, with gold cups the size of fruit bowls over her breasts. Pinky was all in pink, even down to her boots. Her hair was tied back in pigtails, but that was the only girlish thing about her.

It was a well-matched contest. They were both solid, powerful women, although watching them wrestle I couldn't identify them as women. They had too much bulk, too much aggression. The Strangler looked the heavier, but Pinky had more speed and grace in the ring. As the match progressed she began to use her advantages, turning the Strangler's weight against her, ruthlessly following up minor strikes to gain major victories.

It was obvious from the start that Pinky was going to win, but she delayed her triumph with supreme skill, taunting her opponent, humiliating her with technique, and only occasionally resorting to the crude bludgeoning that had characterized the men's contest earlier. It was an awesome performance. She'd let me off lightly at her house. I was almost grateful to her. Almost, but not quite.

At the end, when the referee proclaimed her the winner, Pinky strutted around the ring blowing kisses to the crowd and picking up the flowers that appreciative fans had tossed on to the canvas. Then she ducked under the ropes and was helped into her cloak and headdress by her husband.

She walked away down the central aisle between the rows of seats, hordes of well-wishers and autograph hunters milling around her. James Silvester brushed them away irritably, keeping close to his wife's side. Then, just as they were about to pass directly underneath us, something happened which made me sit up and take notice.

A man in a black lounge suit stepped out in front of them, blocking their path. He had dark skin, a clipped moustache and, although he was only slightly built, a distinct presence which made you notice him, even just a few feet from the overpowering Pinky.

But it was Silvester who caught my eye the most. Or rather his reaction. As soon as he saw the man, he stopped dead, almost clutching his wife's arm for security. I looked down on them from the circle. The sudden fear was clearly visible in Silvester's face.

The man said something to them both. Silvester shook his head almost desperately, as if he was denying some accusation. Then Pinky said something and pushed past. Silvester scurried after her like a small boy clinging to his mother. The man in the black suit turned and gazed after them with hard, unforgiving eyes.

I became aware that Maria had spoken.

'Sorry, what was that?'

'I said, shall we go?'

I nodded. 'Yes, of course.'

I looked back over the brass rail into the stalls. The man

in the suit was putting a coat on, preparing to leave. I wanted to know who he was, and why Silvester was scared of him.

I stood up and pushed past the knees of the people next to us. Maria hurried after me. On the steps I took her arm and almost dragged her down into the foyer. She shook herself free.

'Michael, what is going on? You might at least let me put my coat on.'

She slipped her arms into the sleeves. I watched the spectators pouring out of the hall in a continuous jam which I knew would end at the bar downstairs. The man in the suit was nowhere to be seen.

Maria said suspiciously: 'You seem very anxious to leave all of a sudden.'

'I'm only thinking of you. Come on, let's go for a drink. I know a nice little pub not far from here.'

We went through the main doors. Outside rain was bucketing down. I surveyed the steps below us and the glistening street beyond. Then I saw him on the pavement. He was wearing a black homburg hat now. He waited for a break in the traffic and walked briskly across Division Street.

Maria turned her collar up and said: 'My car's just round the corner. Shall we drive?'

'Oh no,' I said. 'It's a fine night. Let's walk.'

Before she could say anything, I was off down the steps, my sights locked firmly on the homburg hat disappearing into the distance.

We were at the bottom of Carver Street, just entering Charter Square, when Maria finally lost patience.

'I've had enough of this!' she exploded. 'What are we doing? It's throwing it down and we're wandering the streets like a couple of sightseers. I thought we were going for a drink.'

Time for some diplomatic bullshitting. 'I'm sorry,

Maria,' I said placatingly. 'The rain's worse than I thought. Don't worry, we'll soon be inside.'

'Where *is* this pub?'

'Not far now,' I said vaguely.

The man in the homburg turned into the Grosvenor House Hotel.

I said to Maria: 'You're right, we're getting drenched. Let's go in here before we drown. It'll be less crowded than the pub.'

I pulled open the glass doors and let her past me into the shelter of the hotel entrance. This ground floor area was little more than an access point from the street. The main foyer and reception were up above us on the second floor.

The man in the homburg was waiting by the lift. We joined him inside when it came. He barely glanced at us, but I studied him surreptitiously in the mirror on the wall of the lift. Close to, he was older than he'd appeared at first. Mid to late forties, I guessed, and definitely not English. His colour, his complexion, his features all pointed towards a Middle Eastern or perhaps North African origin.

There was a stillness about him which seemed to indicate a man at ease with himself. Composed, collected, someone who kept his emotions in check. It was hard to see him losing his cool, yet there was an aura of menace in that rigid self-control that made me think his temper, when it broke, would not be pleasant to witness.

We let him out first when we reached the main lobby. He crossed to the reception desk and asked for his key. His voice was gentle, almost inaudible, but with a hint of an American accent. I noted the number on the hook as the receptionist took down the key. Five hundred and eight. He went back towards the lift as Maria and I continued on to the bar.

'What would you like?' I said.

'A green ginger wine, I think. To warm me up.'

I ordered the drinks and took my wallet out. It was

empty. Hell, I'd forgotten. I'd used the last of my notes at the Sphinx Massage Parlour. I felt in my pockets and brought out a handful of loose change. It was not nearly enough to pay for the drinks. Not at the prices they charged at the Grosvenor House.

I looked up to find Maria watching me patiently, one hand held out. Slipped between her fingers was a ten-pound note.

'Go on, take it.'

'Look, I feel terrible about this. I forgot to go to the cashpoint.'

'Take it. You bought the tickets, I'll buy the drinks.' She observed me closely. I sensed a question coming I wouldn't want to answer.

'You did buy them, didn't you?'

I played for time. 'Why don't we go and sit down? I see a couple of seats over there.'

Maria didn't budge. 'I might have had my eyes closed most of the time, but that didn't stop me noticing the man next to me scribbling notes on a pad. They were press tickets, weren't they?'

'We had a good view, didn't we?'

'Weren't they?' Maria said.

'Yes,' I conceded sheepishly. 'I was given them.' I felt cheap. And deceitful, and ashamed. But I got over it quickly. You have to in my line of work.

I paid for the drinks and hung on to Maria's change. For safekeeping. Then we crossed the room to a table near the window. Maria slipped on to the sofa beside me and removed her wet coat. Her hair was shining with tiny rain-drops that caught the light like sequins. I took off my sod-den jacket, wondering how she'd managed to stay so annoyingly neat despite the downpour.

'Why?' she said expressionlessly, sipping her green ginger wine.

'What?'

'Why did you invite me?'

I struggled for an answer. 'I thought you might enjoy it.
It was different, wasn't it?'

'That's not quite the adjective I'd use.'

'You ever been to a wrestling match before?'

'No, and I never want to go again.'

Her tone had cooled. I had some ground to make up
here.

'Still, it was fun, wasn't it?'

'No.'

'You're not making me feel any better, you know.'

'Good. You got me here under false pretences.'

I looked down guiltily. 'I know.' Maybe if I agreed with
her she'd forgive me.

'You have the gall to admit it?' There was real anger in
her voice, restrained but there all the same.

I decided it was time to regroup, give her a moment to
reflect before she hit me. I got up from the table.

'Just going to the gents.'

I scooted away across the bar. All-in wrestling had definitely been a major mistake for a date. There would have
to be some serious grovelling before I got out of this one.

When I emerged from the toilets, I made a short detour
to the reception desk. The girl behind the counter turned
on her professional smile long enough for it to reach the
corners of her mouth but no further.

'Can I help you, sir?'

'A man came in about ten minutes ago. Dark coat, homburg hat, foreign-looking. Could you tell me his name?'

'I'm sorry, sir, I'm not permitted to give out information
about guests.'

I tried some charm. 'Come on, I won't tell anyone. Just
his name. It'll be a big help to me. Please.'

She shook her head, unmoved. The charm was letting
me down badly tonight. I took a five-pound note, part of
Maria's change, out of my pocket and put it on the counter.

'Will this help?'

The girl's expression was contemptuous. 'I've told you,

sir, I'm not permitted to give out that kind of information. Now if you'll excuse me, I have other things to do.'

She turned her back on me dismissively. I picked up the five-pound note. What was the world coming to when even hotel receptionists were incorruptible?

As I moved away, I noticed a man in a cheap raincoat sitting in one of the armchairs opposite the desk. He hadn't been there when we arrived. He was reading a magazine, a copy of *Derbyshire Life* from the table next to him. He looked as if he was killing time. He'd probably heard every word of my conversation with the receptionist.

I memorized his face for future reference. He might simply have been waiting for someone, but I had my doubts. I had a feeling he was watching me.

Maria seemed to have calmed down by the time I got back to the table. Her hands were folded demurely in her lap, her mouth relaxed, no longer set in a tight line. The soothing effects of alcohol.

I sat down next to her and did my best to patch things up.

'I want to apologize. I know I was given the tickets but that's not why I asked you out. I didn't think you'd hate it so much, honest.'

She tilted her head on one side to look at me. 'And?'

'And what?'

'What about the rest of it?'

I spread my hands, not understanding. 'What do you mean?'

'I'm not blind,' Maria said. 'We didn't come in here just to get out of the rain.'

I looked as innocent as I could manage. 'Didn't we?'

'You think I didn't notice you were following that man in the hat?'

'Ah.' I'd forgotten how astute she was.

'And I'd like an explanation. While you're at it, you

could also fill me in on your rather crude attempt to bribe
the receptionist just now. With my money.'

So she'd noticed that too. She held out her hand. I took
the five-pound note and the rest of her change from my
pocket and gave it to her.

'Well . . .' I began lamely.

'And don't make something up, Michael. I deserve better
than that.'

I made a clean breast of it. About James Silvester, my
encounter with his wife, how I simply wanted to see Pinky
in action, then got sidetracked unexpectedly when the man
in the homburg confronted them in the hall.

'I didn't plan to follow him. I had to make a decision on
the spur of the moment. That's why I was talking to the
receptionist. I was asking who he was.'

Maria shook her head. She was still upset about something, not just the wrestling.

'When you asked me out, I thought . . .' She stopped.
'Oh, never mind.' She seemed exasperated. 'I think I'd
better go.'

'You don't have to,' I said.

But she was already sliding out from the table, picking
up her coat.

'I'll walk you to your car,' I said.

She didn't say a word to me along our route and I kept
silent myself, sensing it was the wisest course. I wished we
could start the evening all over again somewhere else, but
regrets never bring back lost opportunities.

At her car, I thought she was going to leave without even
a simple 'good night', but she wound down the window
and looked up at me.

I said: 'I know it didn't work out, but I still enjoyed
tonight. It wasn't so bad, was it?'

'No, it wasn't so bad,' Maria said. 'I've always wanted
to spend an evening watching a bunch of muscle-bound,
half-naked retards beating each other to pulp. Then wandering around the streets in the pouring rain for a couple

of hours, before finally ending up in a bar where *I* have to buy the drinks and watch you try to pay off a receptionist with the rest of my money. It's just my idea of a great night out.'

She paused for breath. I started to say something but she held up a hand.

'Don't even try it. You misled me from start to finish, concealing your motives. And you didn't even have the courtesy to tell me what the hell was going on. While we're at it, you didn't have the guts either to tell me how the front wing of my car got dented while you were out in it yesterday. Maybe you thought I wouldn't notice. You, Michael McLean, are a devious, lying, treacherous, spineless skunk.'

She gunned the engine of the Mazda and roared away from the kerb. I watched the car disappear up the street. She was starting to fall for me. I could tell.

CHAPTER 7

Wolds Remand Prison was a two-hour drive away in the picturesque undulating countryside to the west of Hull. A modern brick building with an extensive car park and perspex-covered walkways beyond the fence, it looked less like a prison than a suburban supermarket.

It was run, not by the Home Office, but by a private security firm astute enough to see that here was the business of the future. Privatized privation. An industry with unlimited growth potential, a vibrant, expanding new field that proved beyond doubt that crime does pay. If not for the inmates of the prison, then certainly for the shareholders of the company.

I got there shortly after eleven and interviewed Tony Napier in a characterless room filled with small tables, set out in rows like an examination hall. At each table was a prisoner sitting opposite his visitor, in nearly all cases a woman: wife, girlfriend, mother, one or two weeping quietly, holding hands across the table, condensing their lives and feelings into brief, intense exchanges under the intrusive eyes of the patrolling warders.

I'd seen Tony in court five years earlier, but I remembered his name better than his face. There was, in fact, nothing memorable at all about his appearance. He was neither handsome nor ugly, tall nor short, dark nor fair. Just bland and nondescript on almost every count. The sort of dull, insignificant individual you might pass every day in the street for years and hardly notice.

He was only on remand, an innocent man awaiting trial, so he was wearing his own clothes: a pair of faded jeans and a shiny green nylon shirt. He glanced at me without surprise, or much interest, as he sat down. His eyes had a glazed, resigned look in them as if he expected to be bored by me, but what the hell, it was better than sitting in a cell.

'Hello, Tony,' I said. I pushed a couple of packets of cigarettes across the table to him. 'I brought you something.'

He picked up the packets and stuffed one in the breast pocket of his shirt. The other he opened. He lit a cigarette and looked at me blankly. No thanks, no questions.

'Don't you want to know who I am?' I said.

'Not particularly.'

I had a feeling this wasn't going to be easy. I told him my name and what I did for a living. Then I turned round my notebook and showed him the brief message Harry had written on it for me. It read simply: 'Mike McLean is a good friend of mine. You can trust him.'

Tony studied it momentarily before raising his eyes back to mine.

'So?'

'You know Harry Raymond?'

'A bit. What of it?'

'I just wanted you to know I'm not here to make things difficult for you.'

'That's nice. Thanks.'

I ignored the heavy tone of sarcasm.

'All I want is a quiet chat. About you and Andy Peters.'

I saw a flicker of interest in his boyish face, but it quickly disappeared. He wasn't going to flatter me by showing he cared in the slightest why I was there.

'You did a job together a few weeks back, didn't you?' I said. 'A burglary.'

I shouldn't have been so blunt. He shut off immediately, the old lag's caution about talking to strangers. Especially in a prison visiting room. He was only young, not yet thirty probably, but I could tell he'd been inside before. He was too relaxed, too comfortable in these surroundings to be a first timer.

I couldn't remember whether he'd got a custodial sentence five years ago, even though I remembered the details of the court case quite clearly. It was one of those cases you never forget, a bizarre, entertaining obscenity trial that still seemed preposterous all this time later. It became known as the Snow White Trial, because of the obscene film that formed the central basis of the prosecution.

Two local businessmen, who ran a chain of video shops, had been arrested for renting out under-the-counter pornographic movies. The police subsequently raided a warehouse the two men owned and found not only a stock of hard-core blue films, but a small production line which specialized in making obscene cartoons, apparently very popular in Italy and the Arab states.

The most prominent product, because of its background and associations, was an animated short called *Snow White and the Eight Dwarves*. This looked remarkably like the Disney original but featured an extra dwarf named Horny, a priapic, hugely endowed creature who spent his time flashing Snow White and attempting to rape her. The centrepiece was a mass orgy with all the dwarves involved and the film ended with Snow White in bed with her prince and a naked Horny popping up between them, saying: 'How about a threesome, me on top?'

I'd watched a bootleg copy with Chris Strange and a few other CID officers, and found the whole thing hilarious rather than obscene. The judge and jury had thought otherwise, however, persuaded by the prosecution case that children had seen the cartoons and been depraved and corrupted by them. The two businessmen were sent down. Tony Napier had been just a small cog in the dirty wheel, one of two or three animators employed to make the films. He was a talented artist who could probably have made a career out of it if he'd applied himself. But no doubt burglary was easier.

'You still draw?' I said.

Tony was wary now. 'What?'

'You used to be pretty good, didn't you?'

He inhaled on his cigarette. He had straight, light brown hair which hung down limply over his forehead. He brushed it back out of his eyes, intrigued enough to say: 'Yes, once. What's it to you?'

'Did you do time for that? Snow White.'

He didn't know where I was going, but he liked the subject better than that of Andy Peters. Nostalgia perhaps. More likely pride. He'd been a minor celebrity during that trial, someone with a unique gift for animation that had been widely praised. Even if he had used it to draw a dwarf with a two-foot penis. His name had been in all the papers; for a short while he'd been someone. Now he was just another petty burglar with a record and no prospects.

'Eighteen months, suspended,' he said, a little smugly.

I was right, he was proud of it. I remembered the details more clearly now.

'The judge said you'd been led off the rails, didn't he?'

Tony almost smiled. 'They corrupted me. Picked me up after I'd been kicked out of art school and forced me to work for them. I were young, I needed the money.'

'That's what your lawyer claimed, anyway.'

'It were true. The judge said I deserved a second chance.'

I nodded. 'And what did you do with that second chance, Tony?'

He didn't like that. It was too close to home for him. An unwelcome reminder of what he'd become.

'What the fuck d'you want? I don't have to talk to you.'

'No,' I said. 'But I think you'd better. You don't want to end up like Andy, do you?'

Tony pursed his lips and let the smoke trickle out in a thin stream. His brow furrowed. I could practically see his pin-brain ticking over. He didn't know.

'Don't you read the papers?' I said.

'Why should I read the papers?'

'And no one's told you, have they? Andy's dead. He was murdered three days ago.'

His face went rigid, the flesh colour washing out to leave behind a sickly grey pallor. He licked his thin slit of a mouth, his eyes on me, unfocused.

'What?' he breathed.

'Dead. Someone broke his neck while he was watching a video.' I paused to let it sink in. Then I said: 'Think about it, Tony. You want to go the same way?'

His head jerked upright. 'Now wait a minute. What's it got to do wi' me?'

'That's what I want you to tell me.'

He stubbed his cigarette out violently in the ashtray on the table. He was shocked, maybe just starting to get a little scared. That was the way I wanted him. Scared enough to help me, but not so scared he clammed up altogether.

'I found the body,' I said.

'You? But what . . . ?'

'Just listen. Andy asked me to go and see him. When I got there he was dead. He was going to tell me something. I want to know what.'

'You think I know? Jesus, I've been in here for the past week.'

'But before that you did a job with Andy. What was it?'

Tony gave himself some time, lighting another cigarette and drawing on it deeply. One of the prison warders strolled past us, hands folded behind his back, his boots clunking heavily on the concrete floor. Tony was still reluctant to tell me about the job. I put my elbows on the table and leaned closer.

'I'm not a cop, Tony. Anything you tell me is in confidence.'

'Why're you so interested in the job?'

'I'm interested in anything that might tell me why Andy was killed. He was frightened when he spoke to me. Maybe he had something on his conscience.'

Tony's mouth curled. 'Conscience? Andy?'

'He'd come into some money recently. A lot of money. Did he steal it with you?'

There was no mistaking the surprise on his face. 'Money? We didn't steal any money. Two hundred and fifty apiece, that's what we got.' Another possibility occurred to him. 'That's what he said, anyway.'

I saw where his suspicious mind was leading him.

'Maybe Andy kept the rest for himself,' I suggested, wanting to provoke a reaction.

Tony's face tightened, his teeth clenching into a grimace. 'The little shit! Two hundred and fifty, he said. That's all he gave me.'

'You should choose your friends a bit better.'

'The bastard ripped me off. You sure about the money?'

'He had a house full of brand new electrical stuff. And it didn't fall off the back of a lorry either.'

'I'd have broken his bloody neck myself if I'd known. Have they got who did it?'

I shook my head. Tony was muttering to himself, repeating the same obscenities under his breath. His mind had been diverted down a cul-de-sac and was stuck firmly at the end. All he could see now was the treachery of someone he'd believed was his friend. A treachery which was purely speculative, but which Tony accepted without wanting proof. The mere suspicion was enough to convince him of Andy's guilt.

'What was the job, Tony?' I asked gently. 'I think it's important.'

He looked back up at me suddenly, something else occurring to him. This time fear took the place of indignation.

'What were that about me going the same way? You said something about me going the same way.' His hands were trembling slightly. 'Why would anyone want to kill me?'

'Why would anyone want to kill Andy?'

His voice became more intense, higher pitched. 'I don't know. For God's sake, I don't know. But it's nothing to do wi' me.'

'It's everything to do with you, Tony, if that burglary is somehow part of it all. I want to know who murdered Andy. Don't you?'

He pulled himself together, automatically looking around to make sure no one else was listening. The perennial caution of the old prison hand. Give nothing away unless you have to.

Then he said: 'It were just a simple break-in. An office, that's all.'

Finally, we were getting somewhere.

'Whose office?'

'I dunno.'

'Where was it?'

'Immingham.'

That gave me momentary pause for thought. 'Immingham? What kind of office?'

Tony shrugged impatiently. 'Just a bloody office. They're all the same, aren't they?'

'OK. What did you take?'

'A file. From a metal cabinet.'

'You know what was in it?'

'No. I never touched it. Andy took it.'

'And he didn't mention what was inside?'

'I didn't care. It were just a job to me. Not a very hard job. It were easy money.'

'Let's go back a bit,' I said. 'Whereabouts in Immingham was it?'

'How the hell should I know? Andy had the address. I just went with him in the car.'

'You must have noticed something. A street name, a pub. Come on, Tony, think.'

He jabbed a finger aggressively at me across the table. 'Listen, pal, I don't have to take any shit from you. I get enough of that in here.'

'And you listen to me,' I said, keeping my voice low, but fierce. 'This might have absolutely nothing to do with Andy's death. But if it has, whoever killed Andy might come looking for you next. If you weren't banged up he might have found you already. You understand me? Now I suggest you cooperate with me because I might just get your arse out of the fire. You know anyone else who's going to?'

He was silent for a time. Then he took a breath.

'It were somewhere on the road to the docks. I saw a sign.'

'Good. What sort of building was it? How many storeys?'

'Two. The office were on the first floor.'

'No name on the door?'

'There were a plaque downstairs by the entrance. Brass plaque. I don't remember what it said.'

'Anything else?'

He started to say something, but stopped as one of the warders drew level with the table.

'One minute,' the warder said.

I looked at my watch and nodded at him. It was nearly half-past eleven. I was running out of time.

'Go on,' I said to Tony.

'There were a timberyard, building supplies place across the road. I can't remember anything else. It were dark.'

I hoped that would be enough for me. Tony was putting

his cigarettes away, preparing for the end of visiting time.

'And Andy gave you two hundred and fifty pounds?'

'That were my share. Half, he said, the lying bastard.'

'Who gave him the money? Who hired you?'

'I don't know his name. Some bloke Andy knew from the past. Andy did the deal and delivered the file to him.'

'You sure he did?'

'Well, he said he did.'

'And the man? You have no idea who he was?'

Tony shook his head. 'I only saw him once. From a distance while Andy talked to him.'

'You saw him? What did he look like?'

The warders were moving down each aisle now, making the prisoners stand up. I glanced back at Tony.

'Describe him!'

He took an eternity to reply. The warders were getting nearer.

'Quickly, Tony.'

'I'm not very good with words. Here.'

He snatched the pen from my hand and pulled my notebook across in front of him. He scribbled some lines on the page, sketching in the features of a face with practised skill. He really could draw.

'Time's up,' a warder said, standing over Tony's shoulder. 'Let's go.'

Tony pushed the notebook back to me and stood up. 'That's him.'

'Thanks,' I said, but he was already being escorted away down the aisle; a slight, insignificant figure in a shiny green shirt, returning to the closed world behind the steel doors.

I looked at the face he'd drawn. It was hurried, and little more than an outline, but recognizable all the same. It was the man in the homburg hat from the Grosvenor House Hotel.

I nursed the Lada back to Sheffield and parked in the multi-storey near the Crucible. It was still raining, a depressing drizzle that never seemed to stop, yet never turned into a proper downpour either. It annoyed me. I wanted to yell at the sky: Get on with it, you sod, get the bloody rain out of the way and give us some sunshine.

I took the subway under Arundel Gate and as I came up the steps on to Norfolk Street, I paused to dodge a couple of pedestrians with umbrellas, glancing behind me at the same time. I caught a glimpse of a figure stopping suddenly and turning his back on me. But not fast enough to prevent my seeing his face, and his cheap raincoat. It was the man from the armchair in the Grosvenor House Hotel reception.

I cut along Mulberry Street, resisting the impulse to increase my pace. At the junction with High Street I turned left. Out of the corner of my eye I saw him behind me. I went in through the front entrance of the NatWest bank. I've got an account there, but I usually avoid going into it in case the manager pulls me in for questioning.

I crossed the lobby quickly and ducked out through the side entrance. When I hit George Street I was already running. I took in Chapel Walk and Fargate, slowing down as I reached Surrey Street, then looped round and walked back to the Lyceum Theatre.

In the theatre foyer I recovered my breath, certain that I'd lost my tail. There was a queue at the box office. I picked up a prospectus and leafed through it to see what was on on January 12th. Opera North was visiting for a week and that day there was a performance of Verdi's *La Traviata*. So Crispin May was going to the opera. That fitted. There had been only one ticket in the envelope on his desk, but I didn't think he'd be going on his own. He seemed a social animal, he'd want company. I was interested to see who.

I joined the line and waited. It had to have been an opera, of course. Just my luck. I hated opera. Even wrestling was preferable to an evening of wobbly sopranos and fat tenors.

Then a thought came abruptly. Maria liked classical

music. Handled correctly, this could be my way of re-
deeming myself after the previous night's debacle.

I bought two tickets, charging them to my Visa card to
put off the day of reckoning. They were up in the gods, the
cheapest seats in the house, but they still cost eight pounds
fifty each. Seventeen quid for three hours or so of terminal
boredom and eardrum assault; this really was dedication
beyond the call of duty.

Then I rang Maria's office. Muriel stalled me, wallowing
in the sadistic power of the switchboard operator, until I
threatened to come round and while away the afternoon
with her. She put me through.

Maria's voice was cold. 'I'm very busy, what do you
want?'

'Don't hang up,' I said. 'I want a second chance. Tomorrow night, if you're free.'

'Oh yes? What is it this time? Boxing, Sumo, a ferret
down the trousers competition?'

I kept my nerve. She was quite formidable when she was
angry.

'How does *La Traviata* sound?'

'Don't tell me, she's an Italian stripper?'

'The opera. At the Lyceum.'

There was a silence at the other end of the line. Then
she said: 'Is that *La Traviata* by Giuseppe Verdi? Performed
by singers?'

She wasn't going to get caught a second time. I assured
her it was by Verdi and, as far as I knew, performed by
singers.

'Have you got tickets?'

'I'm holding them in my hand. I paid for them too.'

'And if I say no?'

'I'll have a very lonely night.'

She was cracking. I could sense it by the way her voice
had mellowed. I moved in for the kill.

'I admit last night was a mistake. I want to make it up
to you, Maria. Give me a chance.'

'Don't try to sound pathetic, Michael. It won't get round me.' But she said it half jokingly. I think.

'It starts at seven-fifteen,' I said. 'Shall I pick you up or meet you outside?'

'You've got your car back then?'

'It was written off. But I've got a new one. Souped-up high-performance job.'

'What is it?'

'A B-reg Lada.'

She couldn't stop a small chuckle escaping. It was fatal for her resistance.

'All right, I'll meet you outside. I didn't think you liked opera.'

'Oh yes, love it.'

'Liar,' Maria said, and hung up.

Harry Raymond came in out of the rain. He looked as if someone had thrown a bucket of water over him. His hair was dripping like a greasy mop, the water running down his forehead and the back of his neck. He shivered.

'I'll catch me death,' he said. 'I 'ad to walk all the way from the market, you know.'

I said: 'The fresh air's good for you.'

'I'm allergic to fresh air. If I get a chill on me chest, I could 'ave only weeks to live.'

'Harry,' I said patiently. 'It's rain, not the Satan Bug.'

Harry sniffed and wiped the moisture off his nose with the back of his hand. We were standing in the entrance to the Grosvenor House Hotel.

'Did you bring your tools?' I asked.

'What's this all about?'

'Did you bring them?'

He patted the pocket of his coat. 'In here. But I'm not sure I want to get involved in this.'

'Oh you do. It'll be just like old times.'

'That's what worries me. I'm too old to go back inside.'

I took him by the arm and guided him to the lift.

'They have to catch us first.'

The lift came down as soon as I pressed the button on the wall. We had it to ourselves. On the way up to the fifth floor Harry produced a plastic bag from one of his pockets and took out various bottles and capsules. He swallowed a couple of pills, inhaled noisily on a sinus stick and popped a cough sweet into his mouth. The menthol fumes were enough to knock you out in the confined space.

'That coat of yours is like a branch of Boots,' I said.

'Just precautionary measures,' Harry replied defensively. 'You can't be too careful, all these germs about.'

The lift doors opened on the fifth floor. We stepped out and I checked the number on the room nearest us.

'This way.'

Harry held me back. ''Ang on a sec. Before we go any further, I want to know what we're playing at.'

'I told you on the phone.'

'You said you 'ad a job for me. You didn't say what.'

'Just a door lock. That shouldn't be a problem, should it?'

'You searching someone's room?'

I nodded. 'We'll be in and out in five minutes.'

Harry looked doubtful. 'You sure you know what you're doing?'

'No,' I said.

That was one of my problems. I never knew what I was doing. But it *felt* right, and I have great faith in my instincts. Even when they're wrong.

We walked down the corridor, looking for room 508. I pulled open a fire door and stopped dead. Ten yards ahead of us, the man in the homburg was just coming out of his room. Harry glanced at me and I knew he was about to say something. I gave a brief, urgent shake of the head, continuing walking as the man turned to head for the exit. His eyes caught mine momentarily as we moved aside to let him pass, but he gave no sign of recognition.

We kept going past his door and round the corner at the

far end of the corridor. I drew Harry to a halt and put a finger to my lips. Then I poked a cautious head out to look back the way we'd come. The corridor was deserted.

'That was 'im, wasn't it?' Harry whispered.

'Yes.'

'Jesus Christ, are you crazy? Five minutes earlier and he'd 'ave been inside when we was trying to break in. Why didn't you check at reception to see if his key were missing?'

'I never thought. Still, at least we know he's out now.'

'My nerves can't take this. You realize that just being found in an 'otel with the tools I've got in my pocket is enough to get me a couple of years in the slammer?'

'Don't be such a pessimist, Harry. This is a piece of cake compared to some of the break-ins you must have done in the past.'

'I didn't 'ave you with me then,' he said morosely.

I didn't take offence. Even I wouldn't have wanted to do a burglary with me. I checked the corridor again.

'Come on.'

The door gave Harry no trouble whatsoever. One tool from his pouch and it was open in under twenty seconds. We nipped in and looked around. It was a typical chain hotel room. Bathroom off to one side, twin beds, chair, colour television, tea-making equipment on a tray complete with long-life milk and a small packet of shortcake biscuits.

'What're we looking for?' Harry said.

'Anything that tells me who he is.'

I tried the catches on the suitcase which was lying flat on a slatted platform by the desk. It was locked.

'Give that a go, will you, Harry, while I do the wardrobe?'

There were one or two suits hanging up, an overcoat and a line of pressed shirts. I went through all the pockets but they were empty. He probably had all his valuables in the hotel safe, or maybe with him.

As I searched, I said to Harry: 'I've got a bone to pick with you.'

'Oh aye?' He was still working on the suitcase locks.

'About Crispin May.'

Harry stopped what he was doing and lifted his eyes to mine.

'You went to see him, didn't you? Took no notice of what I said.'

'I had to know, Harry.'

'Why will you never leave well alone?' There was disappointment, maybe concern in his voice.

'You were having me on about him, weren't you?' I said. I still wasn't sure.

'No! I don't joke about people like 'im.'

'I can't believe he's what you say.'

'Believe what you want to, Mike. I won't waste my breath warning you again.'

'But he's only got one arm.'

'How many arms do you need to kill someone? That's why he's called the Bandit. It's short for One-armed Bandit.'

I stared at him. He threw up a hand in a gesture of irritation and said: 'You expect 'im to have a sign stuck to his forehead, eh? If you want to stay in business as a hitman, you'd bloody well better make sure you don't look or act like one.'

Harry turned back to the suitcase, venting his anger on the locks. I watched him, pondering on his words for a time. Then I shook away my thoughts and went through the chest of drawers. There was nothing of any interest inside. Just underwear, socks and handkerchiefs. But it was all expensive stuff, that much was apparent. Whoever the man in the homburg was he wasn't short of a bob or two.

'Take a look at this,' Harry said.

The top of the suitcase was flipped back on its hinges. It contained practically nothing, but Harry was holding something out to me. A passport.

I took it from him and studied it. There was a black and white photograph of the man inside and a lot of visas and stamps on the following pages. He certainly got about.

Germany, America, France, Switzerland, at least a dozen more countries. I'd been right about his Middle Eastern origins. He was an Egyptian. His name was Jawaad al-Nabil.

'Anything else in the case?' I asked Harry.

'See for yourself.'

I rummaged through the few items that remained. A couple of shirts, still in their cellophane wrapping, a book in Arabic, a pair of swimming trunks and some Speedo goggles. A man who liked to keep fit. That was it. I handed the passport back to Harry.

'I'll just check the bathroom.'

I moved away round the end of the beds. Just then the telephone rang suddenly. I started violently, suppressing a small exclamation of surprise. The phone continued ringing. Harry and I both stared at it until it stopped.

'I'm getting nervous,' Harry said. 'Let's get the 'ell out.'

I nodded. 'The bathroom first.'

'You know who 'e is now, don't you? What else do you want?'

'Put the passport back where you found it and lock the case again.'

The bathroom took no time at all to search. There was a washbag by the basin, a shaving kit and various toiletries on the glass shelf above. I ran my eyes over them. Nothing of interest there either. Then I sniffed. There was a distinctive smell in the room. A familiar smell. I went through the toiletries, the canister of shaving foam, the deodorant, the aftershave, holding them all up to my nose. It was the aftershave I recognized.

Harry stuck his head in through the doorway. 'Come on, for Christ's sake. What if he comes back?'

'He won't, he's gone . . .' I stopped, remembering something. 'Shit! He hasn't gone out.'

'What!' Harry's eyes practically left their sockets.

'He was in a suit, wasn't he?'

'So?'

'It's raining outside. His overcoat's in the wardrobe.'

'You mean he's still in the 'otel? Bloody hell!'

Harry took two paces to the door and threw it open. 'This really was insane. Come on.'

I followed him out into the corridor. Harry was about to head straight for the lift but I caught hold of his sleeve.

'Lock the door.'

'Eh? Who cares about the door?'

'Just do it, Harry. I'll keep watch.'

I walked down the corridor and through the fire door, positioning myself on the other side where I could see both Harry and the entrance to the lift. It wasted valuable time, but I didn't want al-Nabil to know anyone had been inside his room. He might remember who'd passed him in the corridor and just possibly recall he'd seen me the night before in the lift. He didn't know who I was, but I didn't intend to take any more chances than I had to. If Silvester was scared of him, maybe I'd do well to watch my step.

I pulled open the fire door and held it ajar with my foot. 'Hurry up, Harry.'

'I *am* hurrying. They're harder to lock than unlock, you know.'

I looked back at the lift. The number seven on the indicator was lit up. As I watched, it changed to six, then five. I was just about to shout to Harry when the figure four lit up, followed by three. I relaxed. It had gone right down past us.

The number four lit up again suddenly. Christ, it was coming back up. I held my breath. The number five glowed bright red. I heard a ping as the lift stopped.

'Someone's coming, Harry,' I called out urgently.

'Nearly done.'

The lift doors slid open. I saw a man in a dark suit start to step out, but I didn't hang around to confirm his identity. I was already through the fire door and running back down the corridor.

'Come *on*, Harry.'

The last tumbler clicked into place. Harry straightened

up. I grabbed him by the arm and dragged him along with me, half running, half stumbling. We rounded the corner just an instant before I heard the fire door open behind us.

Only when we were safely out on to the emergency staircase did I let go of Harry. We leaned back on the walls, panting for breath.

Eventually he said: 'You take some bloody chances, Mike. I 'ope it were worth it.'   .

'Oh yes, it was, Harry.'

I'd just remembered where I'd smelt Jawaad al-Nabil's aftershave before. In Andy Peters' flat the night I found his body.

CHAPTER 8

We all, even the least able among us, have some particular skill which makes us unique; some gift which, however small, undiscovered or apparently insignificant, sets us apart from other people. In my case, it was stirring. Spanners in works, spokes in wheels, fingers in pies, I was world class at the lot. And what this whole business needed more than anything right now was a bit of stirring.

I'd made some progress over the last three days. I knew Andy Peters had stolen a file for the man in the homburg hat, although I didn't know what was in it nor what had become of it. I knew who the man in the homburg hat was. I knew he had some connection with James Silvester, and I knew he'd been in Andy Peters' flat the night he died. Andy had been unshaven when I found him; it wasn't his aftershave I'd smelt. That didn't mean Jawaad al-Nabil had necessarily killed Andy, but it put him pretty high up the list of suspects.

But I felt as if I was bogged down in a quagmire of loose ends and unanswered questions. What I needed was a catalyst to set off a reaction somewhere so I could watch what happened. It was time to light the blue touchpaper and stand well clear.

I telephoned the Titan Works from a call box by the Town Hall and asked for James Silvester. His secretary told me he was at his scrapyard for the afternoon. She gave me the address and phone number, but the address was all I wanted. This was going to be a personal visit.

The scrapyard wasn't hard to find. Even in the relentless grime and dilapidation of the East End it was a landmark of ugliness. A vast open space on the site of an old steel works which was overflowing with stacks of rusty cars, mounds of old fridges and cookers, all the rotting detritus of the disposable society.

I parked on a side street opposite the entrance to the yard and went in on foot. It was growing dark. In the twilight the heaps of scrap iron, the twisted metal shapes, the tentacles of steel, the towering crane and crusher beneath it had a surreal feel, like some enormous abstract sculpture.

I walked towards a light glowing in a Portakabin, occasionally stumbling on the muddy, uneven ground. There were cars parked in front of the cabin and a flat-backed lorry to the side. I pushed open the door and went in.

The light hit my eyes like a flashbulb. I blinked and looked around. The interior was one long room, furnished like an office. Plain and businesslike without many executive trappings.

James Silvester was puffing on a cigar behind a black desk at one end, in shirt sleeves and red braces. Sitting near him was a large, shaggy man with an unkempt beard and a face deeply ingrained with dirt. He looked like a grizzly bear with an attitude problem.

Silvester took a moment to recognize me. Then his moist, fleshy mouth contorted into a mean grin.

'Well, well, so you've come back for more, have you?'

'I don't see Pinky,' I said. 'Or is she hiding in the cupboard?'

'This boy here will do just as well. Won't you, Jeff?'

The grizzly stood up and flexed his hands. His head nearly touched the false ceiling of the cabin. I checked him over. He was filthy from top to toe. Maybe he washed, but not more than once a year. I thought about shouting 'soap', to see if he bolted.

He took a pace towards me. I stood my ground. It took some doing.

'Don't you want to know why I'm here?' I said.

'I can guess. Throw him out, Jeff.'

'I've got business to discuss. Egyptian business.'

Silvester's expression changed. His mouth fell open. I saw his flabby pink tongue inside, saliva on the edges of his lips. Jeff took hold of my lapels. I hoped this gamble paid off, or I could order the wheelchair now.

'Gently,' I said. 'You don't want to ruin your nails, do you?'

He lifted me off the ground to look into my eyes. I could feel the air getting thinner.

'Hold it,' Silvester said. 'Put him down.'

Jeff's face crumpled with disappointment. For a moment I thought he was going to cry, but the tears would've played hell with his mud pack.

My feet touched the floor again. It felt good.

'Well, now we've got the introductions over, let's talk,' I said, heading for the desk.

'Take a walk,' Silvester said to Jeff.

Jeff looked at him, not moving.

'Take a walk,' Silvester repeated impatiently. 'I'll be OK.'

Jeff glared at me. I smiled back encouragingly. 'Off you go. Jimmy and I have things to discuss in private.'

He turned and lumbered towards the door. He moved slowly, as if his body hadn't quite mastered the technique of walking yet.

When he'd gone I sat down on one of the black metal chairs and said: 'He has a way with words, doesn't he?'

'What do you want, McLean?'

'I came to see how you were. Fully recovered from your ordeal the other morning, I hope. You want to tell me who shot at you?'

'You haven't come here to talk about that.'

'Why not? I didn't get much of a chance at your house. How *is* Pinky, by the way? She looked pretty impressive at the City Hall last night.'

Silvester sat back in his high leather chair. There were dark smudges under his eyes and his face and body seemed pudgier than I remembered. He needed a good night's sleep. He studied me calmly, sure of himself but more unsure of me.

'What's your angle?' he said.

'For my story, you mean?'

'*Your* angle. What're you getting out of this?'

He couldn't work me out. In his world there was always a sub-text, an unspoken motive that everyone understood but which never had to be spelt out. He was looking for it in me, automatically mistrusting the surface, convinced there had to be corrupt depths underneath. He didn't understand that the story might be all I wanted.

'You should have given me a quote two days ago, Jimmy,' I said.

'It's James. Mr Silvester to you.' He let his annoyance show. It told me a lot about him.

'It used to be Jimmy though, didn't it? Before you became all grand and bought your stately home. I bet they never called you James in the nick, did they?'

His mouth tightened. His piggy eyes became small and hard, like chips of anthracite.

'Nobody speaks to me like that.'

'What're you going to do? Stick one on me? I thought you'd left those days long behind.'

'Don't be too sure of it.'

The thug in him was not far below the surface. He'd acquired a gloss of money and vulgar sophistication, but the real James Silvester was always in danger of breaking out when he was under pressure.

'You have employees for things like that now, don't you?' I said. 'People like Jeff, or maybe your wife.'

He stubbed out his cigar in the malachite ashtray and leaned forward, putting his bulky forearms on the shiny desktop. 'Don't push me, McLean.'

I smiled at him. I wanted him annoyed. Maybe then he'd say something rash.

'You're not used to it, are you, Jimmy? Someone coming in here and giving you lip. You prefer the arse lickers, the meek little boys who tell you what you want to hear. It makes you feel good, helps you forget the fact you're just another scrap merchant with dirt under your fingernails.'

For a moment I thought he was going to hit me. But he had too much self-control for that. Despite what I'd said, he wasn't just another scrap merchant. He still had the yard, but he'd moved way beyond it in business terms. He knew he didn't have to worry about someone like me. I was a mild irritation, but journalists featured nowhere on his list of threats. Nevertheless, I was an unknown quantity, a loose cannon. He couldn't quite decide how to handle me.

'Do you always conduct interviews like this?' he said.

'Depends who I'm interviewing.'

'You think you'll get anywhere by pissing me off?'

'I can't do worse than I did at your house. I've already got further than that.'

'You won't get any further though.'

'Won't I? I think I will, Jimmy. Why else did you send Jeff away? You want to talk.'

He sneered. 'I've got better things to do than waste my time with tosspot reporters like you.'

I didn't say anything. I waited. If he didn't want to talk he'd throw me out. I watched him casually. He was on

home territory, but he didn't know what to do. His guts
told him to take me outside and punch some respect into
me. But his brain told him to hold back, find out what I
was doing. The violence could wait for another day. Ten
years ago he'd have gone with his guts. Now, he was more
inclined to use his head.

He put his thumbs under his braces, just above his
nipples, and stretched the elastic.

'What is it you want, McLean? Money? You trying to
shake me down for a bit of cash?'

'Why would I want to do that?'

'You look as if you could use some dosh.' He fixed me
with a shrewd, penetrating glare, totting up my net worth
in a single look. 'How much you make in a year? Under
ten grand, I bet. I make that in a month without even
trying.'

'Congratulations.'

'So why d'you do it? What d'you get out of this? Pinky
went easy on you the other day, but it must still have hurt.
You could've got more of the same here but you still came.
Why? You don't look like a stupid bloke to me, but you
sure act like one.'

'If you've got a point, you'd better make it,' I said.

Silvester shrugged. 'Maybe you're in the wrong
business.'

'You offering me a job?'

'No. But we can probably do a deal. How much you
want?'

'To leave you alone, you mean? You got something to
hide?'

'I've got a life to live. And I don't want some arsehole
reporter trying to live it with me, you understand? You
don't take a hint easily, McLean, or you wouldn't be here.
I'm just trying to save us both a lot of hassle.'

He wasn't a good judge of people. Correction: maybe he
was. He just wasn't a good judge of me.

'How much did you have in mind?' I said.

Silvester ran over the numbers in his head. 'Two hundred?'

So that was my price. Sometimes it's good to know what other people think you're worth. Good for your soul, anyway. Maybe not your vanity.

'Is that the going rate for journalists?' I said. 'Or is it the same for everyone?'

'You want it or not?'

I shook my head. 'You just don't get it, do you, Jimmy? You don't see anything beyond the bottom line.'

He was losing patience rapidly. He pulled his thumbs out from behind his braces and said curtly: 'So what the hell *do* you want?'

'To ask you a few questions, that's all.'

'Then ask. Then get out and leave me alone.'

I took my notebook out, going through the motions. I knew I wouldn't get any answers, but that wasn't why I was there. I started with the easy ones to get the rhythm going.

'Tell me what happened when you arrived at work on Monday.'

Silvester rolled his eyes. 'That's been in the papers already. Ask me something new.'

'Did you see who fired the shots?'

'You think that's new?'

'It is to me.'

'No.'

'Any guesses?'

He thought about that one before replying. 'I'm a successful businessman. You don't get to where I am today without making enemies.'

'Most businessmen have enemies. But not many get shot at.'

'Perhaps my enemies are nastier than other people's.'

'Or perhaps you deserve to be shot at more.'

His lips twitched humourlessly, more scowl than smile.

This wasn't what he wanted to talk about, but he had to wait for me to show my hand.

'Envy often leads to violence,' he said.

'You think that's what's behind it then, envy?'

'I don't know what's behind it. I'm as much in the dark about it as anyone else.'

I gave him a look. 'Yeah? You don't seem too worried about it. No police protection, no extra security. What if the gunman tries again?'

Silvester shrugged. 'I'll take that chance. I'm not going to change my life just because someone's got a grudge against me. Whoever it is doesn't scare me.'

'But Jawaad al-Nabil does.'

I slipped it in without drawing attention to it, hoping for a reaction. Silvester took it in his stride. He'd been preparing himself for it since I mentioned the words 'Egyptian business'.

'Who?'

I smiled. 'Nice try, Jimmy, but it won't wash. I saw what happened at the City Hall last night.'

'What's the City Hall got to do with it?'

I went along with him, feeding him some more bait so he knew I wasn't just fishing.

'The man in the dark suit who blocked your exit down the aisle. I saw your reaction to him.'

Silvester frowned. He wasn't very convincing as an actor.

'Oh, him. He was just some fan of my wife's. An autograph hunter. They get in the way all the time.'

'Pinky's big in Egypt then, is she? I'd heard women's wrestling was all the rage among Muslims.'

He hesitated. He wasn't used to this. I guessed it was a long time since anyone had questioned him. He knew bluff wasn't going to work so he fell back on the basic ingredient of his character—aggression.

'You're getting on my tits, you know that, McLean?'

'Yes. And very nice tits they are too. The rest of your

figure leaves a bit to be desired but your mammaries are knockout.'

He pushed his chair back violently and stood up. He'd run to fat but there was still enough muscle there to flatten me.

'Right, you little shit.'

Interview over, I thought. I got up and edged away warily. I'd thrown in the catalyst, Jawaad al-Nabil, but I wanted to be a safe distance away when the chemical reaction began in earnest.

'I know about him, Jimmy,' I said. 'And what I don't know about you and him I'm going to find out. Think about it.'

I pulled open the door of the Portakabin and stepped out before he could reach me. It was not the most dignified of exits, but my dignity tends to go to pieces at the prospect of painful physical violence.

I was relieved he didn't come after me. And even more relieved I didn't encounter Jeff on my return walk across the yard.

Back at the car, I sat in the darkness and waited. I'd stirred the sewer. Now all I had to do was see what turds floated to the surface.

The dark green Range-Rover came out of the yard shortly afterwards. I saw James Silvester at the wheel as he turned right on to the main road and headed towards the city centre. He didn't see me. I started up the Lada and followed him. Was he merely going home, or had I panicked him into doing something foolish?

I knew he wasn't going home the moment he crossed the inner ring road and continued south-west through the suburbs. This wasn't the way to Strines. I kept well back, two cars in between me and the Range-Rover. It was easy enough to stay with him in the slow rush-hour traffic, even in a clockwork Lada.

At Hunter's Bar he turned up Brocco Bank and cut

through the side streets to Endcliffe Vale Road. I held back, no other cars between us now, and watched from a distance as he pulled in outside a low block of flats. He got out and went towards the entrance to the flats.

I drove up slowly and parked directly opposite. Silvester had already gone inside. There was a light on in the front room of the first-floor flat. The curtains were open and I saw a young woman move across in front of the window. She was quite something to look at. Tall, graceful, features close to perfection, shoulder-length black hair that, even from where I was sitting, seemed to glow like polished ebony, and a full figure that the low-cut négligée she was wearing did almost nothing to conceal.

She disappeared from view for a moment, then came back into frame with Silvester following. I saw her lips move but Silvester wasn't interested in talking. He stepped close to her, his hands sliding inside the gaping opening of her négligée. He kissed her. The négligée began to slip down off her shoulders but she broke away in time to stop it. She went to the window and pulled the curtains. I was left to imagine what happened next. Imagining was worse than seeing.

I opened a window to let in some air. So Silvester had a mistress. With a wife the size and temperament of Pinky I was surprised he dared. Yet what surprised me even more was the young woman. It was pretty obvious what he might see in her, but what on earth did a stunning creation like that see in an overweight scrap-metal dealer?

I got out of the car and crossed the road to the flats. I tried the front door out of habit. It was locked. I inspected the panel of bellpushes underneath the entryphone on the wall. There was a name by each button. The first-floor flat was occupied by one Angie Maxfield.

I retreated to the car and backed it up the road a short distance so I could watch the flats without being too conspicuous. I suspected I was in for a long wait. Still, I'd made a bit of progress. I knew Silvester had another woman, I knew her name. And I knew she had lousy taste in men.

It was just under an hour later that they both came out. Angie Maxfield was wearing more clothes now, but she didn't look any the worse for it. Silvester opened the driver's door of the Range-Rover without so much as a glance in my direction. But Angie paused on the pavement and stared across the street. I edged down lower behind the wheel. I knew she'd seen me. Whether it mattered was another question. She got in next to Silvester and the Range-Rover pulled away.

I turned the ignition key to follow them. Nothing happened. I did it again. The engine turned over but didn't start. I tried again, frantically, as the Range-Rover disappeared over the horizon. I got nothing but a high-pitched whine, like the distress call of a dying coot. The Range-Rover had gone. I sat back resignedly. I knew the Lada had been a big mistake. I should have bought a car.

I didn't think the evening could get worse, but it did. It took me twenty minutes to start the car, and then only after I'd resorted to opening the bonnet and wiggling a few wires around. By that time I was frozen through and in a foul temper. I'd have taken it out on the Lada, given the tyres a good kicking, if I hadn't thought it would collapse at the mere touch of a shoe.

I got back to my flat wanting only to eat and sag into a hot bath. But I'd forgotten to go to the shops and the immersion heater wasn't on so there was no hot water. On top of that, there was a rude message from Sam Fielding on my answering machine, enquiring about my overdue feature on the South Yorkshire coalfield, a topic I could not bring myself to even contemplate in my present state of chilled starvation.

To add to my grief, the pile of dirty laundry in the bedroom appeared to have propagated in my absence and was spreading dangerously towards other parts of the flat. If it wasn't contained soon I'd have the environmental health people on my back as well as everybody else.

I switched on the immersion and warmed myself up with a mug of tea, watching television and wondering if I could be bothered to go out for a take-away. I flicked through the channels on the remote control, searching for something bearable to watch. I ended up with a nature programme on BBC2 about hyenas in Africa, nothing but a gory cycle of mating, killing, fighting and dying. I endured five minutes of it then switched it off. It reminded me too much of life.

It was nearly ten o'clock before there was finally enough hot water for a bath. I'd just run it and was preparing to strip off when someone knocked at the door. A heavy, urgent knock. I should have ignored it, but I went through automatically and pulled open the door.

Detective-Sergeant Chris Strange was standing outside. He pushed his beer gut past me into the living-room, the rest of him following a few seconds later. He sat down in an armchair.

I closed the door. 'Come in, make yourself at home.'

'Thanks,' Strange said. 'I have.'

I took the chair opposite him. He stroked his moustache with the forefinger of his right hand and looked around casually, not appearing to take in much but noticing everything. Cops are sneaky that way.

'What do you want?' I said.

'This place doesn't get much better, you know. Every time I come it's the same. You ever thought of painting the walls to hide the damp patches?'

'You moonlighting as an interior decorator now?'

'Just an idea.'

I waited for him to get to the point. He took his time.

'Not disturbing you, am I?'

'I was just about to have a bath.'

'That sounds nice.'

'I'd suggest you joined me, but I don't take baths with strange men. Not on a first date anyway.'

'I'm more of a shower man myself. Quicker, more hygienic. None of that wallowing in your own filth.'

'Yes, I can see that might be a problem in your case.'

Strange adjusted his coat over the prominent mound of his belly. He looked about eight months pregnant. He didn't say anything.

'That all you came for?' I enquired. 'To give me a couple of tips on hygiene and home decorating.'

'I thought you might want to know how the Andy Peters investigation is going.'

'Really?' That wasn't why he'd come but I didn't want to spoil things. 'And how is it going?'

'Slowly. We need some help.'

I watched him. He'd been looking away but his eyes came back to mine. He smiled at me. Never a good sign in a copper.

'You enjoy your trip to Hull?' he said.

Now I knew where we were. 'Hull?' He had the edge on me but I never believe in making things easy for the police.

'Wolds. You and Tony have a nice chat?'

'Word gets about quickly.'

'I know. You can't do anything these days without it spreading all over the place.'

Something had happened, but I couldn't fathom what. 'What's it to you if I go to see someone in jail?' I said.

'Normally nothing. But this time it's different. You're not having much luck at the moment, are you? First Andy Peters, now Tony Napier.'

I went very still. 'What do you mean?'

Strange waited a beat, enjoying the moment.

'Tony was found dead after supper this evening. A couple of hours ago. Someone put cyanide in his coffee.'

CHAPTER 9

They put me in an interview room at police headquarters. A claustrophobic box with no window and about as much charm as a coal bunker. Chris Strange sat down across the table from me and put his hands behind his head.

'You been in one of these rooms before?' he said.

'No.'

'Cosy, aren't they? Just the right size for an intimate little chat.'

'Is that what I'm here for? We could have stayed in my flat.'

Strange mused on that for a short while. 'Yes,' he conceded eventually, 'we could have. But it doesn't have quite the same atmosphere.' He grinned at me maliciously. 'I've wanted to get you in one of these for a long time, McLean.'

'I'm glad I could oblige.' I glanced at the tape recorder on the table. 'Shouldn't you be recording this interview?'

'This isn't an interview. I told you, it's a little chat. The interview comes later.'

I was getting tired of this. I was hungry, dirty. I'd been dragged away from my hot bath, driven down to Snig Hill in the dark, dumped in a poky boxroom, and now Strange was playing party games.

'I don't have to put up with this,' I said. I stood up and walked towards the door. The uniformed constable leaning on the wall blocked my exit. I turned to Strange.

'Am I under arrest?'

'Not yet.'

'Then I'm free to go.'

Strange yawned, but didn't reply.

I went back to the table and leaned down, hands flat on the scratched formica surface.

'It's very late, Chris. I've come down here of my own

volition. I haven't been arrested, I haven't been charged with any offence. I can walk right out that door and you can't stop me.'

Strange sighed. 'I can see I'm going to have to make this official.'

'I think you'd better.'

He told me I was now under arrest, for obstructing the investigation into the murder of Andy Peters. Then he cautioned me.

I said: 'You can do better than that, Chris. You don't have any grounds for holding me.'

'So you can sue us for damages,' Strange said dismissively. 'But the fact remains you're in custody. And you ain't leaving until we get some answers. Now sit down. Take your head out of your arse and look around you. You're not going anywhere unless I let you. You're not even going for a piss without my say so. Sit down.'

There was an edge to his voice which I didn't like. Strange was too experienced a copper to hold me illegally. Something more was going on here than I realized.

I sat down. 'I think maybe I should have a solicitor present.'

Strange shook his head. 'No lawyers, no phone calls even.'

I held my temper. 'You think I don't know what the Police and Criminal Evidence Act says?'

'I'm sure you could cite it word perfect, McLean. You're the sort of awkward bastard who could.'

'I'm entitled to have one person informed that I'm being held and the right to consult a solicitor at any time.'

'Yeah.' Strange picked one of his teeth with his thumbnail. 'But seeing as you're so smart you'll also know what else it says. "As soon as is practicable" I believe are the words in both those sections.'

I knew what was coming. 'Don't tell me. Right now it's not practicable.'

'You catch on quick.'

So much for civil liberties, those checks on official abuse
of power that make our legal system the envy of the world.
None of this made sense. My mind ran over all the permu-
tations, searching for an explanation. It still didn't make
sense.

'We've got twenty-four hours before we have to charge,
or release you,' Strange continued. 'Get used to it, McLean,
you could be here for a long time.'

'What's going on, Chris?'

'You think I know? A lowly detective-sergeant in the
South Yorkshire force. This goes way beyond me. I'm just
the errand boy who was sent to bring you in.'

'So why are you sitting here now?'

'I'm doing you a favour. Giving you a tip. Change the
habits of a lifetime and cooperate. This isn't my show. The
people you're dealing with now are a hell of a lot nastier
than me.'

He held my gaze for a time, letting the message sink in.
Then he broke away and nodded at the constable by the
door. 'Tell Mr Armstrong we're ready.'

A minute, maybe more, passed before the door opened
again and a tall, middle-aged man entered alone. I knew
at once he wasn't a copper. He was wearing a dark blue
woollen suit with a matching waistcoat, expensively
tailored but well-worn and crumpled now. A gold watch
chain hung across his ample belly, and his plump face had
the ruddy complexion of the upper-class claret junkie. He
gave off the stench of a gentlemen's club, a mixture of
cigars, old leather and boiled cabbage.

'Thank you, Sergeant,' he said smoothly. 'You may leave
us now.'

You could cut his plummy tones with a chainsaw. Definitely not a copper. This was the walking embodiment of
the wonderful British Establishment. Strange was right:
they *were* a hell of a lot nastier than him.

Armstrong waited for Strange to leave, then sat down
facing me across the table. He studied me like a zoologist

contemplating some new sub-species, not quite sure how to classify me. Or maybe entomologist would have been more apposite. The superior air of disdain was readily apparent in his face. To him I was an exhibit on a pin, not a person.

'Hi,' I said. 'Who are you?'

He ignored the question. I was the one under the microscope.

'Sergeant Strange has explained the position to you, I trust.'

'Oh yes, he made it very clear.'

'Good. I do hope this interview can be made as short as possible.'

'Me too. We can end here if you like. It's already well past my bed time.'

'Mr McLean,' he said sharply, establishing his authority from the outset, 'I have one or two questions to ask you. I suggest you answer them as fully and as frankly as you can.'

He spoke with the urbane drawl of the public school, but with a subtle hint of menace. Well-bred, beautifully educated, but underneath the sleek patina he had the scruples of a sewer rat.

I gave him a lopsided smile to let him know I wasn't impressed.

'Ask away.'

Armstrong switched on the tape recorder and went through the formalities of noting our names and the time. It all seemed pretty unnecessary considering there were no valid grounds for holding me in the first place. But I was curious to find out what he wanted.

'You went to Wolds Remand Prison this morning, I understand,' he said.

'That's right.'

'You visited a prisoner, Tony Napier.'

I said nothing.

'Didn't you?' he said.

'Sorry, was that a question?'

'Mr McLean,' he said, the first trace of irritation creeping into his voice, 'we are dealing with serious matters here. It would be as well if you cooperated.'

I leaned over the table. He pulled back a fraction, instinctively avoiding getting too close to a pleb like me.

'Then why don't you stop wasting both our times with questions you already know the answers to?'

The corners of his mouth tensed. I thought he was going to make another pompous speech, but he thought better of it.

He said: 'Why did you visit him?'

'Because he was a friend of Andy Peters'.'

'And what did you discuss?'

'Andy's death,' I said. 'Tony didn't know he'd been killed.'

'Did you know Napier?'

'Never met him until this morning. You caught the person who put the cyanide in his coffee?'

I knew he wouldn't answer, but I wanted to ask. Just to let him know this was a two-sided interview whether he liked it or not.

'Was that the only reason you visited him, to inform him of Peters' death?'

'No. Andy had something to tell me before he died. I thought Tony might know what it was.'

'And did he?'

'No.'

Armstrong eyed me narrowly, trying to gauge whether I was telling the truth. 'Did you talk about anything else?'

'Nothing of interest to you.'

'I will be the judge of that.'

Well, he did ask. I told him about Tony's talents as an animator and the saga of Snow White. Armstrong listened carefully, distaste written all over his blotchy complexion.

'I'm not sure it's relevant,' I said at the end. 'Unless you think one of the eight dwarves bumped Tony off.'

'You discussed nothing else?'

'No.'

I'd left out the office burglary in Immingham and the involvement of Jawaad al-Nabil, of course. Those were *my* leads. I was buggered if I was going to give them to this stuffed shirt. Maybe he knew about them already.

Armstrong sat back in his chair and pressed the tips of his fingers together.

'It's strange, is it not, that Napier should be killed on the day you visit him?'

'You think I did it?' I said. 'Poisoned him ten hours or so after I left?'

'No. But I think you know why he was killed.'

I shook my head. 'I've no more idea about that than I have about Andy Peters' death. Why don't you question the other remand prisoners at Wolds? It must have been one of them, mustn't it? Where did they get the cyanide?'

Armstrong shrugged. 'These things can be smuggled in with relative ease. If they can get heroin and cocaine in, they can do the same with cyanide.'

He'd answered one of my questions. His authority was slipping. I tried another.

'What's your interest in all this?'

He wasn't going to be that helpful.

'Andy Peters was murdered as well,' he said, pursuing his own line of thought. 'Doesn't that surprise you? Two petty burglars killed in the space of a few days.'

'Maybe they both upset the same person.'

Armstrong nodded slowly. 'Maybe they did.'

He turned away and gazed at the blank walls of the room. He looked like a harmless old buffer, the sort of pub bore who lies in wait for unsuspecting drinkers to stupefy to death with cricket stories. He probably wore gloves for driving and called women 'the fair sex' as a cover for rampant misogyny. But I wasn't fooled. He didn't get to his position without a brain, even if it was now half pickled in Château Margaux.

He said abruptly: 'You're known to the local police, aren't you, Mr McLean?'

'I have regular contact with them, yes. It's part of my job.'

'And is contact with criminals part of your job too?'

'If there's a story in it, maybe.'

'Did you take anything from Andy Peters' flat?'

'Like what?'

'Answer the question, please.' His politeness was wearing thin.

'I've told the police already. No. Is something missing?'

Armstrong didn't reply. But I knew something was missing. That's why Andy's flat and my own had been searched. I didn't know who'd done Andy's place, but I was getting an idea who'd done mine. And it wasn't the Tooth Fairy. As to what was missing, I could hazard an informed guess: the file from the office in Immingham.

'What is your interest in Jawaad al-Nabil?' Armstrong said.

So he did know about the Egyptian. Now I knew who'd been following me.

I furrowed my brow. 'Jawaad who?'

Armstrong sighed. 'Don't insult my intelligence. The man you followed to his hotel last night.'

'Ah, him,' I said. 'I didn't know his name. I tried to find out but got nowhere. Didn't your man mention that in his report? Careless of him.'

'I repeat, what is your interest in him?'

'Treading on MI5's toes, am I?'

He didn't react. No doubt years of practice at denying what he did. 'Something at the Home Office, old man, desk job, frightfully dull,' was probably all anyone ever got out of him. But I knew he was with Five. He couldn't have been anything else.

'Do you intend to answer my question?' he enquired.

'I saw him talk to someone at the City Hall. Someone I was interested in. I was curious to know who he was.'

'Who was this "someone"?'

'A businessman called James Silvester.'

'Ah.' He let the word out slowly. To me it meant he knew who Silvester was. Now why would MI5 be familiar with him?

'Do you normally follow people around?' Armstrong said.

'Not as often as you. But sometimes.'

'It seems a strange activity for a journalist.'

'I learn things from it. That's how I work. I collect snippets of information then try to piece together the whole picture.'

'And how far have you got with your picture?'

'I've told you everything I know.'

'Have you now?' He studied his fingernails. 'I don't think you have, Mr McLean. From what the local police have told me about you, and my own perceptions of this interview, I am inclined to believe you may well be withholding information.'

'Perhaps if you told me what was going on I could help you more,' I said.

Armstrong forced a tight smile. 'This interview is for our benefit, not yours. If you know anything more about Andy Peters, Tony Napier or Jawaad al-Nabil I suggest you tell me now. Or you may find yourself in detention longer than you would like.'

His tone was mild, but the threat was all too clear. I'd had enough of his supercilious bullshit. The gall was rising in my throat.

'You really think you're going about this in the right way?' I said quietly. 'Hauling me out in the middle of the night and bringing me down here for interrogation as if this were some tinpot South American dictatorship? Everything you've asked me could have been asked at my flat and I might have taken it better. But no, that wasn't the way you wanted to do it. Because you're less interested in my answers than in trying to intimidate me. That's what this is all about, isn't it? Softening me up with a show of power.

You enjoy that, don't you, Armstrong? It gives you a hard-on.'

He winced. Vulgarity always got through to his type better than reason. It was the only way to crack the smug carapace.

'You search my flat, follow me around, detain me on some nonsensical charge. And then when I want to know what's going on you make ridiculous threats about holding me here. You think that will get you any further in whatever it is you're investigating? Or is it just a way of asserting yourself? Showing me what a big boy you are? The important man from Whitehall visiting the provincial peasants to put them in their place.'

Armstrong flushed, but he was too self-satisfied to be remotely concerned about what I thought.

'They are not ridiculous threats, Mr McLean,' he said icily. 'I have every power to detain you.'

'You see,' I said. 'Power. That's what you enjoy, isn't it? You don't give a toss for my rights.'

'You don't have any rights. There's no written constitution in this country, no Bill of Rights. You have no "right" to anything. Any liberties you have are ones *we* choose to give you. And they can be taken away at any time.'

'And who are "we"? People like you and your mates, who went to the right schools and eat in the right clubs? You think that gives you the right to make the rules?'

'I act in the interests of the state.'

'But you equate the interests of the state with your own interests. They're not the same thing, Armstrong.'

He waited a moment, his teeth clenched tight. Then he swung his legs out from under the table and stood up, switching off the tape recorder as he did so.

'I don't think there's much to be gained from continuing this interview. Clearly you are not willing to cooperate, Mr McLean.'

'Not with someone like you,' I said. 'Go back to London.

Have a few ports after dinner and tell your masters that next time they should send a human being.'

Armstrong glared at me, his cheeks puffing with a barely suppressed anger. Then he turned and walked stiffly out of the room.

Chris Strange came in so soon afterwards I knew he must have been waiting in the corridor outside.

'You seem to have upset our Mr Armstrong,' he said.

'Can't think how.'

'You never take advice, do you? You always think you can do it all on your own.'

'God help me if I had to rely on people like Armstrong.'

'People like Armstrong run this country.'

'I know,' I said. 'He told me. Am I being charged?'

'Not for the moment. Come on, we've got a little room waiting for you.'

'I hope it's nicer than this one,' I said.

He led me along to the cell block where a uniformed sergeant filled in the custody sheet and put the contents of my pockets in an envelope. Then Strange escorted me to my cell and unlocked the door.

'In you go.'

I took a step inside. Sitting on the raised plinth that served as a bed were two large Hell's Angels, complete with leathers, chains, swastikas and frontal lobotomies.

'This one's occupied,' I said to Strange.

'We're a bit overcrowded tonight. All the others are full, I'm afraid. But these two will keep you company.'

I knew it was deliberate, but there was no point in arguing about it.

Strange closed the door behind me and turned the key in the lock. I could see his face through the small hatch in the centre of the metal panel. He grinned at me.

'Have a good night.'

The hatch snapped shut. I turned back to find the two Hell's Angels looking at me wolfishly. I took a deep breath.

'Hello, lads,' I said. 'Nice tattoos.'

CHAPTER 10

It was the longest night of my life. The sort of never-ending ordeal we usually only endure in bad dreams. Except this was real. All my worst fears encapsulated in a single harrowing experience. I was cooped up in a seven-by-ten cell with two belligerent Hell's Angels. Two belligerent, *pissed* Hell's Angels, the pair of them having been arrested, I soon discovered, for being drunk and disorderly.

I thought at first it was all part of some cunning plan by the authorities to either beat information out of me or extract it simply by the fear of what these two goons would do to me if I didn't pour out my heart to them. But it rapidly became clear that Biff and Quentin—I had to check that in case I'd misheard—were so terminally stupid even MI5 wouldn't have touched them with the fag end of a Harley Davidson.

They started out hostile, taunting me, swearing, threatening me with various imaginative forms of violence. I played it gently, trying not to provoke them, whilst simultaneously working out how much time I had to make it to the door and scream my head off. They were big, beefy men, their arms bare from the shoulder and heavily stencilled with daggers, hearts and naked women, a veritable exhibition of the tattooist's art. They could have torn me apart without breaking sweat if they'd really felt like it. Fortunately for me, the aggression in them seemed mostly for show, a kind of routine demonstration of anti-social tendencies that they were obliged to keep up as devout, self-respecting Hell's Angels.

After a time I began to ask them a few questions, taking an interest in their lives and what passed for their personalities. I even hinted that there might be a magazine feature in it if they left me alive long enough to write one. This appealed to their vanity as well as taking their minds off doing unpleasant things to me. Having a feature written about them was flattery they couldn't resist and they spent most of the night telling me at laborious length about their various gruesome exploits. By the end I was beginning to wish they'd just beaten me up.

It was eight in the morning when the cell door was finally opened, letting in a welcome gust of fresh air to dilute the beery fumes I'd been breathing in for hours. I knew all about passive smoking but this was my first experience of passive drinking.

A uniformed sergeant took Biff and Quentin out, letting them off with a caution. They shook my hand before they left and said how much they'd enjoyed my company. We almost exchanged addresses and promised to write.

My own turn came an hour later. Chris Strange walked in alone and smirked at me.

'Still in one piece then? You must have more charm than I thought.'

'What would you know about charm?' I said. 'This was all your idea, wasn't it?'

'What makes you think that?'

'It was too crude for Armstrong. But it's just the kind of thing you'd enjoy.'

'You get any sleep? You don't look as if you did.'

'Is that all you've come for, to gloat?' I said.

'You're free to go,' Strange said. It obviously pained him to say it. 'We're not charging you. You're buggering us about for sure, but there's nothing we can pin on you.'

I raised a weary eyebrow. 'Sorry to be such a disappointment. So Armstrong's forgiven me, has he? No more friendly little chats?'

'Nope. You can go. Without a stain on your character,' he added with leaden irony.

'And if I bring an action for wrongful arrest and false imprisonment?'

'You won't. I know you too well for that. You're a pain

in the arse, McLean, but you're not a whinger. You'll take this as one of the hazards of sticking your nose into police business. Now piss off out of here.'

I picked up my jacket and left. They were letting me go. But that didn't mean I was off the hook. Not by a long chalk.

Coffee and toast had never tasted better. Especially when taken semi-submerged in a hot bath. The grime of the police cell, the stiffness in my limbs from a sleepless night on a bench, the budgie's cage taste in my mouth all seemed to disappear as I lay there up to my neck in soapy water.

My mind too felt refreshed. Confused still, but not as foggy as it had been at police headquarters. Things were getting rather more complicated than I'd expected. The death of Tony Napier and sudden arrival on the scene of Armstrong and the posse from MI5 had added a whole new ingredient to the cocktail, changing its nature quite dramatically.

There were now two murders to investigate, and not just simple murders or they would have been left to the police alone. The sharp zest of National Security had been thrown in to pep up the mixture, but I didn't yet know how significant it was, or how its tang would affect the rest of the heady brew I'd spent the last few days trying to taste.

Tony Napier's death had shocked me. He'd seemed a harmless small-time burglar, one of the many dimwits choking up the nation's jails. A typical ineffectual recidivist who'd sampled Her Majesty's hospitality at an early age and appeared intent on booking himself back in at regular intervals for the rest of his life. Yet he had done something, or knew something, which meant he had to die.

It didn't sound like an internal matter to me, another prisoner taking against him. Tony had only been on remand for a few days, surely not long enough for anyone to develop homicidal urges. It had to have been instigated from outside, and instigated by someone with enough clout, or the right contacts, to get cyanide smuggled in and dropped into a cup of coffee. Did that rule out Jawaad al-Nabil, who I was sure had had something to do with Andy Peters' death? He was a foreigner, probably only visiting this country for a short time. Would he have been able to fix it? Perhaps, perhaps not.

But the two deaths had to be connected, and that's where MI5 came in. The missing file was the link. Somehow that was the key to discovering what was going on. Al-Nabil had hired Peters and Napier to steal it, but I had a feeling Andy had kept it for himself. That explained why his flat had been searched, and possibly why he'd been killed.

Where was the file? I hadn't a clue, but Armstrong thought I did. Why else had he let me go? There was no lawful reason for holding me, of course, but that wouldn't have stopped a prig like Armstrong. He'd have locked me up just for the hell of it, to teach me to respect my betters. No, he'd released me because he stood to gain more with me free than in a cell. He was going to see what I did next. Learn from my actions, not what I said—or failed to say— in an interview room.

I got dressed and went out to the car. As I pulled away from in front of the flat, I looked in the rear-view mirror and saw a black Cavalier some eighty yards behind with two men in the front. I hoped they had a full tank of petrol. It was a long drive to Immingham.

My first impressions of Immingham were not good. My second impressions were not much better. It was not a town that grew on you. Small, drab, it clung to the featureless plain on the south bank of the Humber like a benign but unsightly wart, hemmed in by docks, a container port and a sprawling oil refinery that tainted the air with noxious fumes.

The centre was little more than a soulless shopping complex; butchers, newsagents, betting shop, a Kwik Save supermarket. A concrete desert populated by pasty-faced people in raincoats and scarves, heads bowed against the wind and sea mist blowing in from the estuary.

It took me a while to find the office Andy Peters and Tony Napier had burgled. Tony's description had been vague and I had to search the whole area near the docks before locating the two-storey block. It was on the fringes of an industrial trading estate opposite a timber and building supplies warehouse. An ugly concrete edifice, it was no different from the thousands of other dull, functional temples up and down the country in which the gods of commerce are worshipped.

The ground floor was unoccupied, a prominent 'To Let' sign displayed in one of the windows, but a discreet brass plaque by the entrance read: 'Hammond and Silcott, shipping agents. 1st Floor.'

So they'd burgled a shipping agent's office. Interesting. I went up the staircase to the reception area. It was cheaply furnished: a couple of old chairs and a chipboard coffee table. No money wasted on show here. Even the receptionist was reassuringly plain, as if she'd been selected from a warehouse to match the uninspired décor. She had lank brown hair, wire-rimmed spectacles and clothes with the distinctive cut and colour of the school jumble sale.

I told her who I was. She seemed perplexed.

'A journalist? We don't get many journalists here.'

'You had a break-in a couple of weeks ago,' I said. 'I wanted to ask someone about it.'

Her manner changed with a startling abruptness. 'Oh. Well, er, yes I think you'd better see Mr Hammond. I can't talk to anyone about that.'

She fiddled nervously with the buttons of her cardigan, like a schoolgirl caught shoplifting.

'Is he in?' I asked.

'Yes. Yes, he's in. But he might be busy. Well, what I mean is it wasn't important, the break-in. That's all I know.'

She was garbling her words, suddenly on edge about

something. I got the impression she'd had to learn her lines but had forgotten exactly how they went.

'Can I see Mr Hammond?'

'What? Oh, yes, I'll see if he's free. I can't promise of course. Won't you take a . . .'

She jabbed a finger at one of the chairs without finishing the sentence and disappeared hurriedly through a glass door. A short time later she came back out and motioned me to follow her.

'Mr Hammond will see you.'

I was taken into the inner office, and from there into a further office which was as unostentatious as the reception area; everything chipboard, plastic or second-hand.

A short man with a bald pate and tufts of coarse hair above his ears was sitting behind a dark, 'teak effect' desk. He had discoloured teeth and was wearing a scruffy tweed jacket with leather patches on the elbows and a hand-knitted grey waistcoat. He looked as if he'd come in off a park bench.

He ran a cursory eye over me as I entered and waved the receptionist away. He didn't shake hands or offer me a seat. I sat down anyway.

'Now, Mr . . . what is it?' he said in a gruff, rasping voice.

'McLean,' I said.

'Aye. Scottish, are you? You don't have an accent.'

'No. I come from Sheffield.'

'Sheffield, eh? Fine city. Used to go there on business years ago. You know the Grinder's Arms at Darnall?'

'No.'

'Probably knocked down by now. Used to do beer at two-and-six a pint. Ward's ale. Fine stuff. Two-and-six in old money, that is. Half a crown. You old enough to remember old money? No, don't expect you are. So, what can I do for you?'

He opened an old tobacco tin on the desk. It was full of half-smoked cigarette ends. He put one in his mouth and lit it with a match. Maybe he had come in off a park bench.

'You had a break-in a few weeks ago,' I said. 'Could you tell me what was stolen?'

He squinted at me. I saw wariness in his rheumy eyes. 'Nothing.'

'Nothing? Nothing at all?'

'That's what I said.'

'Are you sure about that?'

Hammond nodded. 'It wasn't serious. Probably a bunch of kids mucking around. How did you find out about it?'

I ignored that. 'Did they do much damage?'

'Broke the locks, that's all.'

'Do you have an alarm?'

He hesitated. 'Aye. They did something to that too. Bloody nuisance it was.'

'Doesn't sound like kids to me. What would they know about alarms?'

Hammond changed his story. 'Well, maybe it wasn't kids. Who cares who it was? They didn't take anything.'

'Have you checked?'

'Of course.' He took the fag end out of his mouth and broke down in a fit of coughing. I waited for the barking to stop, then said: 'Are you quite sure?'

His face had turned purple. He poured himself some water from a carafe on the desk and gulped it down. I hoped he wasn't going to die on me.

'Positive,' he said eventually. 'Nothing was taken.'

I was puzzled. Either he hadn't noticed a file was missing, or he was lying. Or Tony Napier was lying.

'You're shipping agents, aren't you?' I said.

'Sixty years in the business. My father ran it before me. It's been in the family since before the war.'

'Do you ship anything in particular?'

'We cover everything. You name the cargo, we'll get it to its destination. Why do you ask?'

'I'm just interested. Did you report the break-in to the police?'

'Certainly. We had to for the insurance.'

'Why would anyone go to the trouble of breaking in and then not take anything?' I said.

Hammond shrugged and took a final suck on his cigarette butt, burning it down to the filter. His fingertips were stained a dirty yellow, the same colour as his teeth.

'We don't have much of value to take.'

'You've got a fax machine out there, a photocopier, word processors. Why did they leave empty-handed?'

'Look, Mr McLean,' Hammond said irritably, 'I haven't the slightest idea. Now, is that all you wanted to know?'

'Thank you for your time,' I said, standing up. I'd got all I was going to from him. Anything else would have been mere conversation. I showed myself out of the office. The mousy receptionist was back behind her desk at the top of the stairs.

I paused by her and said casually: 'You know that file that was stolen during the break-in. Can you tell me what it was?'

She looked at me blankly. 'File? What file?'

It was worth a try. I went back down to the street. The two men in the black Cavalier were parked outside the timberyard opposite.

I let them follow me when I drove off, even slowing to a crawl to let them catch up when they just missed a green light at a crossroads. On the main road out of town I pulled in by a row of shops and went into a chippie for something to eat. When I came out with my cod and chips I strolled back down the line of parked cars to where the men were waiting. I finished my mouthful and tapped on the window. The man in the passenger seat—my friend in the cheap raincoat—wound down the glass.

'Yes?'

'I thought I'd let you know, boys,' I said affably. 'Save you time if you lose me at any more lights. I'm going straight home now. I'll probably stay in, have a cuppa, maybe snatch an hour's sleep, then go out again about quarter to seven. Nowhere interesting though, just the opera. They won't let you in there, at least not dressed like that.'

The man stared up at me. 'What?'

I held out the paper in my hands. 'Here, have a chip.'

I took it nice and easy on the drive home, mulling over my conversation with Hammond, wondering who was telling the truth about the file.

I was none the wiser by the time I got back to Sheffield. I'd driven a hundred and forty miles but to what avail? One short interview which had clarified nothing. Which, in fact, had only made the waters cloudier than they were before.

I had learnt one thing though, I suppose. The stolen file, if it really existed, had something to do with the shipping business. I wasn't sure whether that had been worth a trip to Immingham. But then I wasn't sure anything was worth a trip to Immingham.

CHAPTER 11

Masochism takes many forms, but going to the opera has to be one of the most peculiar. Dressing up to sit crammed in a bucket seat for hours on end, listening to a bunch of overweight hams warbling their way through absurd plots in a language you can't understand. And paying through the nose for the pleasure too. It can't be normal.

'You're such a philistine,' Maria said when I told her this on the way into the Lyceum. 'It's wonderful stuff. Do you know *Traviata?*'

'Not off hand.'

'You'll love it. Really.'

'Where's the bar?' I said. 'I think I'll need a drink by the interval.'

We took our seats in the balcony. The rake was so steep

we practically had to abseil down to them. In front of each row was a metal rail to stop you tumbling out into the stalls far below. It was my first time in the Lyceum since it had been renovated. All rococo trimmings and gilt cherubs. Twelve million quid it cost, and they still couldn't give me any legroom.

'You been here before?' I said.

'Several times. They've done it out beautifully, haven't they?'

'I remember the old Lyceum. I used to come to the panto here when I was a kid. Saw Jimmy Clitheroe in *Aladdin*. I still remember the kitchen scene, Jimmy and Widow Twankey making pastry. They rolled it into balls and played cricket with it, hitting chunks out into the audience. I caught one of them and kept it till it went mouldy and my mum made me throw it away.'

'Jimmy Clitheroe? I didn't think you were that old.'

'I was only about five at the time,' I said, wounded. 'The theatre was much smaller then. They didn't have enough room in the wings so they had to leave the sets outside in the street in between scenes. John Hanson came with *Desert Song* one freezing January and when they brought the sets on stage for the second act they were all covered in snow.'

Maria turned to look at me. 'You know something, Michael? You're a terrible bullshitter.'

I smiled at her. She'd come straight from the office but still looked sickeningly fresh. How did she do it? My own appearance, I was aware, left something to be desired. Shadows under the eyes from my night in the cells, a distinct lack of spark owing to shortage of sleep and too much driving, crumpled trousers and a fraying shirt I'd bought for fifty pence from the Oxfam shop near my flat when I realized in desperation that everything else was in the wash. Well, in the pile awaiting the wash to be exact.

But I was here next to her, wasn't I? The dent in her car and the nightmare outing to the wrestling apparently forgiven and forgotten. That was enough for me at the moment.

I picked up the opera glasses from the holder on the back of the seat in front and scanned the auditorium. We were so high up I needed them just to find the stage. I could see the front section of the stalls and the orchestra pit, but my attention was drawn to a figure entering one of the boxes to the side. It was Crispin May.

He was wearing a black bow tie, frilly white shirt and dinner jacket, the left sleeve dangling loose from his shoulder. His hair looked newly permed, topping the smooth, pinky flesh of his face with a curling wave of silver. I could almost smell the lacquer from the balcony.

As I watched, another figure joined him in the box. I couldn't see the face, but from the bulk and shape I knew it could only be one person. She turned and confirmed my guess: Pinky Silvester. She was wearing a long, loose pink evening gown made of what looked like silk, cut low at the front to reveal her cavernous cleavage. I wondered how many millions of silk worms had given their lives to produce that amount of material.

Crispin May kissed her hand gallantly and held her chair for her as she sat down. So the theatre ticket I'd seen in his office *had* come from Pinky. Was this pleasure, or were they here to discuss business? I went over the possibilities. Discussing another hit on Silvester, discussing a hit on someone else, a chat about interior design—boring, but possible—or a purely social outing to share their mutual love of opera. Maybe Crispin May wasn't gay after all and the two of them were secret lovers. I tried to imagine them in bed together but it was too grotesque to contemplate.

'Who are you looking at?' Maria asked.

I lowered the opera glasses. 'No one in particular. You want these?'

She shook her head. 'Not at the moment.'

I had a last look through the glasses as the house lights went down and saw James Silvester slipping in at the back of the box. He whispered something to his wife and shook hands amicably with Crispin May. Bang went at least two of my theories.

I settled back in the tiny seat, my knees somewhere close to my chin, and made an attempt to stay awake during the opera. It was sung in English which was a bit of a drawback. It meant I understood it.

At the interval we went downstairs to the bar and fought for ten minutes to buy two overpriced glasses of wine. I was dead beat. I wanted only to go home and sleep, but I had to make an effort.

'What do you think?' I said to Maria, suppressing a yawn.

'I'm enjoying it.'

'It's a bit like the wrestling, isn't it? That fat geezer, the tenor, what's his name again?'

'Alfredo.'

'Yeah, well he's got the right build for a few rounds in the ring. And the soprano looks exactly like the Greasbrough Strangler. If they get their kit off in the next half we could see a fair bit of aggro.'

Maria gave me a long-suffering look, one of her specialities, and said: 'If I were you, I wouldn't mention wrestling again, ever.'

I grinned. 'The soprano is pretty big though, you've got to admit. She dies, doesn't she?'

Maria nodded. 'Of consumption.'

'I'm not surprised. She looks as if she's eaten too much already.'

Maria smiled tolerantly. 'That's one of the reasons it flopped on its debut. The audience thought the corpulent soprano they'd cast was hilarious as Violetta.'

'You read that in the programme?'

'I did my thesis on Verdi. At university.'

I was surprised. I knew so little about her really. But then she didn't give much away. 'You did music? I thought . . .'

'That as I'm an accountant I must have done something desperately dull?'

'Well,' I said cautiously, 'it is a bit of a jump.'

'What do I do with a music degree? Except maybe teach.'

'Yes, but accountancy? It's not exactly creative, is it?'

'That depends what kind of an accountant you are,' Maria said drily. 'I wanted a professional qualification. Some control over my career so I didn't end up being told what to do by a man with half my brain. I'm like you really. I don't take kindly to being given orders.'

She took a sip of her wine. She was stronger than she looked, but for all the determination she was still not hard. Independent, probably tough when she needed to be, but not hard.

'How about you?' she said. 'You didn't go to university, did you?'

'You can tell?'

'Just a feeling. Somehow I can't see you amid the ivory towers.'

'I had to get a job straight from school.'

'Through inclination? Or necessity?'

'I had a little grey-haired mother and fourteen brothers and sisters to support.'

'Don't tell me. And you lived in a shoe box and had to work nights down the pit when you were still in nappies.'

'How did you guess?'

'You never give straight answers, do you? Especially to questions about yourself.'

'It's a very boring topic.'

'Only because you don't open it up for discussion. You spend your time asking other people questions, poking your nose into their affairs, yet you don't like it when someone questions you. Do you?'

I was aware of her smoky blue eyes on me, uncomfortably penetrating. I looked away. At the other side of the bar James Silvester was also watching me. He said something to his companions and both Pinky and Crispin May turned their heads towards me. They exchanged a few more words, then Silvester broke off and disappeared into the throng of drinkers.

Maria was following my gaze. 'What a striking woman.'

I looked back at her. 'She is rather eye-catching, isn't she? You don't often see pink barrage balloons at the opera.'

'That's not very nice.' She glanced across again. 'Hang on, isn't that the—'

'Let's go back in,' I said smoothly. 'I think that was the two-minute bell.'

Maria didn't move. 'She's the wrestler from the other night. The one all in pink.'

I was in deep trouble if she worked out I had an ulterior motive for inviting her here. I took her arm and steered her back towards the auditorium.

'Looks nothing like her,' I said firmly. 'And besides, I thought wrestling was a taboo subject.'

Maria said nothing more for the rest of the performance, quietly absorbed in the music. But towards the end, when Alfredo was finally reunited with a dying Violetta, I heard her fumble in her bag for a handkerchief. I turned and saw tears on her cheeks.

On the stage, Violetta, close to death, was giving a locket to Alfredo and telling him to pass it on to the next woman he loved, a tender gesture of almost saintly generosity, tinged with regret at the parting of the ways and made all the more sorrowful by her implied acceptance that he would find someone else after she was gone.

It was a haunting aria. A simple line of melody punctuated by soft trumpet calls from another world. I felt my eyes prickling, a tear welling up and rolling down my face.

When the lights went up at the end we looked at each other mistily. I took Maria's hand and squeezed it. She didn't pull it away.

'I knew you were really a big softie, Michael,' she said.

Well, I suppose sooner or later someone had to find out.

*

We walked back to the underground car park where Maria had left her Mazda. No touching hands now, a couple of feet at least between us, yet I felt closer to her than before. Still a long way to go, but opera was clearly a surer path to her heart than wrestling. I'd better get used to it.

'Is your car here too?' Maria asked.

'I found a meter near the Town Hall.'

'Come back for a coffee.'

'You sure?'

She nodded. I snatched a look at her face but it gave nothing away. I was on my own this time.

There were footsteps in the subway behind us. I glanced round briefly, half expecting to see one of the men from the black Cavalier. But it was a youth in a leather jacket. I didn't recognize him.

I thought nothing more of it until we entered the underground car park itself. Then something made me look round again. There were two of them now, the youth and an older man with a two-day growth of beard and a heavy overcoat. One of his hands was tucked inside the coat. I got the impression he was carrying something. My pulse began to throb on the side of my neck.

Very calmly, I said to Maria: 'Where's your car? Which level?'

'Next one down. Why?'

'Nothing. I may leave you before we get there.'

'What?'

'But I'll see you back at your house.'

She turned, almost stopping, not understanding.

'Keep walking,' I said out of the side of my mouth.

'Michael, what . . . ?' Something behind us caught her eye. She looked back.

'Take it nice and easy,' I said. 'It's me they want.'

'Why?'

'Just get to your car and go home.'

We were walking down the ramp to the next level now.

'Where's your car?' I said.

'Left. By the pillar at the far side. Look, what's—?'

'Lock your door. If they try to stop you, run them down. Understand?'

'But you said—'

'I'm not having them get near you. I'll lead them away.'

'Yes, but . . . but surely they won't do anything to you? Not here. With me present.'

'They'd do it if Mother Teresa and the entire Vienna Boys Choir were here.'

I risked another look back. The two men were less than thirty yards away. They didn't seem in any hurry. Maybe I'd got them wrong. They were just going to their car. Then the younger one grinned at me and I knew there was no mistake.

'You'll be safe inside the car,' Maria said.

'They're not going to let me reach it.'

'Then they'll have to take me on too,' she said defiantly. 'I can hold my own.'

Her mouth was set hard. She had guts all right.

'Listen to me, Maria. When I say the word, run for the car and get in. Don't worry about me.'

'Oh no, I'm not leaving you.'

'Just this once, Maria, do as I say.'

My mouth had gone dry. The footsteps behind us were closer now. They were taking their time, enjoying the slow pursuit, the sensations of fear and panic they must have known they'd induced. But they wouldn't wait for ever. They were dangerous men. More dangerous close to. But I had no intention of confronting them.

'Now!' I yelled.

Maria took off in a straight line, one hand clutching her shoulder bag to her side. I went left, sprinting through the rows of cars. They ignored Maria and came after me. I took the corner at a run and headed down the ramp to the level below. I cut back across the parking area, an open mezzanine floor which was not directly underneath the section above. Through the concrete pillars at the side I heard an engine start up. It had to be Maria. One tiny part of my brain shut off. She was safe. I didn't have to worry about her any more. Just worry about myself.

The two men were still behind me, the young one gradually outdistancing his partner. Another ramp loomed up in front of me. I had a choice. I could head up or down, or continue to the staircase at the far end. I went for the staircase. It was an enclosed space offering no possibility of them outflanking me. And there were more exits from it.

I burst through the wooden doors and paused for breath. Which way? The car park was built into a hillside. From the top it appeared to be underground but there was a way out at the bottom. I opted to go up. It was harder on the legs, but I was only three floors down. The street was nearer if I went up.

I took the stairs two at a time, gasping for air. As I reached the first landing the doors to the parking area were kicked open and a massive figure stepped through in front of me. It was Silvester's tame grizzly, Jeff. He reached out to grab me, but he was slow. I'd already twisted round and stumbled back down the stairs. He came after me, lumbering clumsily in the dim light.

Jeff above me, the two men below. I knew which I preferred to tackle. Down was my only option. Then the youth in the leather jacket came through the doors on to the lower landing. He was alone. He peered around, trying to see which way I'd gone, and in that short space of time I descended the final few steps, jumped into the air and kicked him hard on the side of the head. He tumbled over to the floor in a heap, but he wasn't badly hurt. I skirted round his flailing legs and scrambled down the next flight of stairs. If I could only hold them off long enough, I could be out on to the street at the bottom and away into the maze of the bus station. If my lungs held out. And my legs.

I was clearing four or five steps at a time now, praying I didn't land awkwardly and twist an ankle. I could hear my pursuers up above but only occasionally caught a glimpse of a leg or a hand on the stair rail.

I reached the bottom still in front. I rammed open the exit door and as I came through a baseball bat hit me in the guts. I grunted with pain and doubled up. It was the man in the overcoat. Now I knew what he'd been carrying. He must have come straight down through the car park itself, to cut off the lower exit.

He hit me again on the back and I collapsed on to the concrete, instinctively shielding my head with my arms. The baseball bat thudded into my shoulder. I rolled over to escape the blows. I stood up groggily and backed away. He came for me, his lips curled back from his mouth in a savage snarl. I dodged the next blow and toppled out into the street. He paused as Jeff and the youth emerged from the staircase to join him. There were three of them now. I had nowhere to run, no energy even to try.

Jeff pushed the others aside and lashed out at me with a fist like a frying pan. If it had connected fully it would have broken my jaw, but I jerked back in time and it caught me only a glancing blow. It was still enough to knock me sideways on to the pavement. I turned over, twisting my head round.

It was then I heard the engines.

The roar of motorbikes. Then a shout. I saw Jeff and the others turn as a tidal wave of black leather and steel helmets engulfed them. I recognized the two figures at the front before the scene disintegrated into a mêlée of chains, knives and flying fists. It was Biff and Quentin.

For the first time in my life, I was glad to see a bunch of Hell's Angels.

CHAPTER 12

'Michael, thank God! I was so worried.'

Maria pulled open the door to let me in, touching my arm momentarily in a gesture of concern.

'You all right?'

I nodded. 'I could do with a coffee.'

'Of course. Come through.'

We went along the hall into her warm kitchen, a cluttered, homely room that smelt of spices and fresh herbs. Maria put the kettle on and spooned coffee into a glass cafetiere. I slumped down on one of the pine chairs and watched her wearily.

'I phoned the police from a call box as soon as I got out of the car park,' she said. 'Did they find you?'

'No.'

'You've been so long.'

'I was buying a pint for eight Hell's Angels.'

She paused in what she was doing. 'What?'

I told her what had happened. She listened quietly, wincing when I got to the baseball bat.

'But you must be hurt. Have you been to the hospital?'

'I'm OK. A bit bruised, nothing serious. Biff and Quentin showed up before things got really nasty.'

'Biff and Quentin?'

'Two of the Hell's Angels. I met them in a police cell last night.'

Maria took a while to absorb all this, filling the coffeepot automatically with hot water while she did so. Then she said: 'A Hell's Angel called *Quentin*?'

'I should've phoned you from the pub. The least I could do was buy them a drink.'

Maria picked up the cafetiere and put it on a tray with some milk and a couple of mugs.

'Let's go through. It's more comfortable next door.'

She waited until I was settled on the settee in the living-room, half sitting, half lying on the cushions before saying: 'I think you'd better start at the beginning.'

'You know the beginning. You were with me.'

She passed me a mug of coffee. 'You know what I mean. The whole thing. Who were those men?'

'The two behind us I'd never seen before. The third, the one on the staircase, works for James Silvester.'

'But how did they know you'd be in the car park at just that time?'

'They followed us from the Lyceum. Silvester saw me in the bar at the interval. He must have phoned them and told them to wait for me outside.'

'Silvester?' Maria screwed up her nose, thinking. 'Was that the man . . . wait a minute, Sil*vester*? I know that name. It *was* the wrestler, the woman in pink!'

She glared at me. I wasn't going to come out of this well, I could feel it. Silvester's goons angry I could cope with, but Maria angry was a different matter altogether.

'Oh yes,' I said desperately. 'Now you mention it, maybe it was her.'

'You've done it to me again, McLean,' she said softly through gritted teeth. 'What did I call you the other night? Devious? Lying? Treacherous?'

'I think you added spineless too,' I said helpfully. Best to confess your sins in circumstances like this, then hope for expiation.

'You *knew* all along it was the wrestler. And it wasn't a coincidence she was there. That's the only reason you went.'

'That's not true,' I protested. 'How would I know she was going to be there? I went because I wanted to make it up with you. I knew you liked music.'

'So why did you pretend not to recognize her in the bar, if you didn't have a guilty conscience?'

'Because I didn't want you to think I had an ulterior

motive for being there. It was pure chance we saw her.'

Maria took a sip of her coffee, her eyes never leaving my face. I assumed a look of saintly innocence.

'And stop doing that,' Maria said irritably. 'We both know you're no angel.'

'I'm telling you the truth.'

'If I had any sense I'd throw you out now. I can't believe a word you say.'

I waited. She didn't do anything. I sensed I was in the clear. There was circumstantial evidence against me, but not enough for a conviction. I adjusted my position on the settee and flinched as a sharp pain shot through my shoulder where I'd been hit with the baseball bat.

'And don't think you're going to get any sympathy from me,' Maria said. But her tone was gentler. She was giving me the benefit of the doubt.

I rested my head on a cushion. I'd almost dropped off a few times at the opera. Now I was finding it increasingly hard to stay awake as the exertions in the car park caught up with me. I drank some coffee, hoping it would clear my brain.

Maria was watching me. The flare in her eyes had subsided, the cool smoky blue back in place.

'So are you going to tell me, or not?' she said.

'If you want to know.'

She sighed impatiently. 'Of course I want to know. Do you have any idea how worried I was in that car park?'

'I made sure you were safe, Maria. I'd never have let them touch you.'

'About *you*, you idiot. Not me. I was worried about you being hurt by those thugs.'

'I could handle it.'

'Michael, if some Hell's Angels hadn't happened to be passing, you'd be lying unconscious in a gutter right now. Or worse. It's quite clear you can't "handle" it. Now what's going on? Why would this man Silvester want you beaten up?'

'Because he doesn't like me very much. I told you about him at the Grosvenor House.'

'You told me he'd been shot at, and his wife had kicked you out of their house. That doesn't explain why he sent three men after you. Or have you been up to something since then?'

I explained about my visit to the scrapyard in the East End, outlining the gist of my conversation with Silvester.

'You certainly like to push people, don't you?' she said when I'd finished. 'But I don't get it. What's the connection between Silvester and this Egyptian fellow?'

'I don't know. I thought I might find out if I got under Silvester's skin a bit.'

'If you put yourself in the firing line you mean.'

'I didn't expect it to turn out quite like that.'

Maria shook her head. 'I really don't understand you. You knew what he was like. Did you really think he'd do nothing after you'd announced your intention to stick your nose into his business?'

I shrugged. 'I thought it might help me crack the story.'

'All it seems to have cracked is a few bones in your body. You don't even know there is a story in all this.'

'Oh, there's a story all right. I just don't know exactly what it is yet.'

Maria crossed her legs. She'd changed out of her work clothes and was wearing a pair of loose black leggings and a baggy jumper that somehow concentrated your mind on what might be underneath it.

She waited. 'Is that it?'

'Pretty much.'

Those cool eyes stayed on my face. 'I want the whole thing, Michael. Not just the bits you feel like telling me. I was with you tonight, remember? I think you owe me the rest.'

'Well, I've filled you in on Silvester. There's not much more to say about him.'

'And the Hell's Angels you met in a police cell?'

'Biff and Quentin? They were drying out after a few too many drinks. I just happened to be put in with them. They kept me awake all last night recounting their life stories.'

'And?'

'You wouldn't want to hear them. It was nothing but booze, violence, bikes and women. In that order.'

'Are you going to stall all night? You think I'm interested in a couple of Hell's Angels? Why were you in a police cell?'

'Ah. It gets a bit complicated here.'

'I've got time,' Maria said patiently.

'And I don't want to get you involved.'

'You should have thought of that before you took me to a wrestling match and the opera, both times, it would seem, as some kind of cover for your dubious activities.'

'That's not how it was.'

'You *used* me, Michael. Now cut the crap, or I'll dig out my old school hockey stick and finish the job those three heavies started.'

I couldn't work out whether she meant it or not. I decided not to take a chance. I told her about Andy Peters and Tony Napier, my visits to Wolds and Immingham and my interview with Armstrong.

At the end she said: 'I see what you mean about complicated. But you haven't done anything illegal, have you?'

I'd left out the little matter of breaking and entering at the Grosvenor House Hotel. You can take confessing your sins too far.

'Not a thing,' I said virtuously.

'So why did they put you in the cells?'

'Pure malice. I upset Armstrong. Made a rude comment about his old school and his club. They get very sensitive about things like that these toffs from MI5.'

Maria's eyes jerked back to mine suddenly. 'MI5? They're involved in this?'

'So it would seem. Why, I don't know.'

'Did he tell you that?'

I shook my head. 'They don't go around advertising the fact. But he wasn't a cop, or Special Branch. That only leaves the Security Service.'

'And what are the implications of that?'

I gave this some serious thought. 'The implications? Probably that I'm in deep shit.'

Maria finished her coffee and put the mug down carefully on the arm of her chair. She was studying me shrewdly.

'You're enjoying this, aren't you?'

I started to deny it but she interrupted me.

'Come on, Michael, I know you are. There's nothing you like more than getting up people's noses.'

'I'm just quietly going about my job. I never deliberately upset anyone.'

'I suppose it just happens by accident, does it?'

'Mostly.'

'So how come you end up in a cell overnight?'

'It was wrongful imprisonment. They released me, didn't they?'

She said nothing for a time. I suppressed another yawn and watched her drowsily, wondering if I'd get away with making a pass. If I could manage a pass in my exhausted state.

She looked so maddeningly composed. Legs crossed, tilted sideways at an angle so the toes of her left foot were practically tucked round her right calf. I've never figured out how women do that. The shapeless jumper at least three sizes too big, the sleeves pulled up to reveal slim wrists, one encircled by a band of silver. Her beautiful face in repose, smooth, clear-eyed, one hand resting on her chin, a finger touching her lips pensively. More than enough to make a grown man weep.

I estimated my chances of getting across the room, leaning down and stealing a kiss before she knew what was happening. Not good. There was something in her manner that urged caution. A distance, an aura of self-possession that made her hard to get near. Yet underneath it all, I felt, there were doubts, insecurities, a hidden vulnerability that only the warmth of human contact could dispel. Don't rush it, she seemed to be saying. Maybe one day, but not just yet. I've always been an optimist.

'Do you have any idea who killed those two men, the burglars?' Maria asked suddenly.

'Nothing concrete.'

'Whoever did the second murder, the one in jail, must have been pretty desperate.'

I nodded. 'And pretty well connected. Not just to get the cyanide in and into Tony's coffee, but to get hold of the poison in the first place. You don't just go into a chemists and buy a jar of cyanide off the shelf.'

'You think it's all linked to that file?'

'I can't see what else.'

'But the shipping agent said nothing had been stolen. What if—what's his name, Tony?—what if he lied to you?'

'I've considered that, but I don't think so. He gave me all the right information: the location of the office, first floor, opposite a timberyard. It all fits. You see, there *was* a burglary there. Even Hammond admitted that. And Tony must have done it to know the details. So why should he lie about taking a file?'

'Why should the shipping agent lie?'

'I can't work that out.'

Maria pursed her lips. 'If it's all true, where's the file now?'

'That,' I said, 'is what we all want to know. Me, Armstrong and whoever murdered Andy and Tony.'

She uncrossed her legs and leaned forward, resting her forearms on her knees. Her expression was serious.

'Michael, don't you think you should leave all this to the police, or MI5?'

I shook my head. 'I've got a personal interest in this. Not simply for the story, but for Andy Peters. I found him, Maria. Dead. You don't forget that. And I'm going to find out why he was killed.'

I thought she was going to argue with me, but she just looked away, staring at a bright Dufy print of the bay at Nice which hung above the fireplace. Then she stood up and came towards me.

'I won't be long. Help yourself to more coffee.'

She passed by the end of the settee. Her hand brushed my shoulder.

'Be careful, Michael,' she said.

By the time I turned my head she had gone from the room. I rubbed the spot where she'd touched me. The slight imprint of her fingertips remained, as cool and elusive as she was.

I closed my eyes, listening to her footsteps on the stairs, a door opening somewhere at the back of the house. The sounds seemed to merge together so I was no longer conscious of the difference; then disappeared altogether as an enveloping silence seemed to fold itself around me, closing out the world.

I wondered vaguely if she'd come back down, sit beside me, let me hold her . . . then the silence seemed to seep gently inside me, obliterating everything except the outline of her face. Then that too, in time, faded away to nothing.

CHAPTER 13

When I awoke it was morning. Light filtered in through a gap in the curtains, casting pale shadows across the duvet that covered me. It took me a moment to realize where I was, the unfamiliar room, the smells, the sounds of a different house.

I sat up, remembering the previous night. I couldn't believe I'd dropped off and slept through without interruption. Even in my own bed I rarely did that. I threw off the duvet and emerged in my crumpled clothes, stretching to ease the stiffness in my shoulder and back. They still hurt from the beating with the baseball bat.

There was a note on the coffee table next to the settee. I picked it up and read it. *I didn't want to wake you. Help yourself to breakfast etc. Call me.* It was signed *Maria*, but with a cross after the name. A kiss. Only on paper, it was true, but maybe I was getting somewhere after all.

I sat still for a while, contemplating what might have happened if I hadn't fallen asleep. Then I roused myself. You can dwell too long on regrets.

I folded up the duvet and took it upstairs. I had no idea where it belonged so I just dumped it on the bed in the small front room. Then I went into the bathroom and washed. I still felt weary despite the full night's sleep. Middle age catching up on you, McLean, I said to myself in the mirror, wondering if the bags under my eyes were merely temporary or the first signs of the imminent collapse of my entire body.

I rubbed my skin dry with a big fluffy towel from the pine rail above the radiator and looked around, considering taking a bath or shower. It was such a warm, welcoming room, above all such a female room, that I could happily have moved in and settled down for a few years. Even the line of handwashed tights hanging over the bath like small skinned animals were somehow appealing. The earthy, practical side of a woman amidst all the perfumes, talcs and scented soap. I pictured Maria in here, emerging from the tub, wrapping a towel around herself . . . I went out quickly before I had a seizure.

The wind was blowing from the north-east, cutting through exposed flesh like a razor. But at least the sun was shining, washing the streets and houses with wintry splashes of colour. I drove home, stopping at a bakery on the way, and had hot rolls oozing with melted butter for breakfast. Then I telephoned the Grosvenor House Hotel and asked for Jawaad al-Nabil. The receptionist told me he'd checked out that morning, leaving no forwarding address.

I rang three more hotels on the off chance he'd simply moved somewhere else, but they'd never heard of him. Either he'd left town or gone to ground. One avenue of enquiry blocked. I tried another. Gordon Crieff was more helpful.

'The Andy Peters case,' he said. 'We think we've found a witness.'

'Yeah? Who?'

'A woman who lives on the second floor at Park Hill. Came home from bingo the night Peters was killed and met a man she'd nae seen before coming out of the lift. Definitely not a resident.'

'What makes you think he had anything to do with the murder?'

'It was about the right time. Somewhere between half ten and eleven. And we've done a check. No one in the flats had a visitor answering to his description that evening.'

'You releasing the description?'

'It's nae very full, I'm afraid. It was dark outside the lift and the woman only saw him briefly. In any case, he was wearing a balaclava so most of his head was hidden.'

'She didn't see his face?'

'Some of it. Where it wasnae covered by the balaclava. He was black.'

'What?'

'That surprise ye?' Crieff said.

'No. Is she sure? He wasn't just dark-skinned?'

'She's nae certain about a lot of it. But that's what she says. He had a black nose and cheeks. She couldnae place his age but she thought he was youngish, from the way he moved. Tall, probably over six feet, and well-built.'

'Anything else?'

'Just one thing. She said he ponged a bit.'

'What of?'

'Sweat, she thought. She caught a whiff as he came out, and the lift stank of it.'

'Makes a change from piss, I suppose,' I said. 'Made any progress in finding him?'

'Not so far.'

'Thanks, Gordon.'

'Ye want the other stuff? The dailies.'

'Anything interesting?'

'Only a brawl near the bus station last night. Bunch of Hell's Angels beat up three blokes, put them in hospital.' He reeled off the names of the victims and I scribbled them down automatically in my notebook. 'We dinna know why. Just one of those senseless attacks. We think it might be linked to a phone call we got just before it happened. Some hysterical woman claiming a friend was in danger in the car park above Pond Street. She dinna give a name so we don't know if he was one of the three.'

I smiled but didn't enlighten him. Maria hysterical? That would be the day. I hung up and thought about the description Crieff had given me. It didn't appear to fit anyone I'd encountered in the past few days. Certainly not Jawaad al-Nabil. He was quite short, five feet eight at the most, slightly built and so immaculately turned out it was almost impossible to imagine him actually sweating, never mind reeking of it. But I still wanted to talk to him. If only I knew where he was.

I made a list in my notebook of all the people I could think of who were connected, however slightly, to James Silvester, Andy Peters, Tony Napier and Jawaad al-Nabil. I'd spoken to them all, with one exception: Silvester's alluring mistress, Angie Maxfield. She probably had nothing to do with any of this, but it made sense to check her out.

Besides, I had no other pressing business this morning, unless you counted the tiresome grind of actually earning a living: finding some news to hawk around the Nationals or finishing the feature on the decline of the South Yorkshire coalfield. I had a feeling that paying a call on Angie

Maxfield would be infinitely more fun than either of those.

The black Cavalier and my two tails were nowhere in sight outside, but parked up the street was a dark blue Carlton saloon with a lone man in the driver's seat. It was a poor choice of car. No one in this neighbourhood owned a Carlton. Even the drug dealers, who had the money, would have curled up and died at the mere thought of such a staid, middle-class vehicle. The poor guy might as well have put a flashing sign in the windscreen saying 'Government Official on Surveillance Duty'.

I drove off in the Lada, the Carlton following predictably a short distance behind. I wondered where MI5 had been when Jeff and his chums came for me in the car park. That's the trouble with civil servants: they're never around when you want them. But it was still an interesting point. They'd been following me all day, yet in the evening, after I'd helpfully told them I'd be at the opera, they'd disappeared mysteriously just at the moment the goons emerged from the woodwork to rough me up. Another coincidence, or something more complex?

Angie Maxfield was just coming out of the entrance to her block of flats when I pulled in across the road. I left my engine ticking over while I watched her get into a sporty yellow Peugeot 205. She was wearing skin-tight black trousers, calf-length boots and a leather jacket, her dark hair tied up loosely at the back of her head with a silver ribbon. I saw her breathtaking face in profile as she drove away. It was going to be tough keeping an eye on her, but I braced myself manfully for the ordeal.

And ordeal it turned out to be, for she spent the entire morning shopping for clothes. Next, Principles, Wallis, House of Fraser, half a dozen others, she went into them all, spending an eternity fingering the rails, holding up skirts, trying on outfits, even occasionally buying one. It brought back painful memories of my marriage, the Saturday excursions into town 'just to buy a blouse' that turned into gruelling eight-hour endurance tests as my wife forced me into every shop we passed and still managed to end the day without finding anything she liked.

It was nearly one o'clock when Angie finally stopped for a break at the self-service restaurant in Cole Brothers, the store from which Andy Peters had bought his collection of new electrical hardware. I was relieved. So were my legs. It was an exhausting business tailing someone round women's clothes shops. Even the lingerie departments had begun to pall after a couple of hours.

Angie sat down at a table with a glass of orange juice and a ham salad. I paid for my chicken sandwich and pot of tea at the counter then wandered over towards her. The restaurant was crowded. I paused, pretending to look for somewhere to sit.

'Excuse me, is this seat taken?'

Angie looked up at me and shook her head. 'Feel free.'

I sat down opposite her and poured some tea. She ignored me, picking at her salad as if she didn't really want to eat it. Close to she was even more beautiful. Too beautiful in fact. The perfection of her features, the oval face, the delicately carved nose and lips, the flawless complexion gave her an artificial look. No defects, no blemishes to make her human. She was lovely, but strangely characterless, like a classical sculpture on a plinth.

'Busy morning?' I said.

Her head lifted. 'Pardon?' She saw I was looking at the pile of carrier bags by the table. 'Oh, yes.'

She smiled. Her teeth were a dentist's dream. I started to wonder vaguely if any part of her body was imperfect, but stopped myself. It played hell with the concentration.

'I'm taking advantage of the sales,' she explained. 'In my line of work you need a lot of clothes.'

I took the opening she offered. 'What do you do?'

'I'm a model.'

I feigned an interest, asking a few more questions, encouraging her to open out. Not that she needed much encouragement. She seemed quite happy to talk, particularly about herself. She was not the least bit curious about me, which suited me fine. The fewer questions I had to answer the better.

She was chatty, forthcoming, self-absorbed, her conversation—in sharp contrast to her looks—that of a young girl not a woman.

'Of course it works out terribly expensive, all these clothes. But I have to do it. It's an investment really. I must spend thousands a year on outfits. You know how it is.'

I nodded sympathetically, gauging how much I'd spent on clothes in the past year. Fifty quid maximum maybe, fifty-one if I included the suit from Dr Barnardo's.

'But my looks are my life. If I don't look nice, who's going to give me any work? My agent says it's money well spent if it furthers my career.'

'Are you busy?'

'On and off. I've done a few catalogues, mail-order, that kind of thing, but there's no future in that. My agent's trying to get me some magazine covers. That's where the money is.'

I let her babble away, but as I listened to her, it occurred to me that she was behaving rather strangely; being just a bit too talkative, too friendly for a casual chat between strangers over lunch. I got the feeling she'd almost been expecting me.

I thought back over the morning. I'd been very careful about following her. I was sure she hadn't seen me. I'd kept well out of sight, and in any case she'd been so absorbed in her search for clothes she wouldn't have noticed if a troop of Household Cavalry had been behind her. Nor could she have recognized me from that evening outside her flat. She'd seen my car, but it had been too dark for her to have seen my face clearly. I began to wonder if she was quite as naïve as she sounded.

'Anyway,' she said, wiping her lips with a paper napkin,

'I can't spend all day nattering to you, can I? I must get off.'

She pushed the half-finished salad away and gathered her belongings together. 'It was nice talking to you.'

I had to make a decision. I'd found out plenty about her, most of it inconsequential, but hadn't even begun to probe her about Silvester which was the whole point of talking to her.

'Maybe we could continue another time,' I said.

She paused, one arm halfway through the strap of her shoulder bag. Her gaze was blank, non-committal.

'What did you have in mind?'

'How about dinner tonight? Are you free?'

She gave it some thought. 'I could be.'

I offered her an added incentive. 'I know a few people in the magazine business. Maybe I could put you in touch with a couple.'

What are you doing, I thought. You sound like the archetypal dirty old man. Sleep with me and I'll give your career the break it needs. But it seemed to work, for Angie said: 'OK. Where and when?'

I arranged to pick her up at eight, then watched her collect up her carrier bags and leave the restaurant. I looked around for my tail from MI5. He was nowhere in sight but that didn't mean I wasn't still under surveillance. By now they'd have swapped over several times, particularly as they knew I was on to them.

I finished off what remained of my stewed tea and thought about Angie Maxfield. She must have been twenty-two or twenty-three years old. Not quite young enough to be my daughter but not far off. Why had she accepted my invitation? An invitation from a man she barely knew, a fifteen-minute acquaintance who had told her nothing about himself. She was not the brightest woman I'd ever met but someone her age should have had more sense than to say yes. Yet she hadn't. Why not?

If Silvester was anything to go by she liked older men,

but that wasn't a good enough explanation. Although I had my vanity, I was well aware I was less than irresistible to women. You could number my relationships on the fingers of one hand, fingers and thumb if you counted my ex. At parties—not that I was ever invited to any these days—I never got off with anyone. I was always the guy in the corner no one wanted to dance with, who spent the evening in the kitchen talking to the computer programmer and the girl with acne and who slunk off home early and alone. Yet here was this stunning model accepting my invitation to dinner. It was just a bit too good to be true. And too easy.

Something very peculiar was going on. I wondered if Silvester had noticed me following him to Angie's flat and warned her about me. Worse than that, maybe he'd briefed her on what to do if I approached her. I'd started the day tracking Angie. Now I began to wonder if our roles had been reversed and she was the bait to lure me within reach of the hunter.

I telephoned Maria at her office as soon as I got home.

'You busy?'

'Nothing that can't wait,' she said.

'I wanted to say sorry for falling asleep on you last night.'

She laughed softly. 'That's all right. It made quite a change. The men I've been out with, it's usually me who falls asleep.'

That gave me a sudden pang. There had to be others, of course. Why shouldn't there be? But I didn't want to know about them. I kept my voice light.

'Thanks for covering me up with the duvet.'

'It was the least I could do. You looked settled in for the night.'

'You should have woken me.'

'I thought you needed the sleep. By the way, I never said thank you for the opera. I loved it.'

'Any time.'

For a moment there was silence. Then Maria said: 'Why

don't you come round tonight? I could cook us something.'

My heart sank. Isn't that always the way? You commit to one thing, then something you really want comes up.

'Hell, I'm sorry. I'd like that, but I'm working tonight.'

'Not to worry,' Maria said. I listened for any hint of disappointment. If it was there I couldn't detect it.

'Another time, maybe,' I said.

'Sure,' she said. But she didn't suggest an alternative.

I put down the receiver knowing I'd made the wrong choice. Knowing which one mattered to me above all else. I should have accepted, then called Angie Maxfield and cancelled our dinner date.

I picked up the telephone again to dial Maria's number. There was a whirring sound on the line, a distant noise as if it were coming from the end of a long tunnel. Then the words: '*Another time, maybe. Sure.*' My own voice, then Maria's played back to me like a tape recording. I lowered the receiver back on to its rest and held it there for a while.

I suppose I should have guessed, but it still came as a shock. If I was being watched by the Security Service they'd hardly ignore my phone. It had probably been tapped for days. I resented that. It annoyed me more than the men in the cars outside. They at least had faces, a human side I could recognize. But this was a machine eavesdropping on my life and I didn't like it.

I spent the next few hours washing shirts in the sink and reviewing my progress on the Peters, Napier and Silvester fronts. I was way out of my depth, floundering around in waters that could easily drown me if I wasn't careful. But I couldn't bring myself to retreat to the shallows and hand over everything I knew to the police and the spooks from MI5. Cooperating with the authorities was complete anathema to me. Why else was I a journalist?

The missing file preoccupied most of my thoughts. I had to find it. But Andy Peters' flat was also uppermost in my mind. I had a feeling I'd overlooked something there, something important. Whatever it was, I'd seen it, but not noticed it. I reran the events of that night in my mind. Entering the flat, finding Andy's body, checking the kitchen, the bedrooms. Somewhere in the confusion of memories was a vital piece of information, but I couldn't identify what it was.

I was no nearer an answer by the time I'd changed and was ready to go out for the evening. Before I left I picked out two numbers from the phone book at random and dialled them. When someone answered I said in a cryptic, mysterious voice, imbued with controlled panic: 'Don't say anything, you know who this is. They're on to us. Close down the operation immediately and take the first plane to Argentina.'

Then I consulted my contacts book and called the private line of the Bishop of Sheffield. I gave him the same message and hung up. That should keep the phone tappers busy for a couple of hours, I reflected as I went out to the car. I hoped the bishop had a good explanation.

Dinner with Angie Maxfield was a sorry affair. My fault, not hers. We went to the Frog, my favourite French restaurant near the cathedral which was run by an ex-miner from Wath-upon-Dearne called Ollie Robinson. On the way in we met Maria.

She was just leaving, having already eaten with a female companion I didn't recognize. Five minutes later and we'd have missed each other. There was no missing each other now.

She looked at me, surprised, about to say something. Then she noticed Angie. It was pretty hard not to notice Angie, given the spray-on white dress she was wearing. Maria gave her a long appraising glance then her eyes came back to mine. I saw the hurt in them, a momentary pain that she quickly obliterated.

'Hello,' I said awkwardly. She didn't say anything. There was no point in trying to explain, not in the bustle of a crowded restaurant. It would only sound feeble.

Maria pushed past me to the exit. 'Don't work too hard,' was her parting shot.

After that the heart seemed to go out of the evening. Angie didn't notice the change, she was too wrapped up in herself to be aware of the moods of those around her, but for a time I lost all interest in her and anyone else except Maria.

I'd well and truly blown it. Rejected the chance of dinner with a woman I cared about for an evening out with a vacuous, overdressed china doll. The damage was probably irreparable. I was all those words Maria had thrown at me: lying, devious, treacherous. And she'd caught me *in flagrante*. An innocent party in truth, but she'd never believe that. Not from me.

Angie prattled away about her schooldays and career throughout the first two courses, running on automatic pilot without the need for any significant contribution from me. But when we reached the dessert I pulled myself together. I'd had a purpose in bringing her here. It was about time I concentrated on it.

'Do you know what I do for a living, Angie?' I said.

She looked slightly startled, as if this question had never occurred to her.

'No, what?'

'I'm a journalist.'

'Really? I met a journalist in Wales last summer. On a photo shoot for some hiking clothes. Anoraks, boots, that kind of thing. I had to pose by rocks and waterfalls looking all rugged and outdoorsy.'

The thought of Angie looking rugged and outdoorsy briefly diverted me. Somehow it wasn't very convincing.

'Do you want to interview me?' she asked. 'Is this what all this is for? Which paper are you on?'

Why did everything always come back to her? 'Angie,' I said firmly, 'just shut up for a minute, will you?'

She fell silent, frowning at me. I'd have preferred to get the information out of her by stealth, but there really wasn't a way of probing her subtly on this matter. It was frontal assault or nothing.

'I'm making a few enquiries about a friend of yours,' I said.

'A friend?'

'James Silvester.'

'Oh.'

She didn't seem particularly surprised. I reminded myself not to underestimate her. It was more than a possibility that Silvester had put her up to this; that she was here to find out exactly how much I knew about him. I'd have to be careful I found out more than I gave away.

'How do you know about him?' she said stiffly.

'Never you mind.'

'It's none of your business. It's personal.'

'I'm not interested in that side of it. I want to know what he talks to you about. The things he says. About his work, his business deals, his friends, his enemies.'

'Is that the only reason you asked me out?'

'Well, it wasn't for your conversation,' I said cruelly.

She pouted childishly. 'That's a horrid thing to say.'

'I know, I'm a horrid man. So why don't you humour me and tell me about Silvester?'

'I told you, it's none of your business. I thought you were going to get me some magazine work, not interrogate me about my private life.'

'You've spent the last hour telling me about your private life.'

'Not that kind of thing. Not about my friends.'

'What do you see in him, Angie?' It wasn't the most important question on my mind, but I still wanted to know the answer. I've never understood why young, beautiful women sleep with ageing unattractive men. Maybe the women themselves don't understand.

Angie picked her clutch bag up from the empty chair next to her and started to get up. I caught her wrist and held on to it tight. She bent down towards me and whispered fiercely: 'You want me to scream?'

I kept hold of her wrist. 'You want me to tell Silvester's wife about you and Jimmy?'

Her face went rigid. It really was a beautiful face. I wished I could have liked it more.

'You met Pinky?' I said.

Angie sat down heavily and glared at me. I let go of her arm. There was a faint red mark on the skin where my fingers had been.

'Now let's settle down and start again.'

Angie ran her tongue over her lips. 'You wouldn't tell her?'

'Not if you cooperate.'

'She'd kill me. James says she's violently jealous.'

'I can believe it. She's violently everything else. Now why don't we have a coffee to round off the evening?'

She nodded sullenly. I ordered the coffees from Ollie who stood over our table and wrote it down very slowly, his eyes fixed on Angie's cleavage. Sex, the fools it makes of us all.

I waited for the cups to arrive, letting Angie calm down, before I said: 'Does Silvester know you're here tonight?'

'Of course not. Do you think I'd tell him?'

I watched her carefully. If she was lying she was good. Maybe Silvester wasn't part of this.

'Why did you accept my invitation?'

Angie shrugged. 'Why not? I like going out for dinner.'

'You do it with other men?'

'Why shouldn't I?' she said defensively. 'I'm not handcuffed to anyone in particular. James is no fun. He always wants to stay in when he comes to see me.'

I bet he did. 'Is that often?'

'Couple of times a week. Look, I thought you weren't interested in that side of it.'

'What does he talk about to you? His work?'

'He never talks about work.'

'All men talk about work,' I said. 'It's almost their only topic of conversation.'

'Well, I don't listen much. It's too boring. All about scrap metal and deals. He's got a factory or something too.'

'A foundry.'

'Yeah. What's a foundry, anyway? It doesn't mean anything to me.'

'Has he mentioned any deals to you recently?'

Angie squinted at me, the cup of coffee poised midway between table and lip. 'Why're you so interested in him? What's he been doing?'

'Has he mentioned any deals?'

'Not that I can remember. I'm not good with facts like that. Do you really know some people who could get me on the cover of a magazine?'

I nodded, wondering what Sam Fielding would say if I suggested he put her on the cover of the *South Yorkshire Industrial Bulletin.*

'Did he say anything about being shot at in his car?' I asked.

'Did he or what! He talked about nothing else for hours. He was furious about it.'

'He have any idea who pulled the trigger? A name?'

Angie hesitated. This was it. I pressed her. 'Did he?'

'Not a name. At least I don't remember a name.'

'Then what?'

'He just said it was "that bloody wog". He went on and on about him. But I don't think he mentioned a name.'

I gave myself time to reflect. 'That bloody wog.' Who did Silvester mean by that? Jawaad al-Nabil? Did he count as a 'wog'? Probably, to a man like Silvester. Or was it the black man the police witness had seen coming out of Park Hill flats? That was the trouble with racist terms like 'wog'. They could apply to virtually anyone with dark skin.

Was there a key player in all this, I wondered, whom I had yet to meet? A black man who had killed Andy Peters and attempted to kill James Silvester, and then disappeared mysteriously.

I said to Angie: 'Did Silvester say why this man should shoot at him?'

'I don't think so.'

'Have you ever heard him mention the name Jawaad al-Nabil?'

Angie shook her head. 'Who's he?'

'It doesn't matter.'

She regarded me inquisitively. 'What's this got to do with you, a journalist?'

I wondered when she'd start to probe me. 'I'm just curious,' I said evasively.

'Come on, I've answered your questions. You can't leave it at that. Is James in trouble?'

'That's hard to tell.'

She persisted. 'What's he been doing? I think you should tell me. I don't want to get mixed up in anything funny. I've my career to think of. Are you doing a story about him?'

I brushed the questions aside. 'Finish your coffee. I'll take you home.'

'I want to know.'

'Just finish your coffee, Angie.'

I went to the bar and paid the bill, then waited for her to join me. On the way to the exit I said: 'You knew who I was at lunch time, didn't you?'

It caught her off guard. For an instant she was flustered. 'What d'you mean? Of course I didn't.' But she was lying.

I smiled at her. 'Jimmy told you to come tonight, didn't he? Why?'

'I told you, he doesn't know I'm here. Now are you going to take me home or not?'

I dropped her off outside her flat in the pouring rain. She didn't invite me in. I was on edge, expecting something to happen. But nothing did. Maybe I'd got it all wrong.

'I'll know better than to talk to strangers in a restaurant

again,' Angie said vehemently before she slammed the door.

At least she'd learnt something. I watched her walk in through the front entrance. The outside lamp wasn't on, but in the reflected glow from the staircase light I caught the faintest movement in the shrubbery beyond the gateway. Was it a shadowy figure? Or just the breeze in the undergrowth? I tensed, peering out into the darkness. But there was nothing there. Nothing I could see anyway.

I put the car in gear and drove off feeling vaguely unsettled. No one followed me, no anonymous men in cars, but still something didn't feel right. It would be nearly twenty-four hours before I finally realized what. But by then it would be too late.

CHAPTER 14

It took a real effort of willpower to get out of bed next morning. I'd slept badly, haunted by the hurt in Maria's eyes at the restaurant. But I forced myself up, threw on some clothes and padded through into the kitchen in my bare feet to make some coffee.

The lino floor was ice cold under my toes. I hopped across, trying to avoid too much contact with the frosty tiles, and filled the kettle with water. I switched it on and scuttled back to the warmth of the carpet in the bedroom.

I pulled on some socks, then slipped my thawing feet into my shoes. The leather was still damp from the previous evening's rain and the tops were splashed with blobs of mud. I bent down to tie the laces and stopped in midmovement. I knew suddenly what I'd overlooked in Andy Peters' flat.

His shoes had been spattered with a curious white substance. I'd assumed at the time it was paint but now I realized what it really was. I put on my windcheater and left the flat in a hurry to find a secure phone.

The nearest kiosk had been vandalized, the cash box forced open with a crowbar. It took me five minutes to walk to the next phone. To my relief, it was working. I called Harry at his shop.

'This is a bit early, isn't it? I've only just got in,' he said.

'I need some help, Harry.'

'I'm not doing no more breaking and entering, if that's what you want,' he said immediately.

'This is all strictly above board. Did Andy Peters keep pigeons?'

'What?'

'Pigeons.'

'That's a funny question.'

'Did he?'

'Well, yes. At least I know 'e used to. Why?'

'Do you know where he kept them?'

'Up beyond the flats.'

'Will you show me? Now.'

'I've got a shop to run.'

'Please, Harry. It'll only take you half an hour.'

'Why're you interested in 'is pigeons?'

'I'm in a call box and running out of money.'

Harry sighed heavily. 'All right. Come and get me.'

I walked back to pick up the car from outside the flat. As I opened the door of the Lada I became aware of a figure getting out of another car parked on the opposite side of the road and walking towards me. I turned to look, expecting some government stooge, but it was Hughie O'Donnell.

'The keys, Mike,' he said.

I stared at him, not understanding. He held out his hand.

'The keys. To the Lada.'

'What?'

'You knew, didn't you? I don't like to be taken advantage of.' His voice was gentle, but deeply wounded.

'What are you talking about, Hughie?'

'Your cheque bounced. The bank sent it back yesterday. The keys, please.'

I was taken by surprise. Maybe I should have guessed, but I never had any accurate idea of how much was in my account.

'You're kidding? Look, I didn't know.'

'I trusted you. This upsets me terribly, Mike. I never thought you of all people would do such a thing to me. I thought you had some integrity.'

'There must have been a mistake. Let me keep the car and I'll find the money for you from somewhere.'

'The keys.'

Reluctantly, I handed them over. Hughie beckoned across the road. One of his mechanics got out of the car and joined us. Hughie gave him the keys.

'You got any belongings inside?' he asked me.

I shook my head.

'You shouldn't have done it, Mike. It's not a nice thing. This will be on your conscience for a long time. When I go to church this evening I'll say fifty Hail Marys for you.'

He walked back to his car and drove away, shaking his head sadly. I really had plummeted to the depths when a used-car dealer started saying prayers for my soul.

I took a taxi to Harry's shop, using up almost the last of my cash. A red Montego with two men in the front followed me all the way. The spooks were certainly getting through the cars.

I made Harry come out with me through the rear of his shop and halfway round Castle Market, dodging in and out of stalls. He panted after me, struggling to keep up.

'What the 'ell's going on?' he demanded. 'Me legs can't take much more of this.'

'Just making sure no one follows us.'

'Why should anyone follow us to a bleedin' pigeon loft?'

'You wouldn't want to know, Harry.'

'Is this going to get me a bad name with the law?'

'You've got a bad name already,' I said.

We caught the bus up City Road to Skye Edge and walked along the barren hillside to a scrap of muddy open land with four or five ramshackle wooden huts on it.

'Those are the lofts,' Harry said as we approached.

'Which one was Andy's?'

'I dunno.'

'I thought you said you knew.'

'I said I knew where they were. Not which one were which. He might not have had one any more. It were a few years back that I knew for certain he kept pigeons.'

We stopped outside the first hut. I shielded my eyes and peered in through the window. Inside I could dimly see rows of birds in small compartments. Their cooing was clearly audible through the cracks in the planks. I turned back to Harry.

'It could be any of these.'

He shook his head. 'I know which one it is.' He screwed up his nose. 'You smell it?'

I sniffed the air. The wind was gusting strongly up the hillside but I could discern a faint, unpleasant odour underneath.

'What is it?'

'Come over 'ere.'

Harry walked away from the hut. The odour became stronger, a sharp, fetid stench that turned the stomach. I tried hard not to inhale.

Harry stopped. 'It's that one over there. The last one. I wouldn't go any nearer if I were you.'

It dawned on me then what the smell was. The sickly, rancid aroma of decomposing flesh.

'Jesus, you don't think . . .'

'The whole lot of 'em. No one's been up here since Andy died.'

I took my handkerchief out and held it over my mouth and nose. Harry put a restraining hand on my arm.

'You know what it'll be like in there, don't you?'

'I have to get inside. Whatever it takes.'

I crossed the strip of open land towards the last, most isolated of the five huts. Even through my handkerchief the reek of death was overpowering. I looked in through the grimy pane of glass by the door. There was nothing moving inside; just patches of grey and white, unidentifiable shapes lying still in the gloom.

I examined the door. It was fastened by a padlock. I tugged at the hasp. It was rusty and far too solid to break. But it was only as strong as the wood it was screwed into and that was old and rotten.

I lifted my foot and smashed the heel of my shoe into the edge of the door. The wood splintered but held. I kicked it three more times and on the final blow the wood disintegrated and the screws of the hasp came free.

I pulled open the broken door and a blast of noisome fumes hit me full in the face. I turned away, coughing, trying not to retch. I'd never smelt anything like it, the pungent vapours of putrefaction but with a piercing edge of ammonia that burned the inside of my nostrils.

I braced myself, holding my breath, and ran inside. There was a gate covered in wire mesh just a few feet beyond the door. It wasn't locked. I pulled it open and moved through into the enclosure beyond. I took a shallow breath. The atmosphere was even worse here. In small bays along the back wall were the bodies of dead pigeons, tiny bundles of feathers and decaying tissue throbbing with voracious maggots and worms. Clouds of flies rose up and buzzed around my ears. I grimaced and tried not to look at the half-eaten carcasses.

The floor was two inches deep in droppings and straw. My shoes squelched through the sticky white gunge. It turned my guts even more than the stench. I looked around. It had to be here somewhere. Maybe not too well hidden. Andy would have felt it was safe here, away from his flat, within easy reach if he wanted it, but a place known only to him and a few friends.

I squinted into the bays where the birds were lying. I could see nothing. Besides, he wouldn't have put it anywhere the pigeons could rip it apart or shit on it. It had to be better protected than that.

I turned my attention to the near side of the enclosure, where there was a mound under a plastic sheet by the wire mesh fence. I lifted up a corner of the sheet. Underneath were sacks of straw, pigeon feed and a large plastic camping canister of water. I moved them all aside and examined the floorboards below.

One of them was loose. I hooked my fingernails into a crack and lifted out a small section of plank. There was a space underneath, just big enough to hide a small parcel in. But it was empty.

Harry appeared in the doorway, a handkerchief over the lower part of his face. He took in the scene inside.

'My God,' he mumbled. 'Poor little bastards.'

He saw me down on my knees. 'You crazy? Get out of here before the smell knocks you out. What're you doing, anyway?'

'Looking for something.'

'You find it?'

I shook my head. 'If it was here, it's gone.'

'Come on then. Jesus, you could catch anything in here. What's that disease called? Sitta something.'

'Psittacosis. You get that from parrots.'

'Parrots, pigeons, they're all the bloody same to me.'

I stood up and came out of the enclosure, disappointed. I'd been so sure it was here. But there was nothing. I felt slightly faint from the fumes. I shook my head, trying to clear my mind.

Then I saw something glint above the door. Something metallic.

Harry had taken my arm. 'You OK? Come on.'

I shook myself free and reached up. There was a narrow shelf above the lintel. My fingers touched something smooth. I grasped it and lifted it down. It was a thin

imitation leather briefcase, without handles but held shut
by a zip fastener. I stared at it.

'You hear me?' Harry said. He pulled me outside and
dragged me a distance away from the hut. I took a deep
breath, cleaning my lungs out with the fresh air. I still felt
nauseous. Then I opened the zip on the top of the briefcase.

Inside was a cardboard folder containing a number of
documents. I flipped through them and saw the heading
'Hammond and Silcott, shipping agents'.

'That it?' Harry said.

I nodded weakly. Then I turned away and threw up in
the mud.

The documents in the file seemed innocuous enough. They
were shipping records for a cargo of steel castings which
had been sent from Immingham to Bremen two months
earlier on board a Norwegian ship named *The Sunndal*.

The company sending the cargo, Poseidon Steel Ltd, had
an address in Sheffield but I'd never heard of them. The
cargo was described in more detail on one of the sheets:
'maraging steel pipes for use in the chemical industry,' it
said. I didn't know what maraging steel was, but as I was
reading the file in the central reference library I looked it
up in a book on metallurgy. It didn't help much.

It was puzzling. I was unfamiliar with the shipping business, but nevertheless I could see nothing particularly
special about the documents. Why had Jawaad al-Nabil
hired Peters and Napier to steal them, why had Andy hung
on to them and why were various parties, MI5 included,
so keen to get their mits on them?

I thought it over for a long time, then put the file back
in the briefcase. Before I left the library I checked a few
facts in some more reference books and made brief notes.
The pieces of the puzzle were obstinately refusing to fall
into place, but I knew one person at least who could help
me.

Sam Fielding was, true to form, attempting to light his

pipe when I walked into his tatty office. I helped myself to a chair and waited for him to stop puffing.

'Sorry about that, Michael,' he said eventually. 'Damn thing needs a good clean out. Probably a blockage in the stem.' He pushed his chair back and peered at me. His eyes, behind the thick spectacles, were blurred and magnified into bulging white orbs.

'I'm glad you came in. I rang you this morning, left another message on your machine.'

'Oh yes?' I said warily. I could guess what was coming.

'That article you said you'd post never arrived.'

'Didn't it? The Royal Mail's getting worse.'

'Have you a copy of it? I need it urgently.'

'Of course. I'll send it off to you as soon as I get home. I don't suppose there's any chance of the money now?'

'You need it?'

'I've got a temporary cash-flow problem.' Temporary, going on permanent.

Sam took a cheque book out of the desk and filled one in. He handed it to me. 'That do?'

'Very nicely, thanks.'

'Was that the only reason you came in?'

'No. I wanted to tap into your encyclopaedic knowledge of the steel business again.'

'Happy to oblige.'

'You heard of a company called Poseidon Steel?'

'Yes. You still sniffing around James Silvester?'

I started. 'What? Silvester?'

'You knew he owned Poseidon, I assume?'

'No, I didn't. Tell me more.' Suddenly one or two things were beginning to make sense.

'Well, it's the parent company for most of his business ventures. Poseidon owns the Titan Works in Attercliffe, that's no big secret. What's the problem?'

'They own anything else?'

'Silvester's scrap metal business, of course. He moved it under their overall umbrella when he bought Poseidon.

Also, I believe, a small electroplating company at Tinsley.'

I sat bolt upright. 'Electroplating?'

Sam nodded. 'That's not so peculiar, is it? There's lots of them around.'

I thought about the notes I'd made in the reference library. It was only circumstantial evidence, but I was pretty sure now Silvester had more than just dirt on his hands.

'What's maraging steel?' I asked.

Sam smiled. We were in his element now. I knew I was in for a broadside of obscure technical data.

'It's a very low-carbon martensitic steel. About eighteen per cent nickel, plus cobalt, titanium and molybdenum.'

I wished I hadn't asked. 'Sam, can I have this in English, please?'

'I'm trying to keep it simple. It's generally produced by vacuum melting and exhibits much higher levels of toughness than conventional high-carbon martensitic grades of equivalent strength.'

'In other words,' I said, translating on the hoof, 'it's bloody strong steel.'

Sam pulled a face. 'You could put it like that. Very crudely. But I hadn't finished explaining it to you.'

'You've told me more than enough,' I said hurriedly. 'Does Poseidon make it?'

'They probably have the capability if they wanted to.'

'And export it to Germany?'

Sam shook his head doubtfully. 'I don't know about that. As raw steel, you mean?'

'As pipes, for the chemical industry.'

'Pipes? It's possible, I suppose. But the Germans have facilities for making things like that for themselves. Why should they import them from us?'

Why indeed? I thought. And why should James Silvester send them a cargo of the things? Unless . . . unless they weren't actually for the Germans.

'The chemical industry, you say?' Sam asked, frowning.

I nodded. 'Is that odd?'

'Maybe. Maraging steel's a very specialized product. Not easy to make and much more expensive than conventional low-alloy engineering steels. You don't waste it on products that don't need it. It's usually used selectively where its strength is vital or where weight saving is of paramount importance.'

'On what kind of things?' I said.

'Well, in tooling. Or for gears, die-castings, shafts, bearings.'

That was a dull list.

'Anything else?'

'Well, it's also used quite extensively in the aerospace and weapons industries.'

Now that was much more interesting.

I left the file with Sam for safekeeping—my flat was just a little too vulnerable to risk—and went home to finish off my colour piece for him on the decline of the South Yorkshire coalfield. It was an unwelcome chore but I had to get it out of the way, particularly now I'd been paid for it.

I made myself a pot of strong tea and a couple of toasted pikelets in the kitchen, to fortify myself for the ordeal. There was a chill draught blowing in from a tiny gap at the bottom of the sash window. It had never closed properly. I rammed it down into its frame and took my mug and plate through into the living-room.

The feature took me just under two hours to complete, a long time by my standards. It would've taken less, but it was so tedious I kept falling asleep at the typewriter. I sealed it in an envelope and took it out to the postbox at the end of the street. It was dark now, the night closing in with its dank, enveloping shroud.

I went back into the flat shivering and sat in front of the gas fire. I was just dozing off when the telephone rang. I could reach it without leaving my armchair.

'Yes?' I said sleepily.

'Is that Mike McLean?'

I woke up quickly. It was Angie Maxfield's voice.

'Yes, it's me.'

'You know who this is, don't you?' She was speaking softly, intensely, her voice quavering slightly. She sounded frightened.

'What is it?'

'I need to see you. Now.'

'Why?'

'I can't say on the phone. Just come round. Please.'

The line went dead. I kept the receiver in my hand as if hoping for more. It was uncanny. There were so many similarities to the call I'd received from Andy Peters. The same request, the same tone of urgency and fear. I'd trusted Andy even though I'd only met him once. I wasn't so sure about Angie.

There was a fair chance I was being set up by Silvester. But there again Angie had seemed genuinely scared. She might just have something important to tell me. What did I have to lose by going? It might be a trap. But if it was, I was at least walking into it with my eyes wide open.

CHAPTER 15

I had the taxi driver drop me a hundred yards from the entrance to the flats. I waited in the darkness beneath a high wall for a few minutes, watching the street in front of me. There was no one about, no parked cars I recognized. Crossing the road, I walked towards the flats, every sense alert to the slightest sign of danger.

The foyer was brightly illuminated, the lamp in the porch outside working tonight. I held back, still unsure about going in. The curtains to Angie's flat were drawn, a light on behind. I saw nothing move. No strange shapes silhouetted on the thin material, no dark, waiting faces peering out.

Sooner or later I had to make up my mind. I had a last look around, and went into the entrance.

The front door wasn't fully closed. The catch was just touching so it didn't engage. Fortuitous, or carefully planned? I pushed it open a fraction and slipped through the gap, holding the door so it swung back gently into its original unlocked position. I might have to exit in a hurry and I didn't want any obstacles in the way.

I went quietly up the stairs, keeping close to the wall so anyone looking down the stairwell wouldn't see me. The first floor landing was deserted. I approached the door of Angie's flat and listened outside it. Not a sound. That struck me as peculiar. Who lives in total silence? No television on, no record player, not even the pad of feet or the chink of pans in a kitchen.

I swallowed hard a couple of times, trying to ignore the pounding in my chest. I reached out to ring the bell. And stopped. I'd got this far unannounced. There was no point in spoiling it now. I took hold of the door handle and depressed it slowly, pushing inwards at the same time. I'd expected resistance, but it swung open easily. I let go and stepped back, getting ready to run if Silvester or any of his goons appeared.

There was a small entrance hall inside with two doors opening off it. Both were ajar. I pushed the one nearest me. It was the bathroom. The light was off but I could see there was no one inside. Water glinted in the bath tub. I dipped the tips of my fingers into it. The water was still warm, scented with bath oil.

I moved to the other door and tapped it open with my foot. The living-room beyond appeared to be unoccupied too. I listened hard again. Still no sound.

The room was big, one side half partitioned off to form a compact kitchenette and dining area. There were no obvious places for anyone to hide. That left only the bedroom. I stayed where I was and called out.

'Angie?'

I waited, then moved softly around the perimeter of the room towards the door at the far end. That was closed. There was nothing to be gained by being cautious now. Besides, I had a feeling the whole flat was empty. I threw open the door and looked in.

The sight that met my eyes was such a shock I recoiled as if hit by a piledriver. Angie Maxfield was lying on her back on the double bed. The powder blue, towelling bathrobe she was wearing gaped wide open. Underneath it she was naked, but I noticed that only subliminally. What caught the attention was the knife handle protruding from her chest below her left breast.

It was an ordinary kitchen knife. I had one myself almost the same. My stomach knotted but I forced myself to look at her. Blood had trickled down her ribcage and on to the cover of the bed. From the way it glistened I could tell it was only just beginning to congeal. Her beautiful, perfect face was frozen like a frame from a film, her eyes unblinking, no breath of air escaping her lips. A motionless body, the warmth draining away from it, the pulse of life silenced by that thin blade of steel.

An immense feeling of sadness overwhelmed me. She was young, just setting out on her path with the buoyancy and optimism of a child. Yet now the world had ended for her. That heart-rending beauty would never have the chance to grow old and wither. It was forever captured like a still-life drawing on a pad. Though not a still life, but a still death.

I could bear to look no longer. I turned and went back out into the living-room. The feeling of nausea was with me still, the aftereffects of shock, but my mind had started functioning more clearly, overriding the physical sensation of sickness. I wanted to know who'd killed Angie. And why. Those same two questions again. I'd asked them after Andy Peters and Tony Napier had died. Now I was asking them a third time.

A flash of blue light caught my eye through the curtains. I pressed myself against the wall and peeked out. A police car had just pulled in outside the flats, the beacon still revolving on its roof. Two uniformed officers got out, pulling on their caps. One of them glanced up at the windows.

I ducked back. The blood was throbbing in my veins. Throbbing with fear. The police hadn't arrived by chance. They'd been tipped off. I'd been set up all right, but not in the way I'd expected.

I went out to the landing. I could stay and explain what had happened, of course, but I didn't give much for my chances of convincing anyone. There was a body in the bedroom, dead only a matter of minutes, and I was the guy on the spot. What's more, I'd already found one corpse in a flat. They'd think I was making a habit of it. And if I was in a police cell I wasn't going to get much nearer finding out who the killer was.

I heard the front door creak open, the footsteps of the two coppers in the foyer. I looked up. I could hide on the next floor, or the one above that, but if anyone came out of the other flats or the plods chose to check upstairs first I was done for.

They were coming up now, murmuring to each other. I retreated quickly into Angie's flat. There was no way out from the living-room. The bedroom was the only possibility. I went through, averting my eyes, wanting instinctively to cover the lifeless figure on the bed. The window looked out on to a garden at the rear. I opened it as quietly as I could and climbed over the sill.

The voices of the policemen were louder now. One of them called out. I knew they were coming in behind me. I lowered my legs out into space, hanging from the full extension of my arms, and let go. My feet sank into soft earth as I hit the ground. I rolled over and stumbled upright. There was a wall at the bottom of the garden but just bushes down the side. I pushed through the thick undergrowth and crouched down, looking back towards the flats. One of the policemen came into view at the bedroom window, talking urgently into his radio.

I crept away into the next garden, then clambered over a fence and a couple of walls, and emerged through a drive on to one of the side streets off Endcliffe Vale Road. I straightened my dishevelled clothes and ran a hand through my hair before walking briskly away down the hill. I wanted to be as far away as possible when the police reinforcements arrived. A man can take only so much excitement in one evening.

It took me forty minutes to walk back to Burngreave. I was down to my last handful of change so a taxi was out of the question. I could have caught a bus, but I had a feeling I ought to conserve every penny I had. Besides, the fresh air did me good. It helped me think.

I held back on the final corner before my flat, and was glad I did. Poking a cautious head round the brick wall, I saw a line of vehicles parked up the street. Two of them were marked police cars. Chris Strange and the MI5 man, Armstrong, were coming down the steps from my front door. They hadn't wasted much time.

I retreated to the safety of a nearby alley and considered what I should do next. Turning myself in was clearly not an option. The authorities would know by now from their phone tap that Angie had rung and asked me to go round. It wouldn't take them long to find the taxi driver who'd dropped me off near her flat.

I was going to have some very awkward questions to answer and neither Strange nor Armstrong were likely to be very understanding. Even if they weren't convinced I had any part in Angie's death, they'd still bang me up to 'help with their inquiries'.

There was only one option which made sense. I had to stay out of sight for a while, try to sort things out myself, but where could I go? I thought of Maria, then ruled her out at once. My phone conversations with her had been monitored. They knew all about her and would no doubt be waiting for me if I showed up on her doorstep. In any case, after our last unfortunate meeting at the Frog she was hardly going to be too sympathetic towards me or my predicament.

Harry was out because my friendship with him was also known to the police. In fact, just about everyone I could think of was ruled out for one reason or another. It was safer not to trust anyone at all.

That still left me with the same basic question. Where was I going to hole up until morning? I needed somewhere sheltered, close by, a place the police wouldn't dream of looking for me.

My first night in a mausoleum. The bed was a bit hard and the atmosphere on the creepy side, but it was out of the wind and well off the list of haunts the flatties would automatically think of searching.

I'd found it by chance in Burngreave Cemetery, trying to keep off the streets in case a passing police car or an inquisitive pedestrian wondered what I was doing wandering around in the middle of the night. There'd be an alert out for me by now, I was certain of that.

It was an ancient, ugly, decaying Christmas cake of a tomb. A monument to Victorian vulgarity, eight feet high with carved cherubs and angels adorning the top and sides. At one corner the marble structure had collapsed, leaving a gaping hole through which I'd crawled. Inside there were two huge stone plinths covering the last remains of Thomas and Elsie Parkinson. I slept on top of Elsie, but she didn't give me any trouble.

I was pretty relieved, however, when morning arrived. I'd dozed fitfully for a couple of hours but the accommodation and temperature were not really conducive to a peaceful night's sleep. I crawled out into the daylight and jogged round the cemetery in a futile attempt to warm myself up. All it did was jar my half-frozen bones and wear me out unnecessarily. What I needed most was a hot drink and somewhere out of the cold to recover for a few hours.

The café I found on Barnsley Road was just perfect. Steamy, full of workmen having breakfast, no one taking any notice of a single man with crumpled clothes, bleary eyes and a smudge of stubble on his face. I stayed there half the morning, stretching out a few cups of tea and a bacon sandwich. I could have done with more to eat but my cash was dwindling fast. I couldn't afford to blow it all on one meal.

The walk into town killed another hour or so. I bought the midday edition of the *Evening News* and read it on a bench in the Peace Gardens by the Town Hall, sitting next to a dirty, semi-comatose tramp.

The murder of Angie Maxfield was on the front page. Just the bare facts padded out with quotes from unnamed police officers, neighbours, Angie's agent, anyone the reporter could get hold of who'd known the dead woman. The police weren't giving much away, that was clear to me.

My name was mentioned in the story, in the indirect, coded fashion in which suspects are always identified in news reports. 'The police are anxious to interview freelance journalist, Mike McLean, who is believed to have important information which might assist them in their investigation.' Sub-text: 'This is the guy who did it.'

I was in a dilemma. I'd chosen to stay out of the way, an action which could only increase my guilt in the eyes of the police. Yet now I wasn't sure what to do with my freedom. There was no point in simply walking the streets hoping for inspiration to strike. If I wasn't going to go in and tell the authorities what I knew, I had to put my knowledge to some positive use myself. In other words, do something. But what?

I stared at the newspaper on my knee. There was a photograph of Angie Maxfield spread across three columns, a modelling snap they'd probably got from her agent. It made her look even younger, like a teenager even: guileless, innocent, malleable. I wondered who would have wanted to kill such a harmless child. What manner of person could have brought themselves to ram a kitchen knife into her chest and walk away?

I thought of James Silvester. He was hard, violent, but Angie had been his lover. What reason did he have to kill her? Maybe he had nothing to do with it after all. Maybe the call from Angie had been genuine and someone else had silenced her before she could talk to me. No set-up, no premeditated plan to implicate me in the death. I'd just shown up at the wrong time.

My eyes drifted away from the photograph to the single column of text down the right-hand side of the page. It was another story, a brief court report. I barely took in most of the words but two in particular stood out. A name: Jason Kinsella. I'd never heard of him but the surname was familiar. I read the report again. It covered a straightforward remand hearing at the Magistrates' Court; Jason Kinsella, 24, unemployed of Robey Street, Grimethorpe, charged with two counts of assault occasioning actual bodily harm. Remanded in custody for a further seven days. It was the 'further' that made me sit up and start thinking.

I took out my notebook and riffled through the pages until I found the three names Gordon Crieff had given me. The names of the heavies who'd chased me through the car park and ended up in hospital after an unfortunate encounter with a chapter of Hell's Angels. Kevin Stokes, Russ Conningsby and . . . Jeff Kinsella. Not a very common name. I wondered if by any chance the two were related.

I folded the paper and gave it to the tramp next to me. He stuck it inside his threadbare shirt. There's nothing quite like newsprint next to the skin. As he did so, I caught a pungent whiff of body odour, the sour smell of decomposing underpants. I edged away along the bench and stood up. The tramp muttered something and I glanced down at him. His gnarled face, smeared with filth, jarred something suddenly in my memory. I realized then who the black man seen leaving Park Hill flats had been.

I went round the back of the Town Hall to the row of payphones on Surrey Street. I counted my change: about one pound fifty in silver. That was it.

I put a ten in the slot and rang the office of the *News*. The chief court reporter, Stan Waxman, would be having his sandwiches at his desk about now. He was a creature of habit, his days marked out for him by the rigid timetables of the Crown and Magistrates' Courts. I told him who it was.

'The police want to see you,' he said reprovingly.

'Yeah, I know. Listen, Stan, did you do the remand hearing on the front of the midday edition, a Jason Kinsella?'

'Yes.'

'Fill me in on the details.'

'I don't remember them. You any idea how many of these I do a day?'

'Do me a favour. Check your notes.'

There was grumbling at the other end of the line. I could picture Stan with his cheese and pickle sandwiches unwrapped from their foil in front of him. It was always cheese and pickle. Crumbs on his toothbrush moustache, his tie stained with splashes of tea, his brain slowly atrophying after thirty years of tedium as a full-time court reporter. I fed another ten pence into the slot.

'You found them yet?' I asked.

'Hold your horses. I'm deciphering my shorthand.' Three decades in the business and he still couldn't read back his Pitman. 'It was an assault case. Unprovoked attack.'

He outlined the facts of the case for me. I watched the money tick away on the electronic display in front of me. Nine, eight, seven . . . I couldn't afford another ten.

'Which jail's he being held in?' I asked.

'There's only one for remand prisoners. They're all sent there from Sheffield.'

'Which one?'

Four, three . . .

'Wolds.'

The display flashed to zero and the connection was cut. For a moment I stood there, another piece of the jigsaw falling into place. Then I pushed in more coins and called South Yorkshire CID.

'Strange,' a voice said wearily.

'I gather you're anxious to interview me,' I said.

A beat. Then the same voice, suddenly alert. 'Where the hell are you, McLean?'

'It wasn't me, Chris. You know that.'

'I think you'd better come in. The longer you wait, the worse it'll be.'

'You planning to charge me?'

'I don't have a choice.'

'You don't believe it was me, do you?'

'I believe the evidence.'

'All circumstantial.'

'Listen, McLean, you're up to your eyeballs in this. We know she called you, we know you went there, we know you were in her flat—your fingerprints are on the door handles—and we know you left through the bedroom window. There's a couple of shoe prints in the soil immediately below which are almost identical to a pair we found in your flat.'

'That doesn't prove I killed her.'

'Then how do you explain your fingerprints on the knife?'

I fell back hard against the side of the kiosk. *What?*

'The knife. Your dabs are all over it.'

I realized then why it had looked so familiar. It was *my* knife. From my kitchen. And I knew also why the window in my flat had been partially open yesterday afternoon. Stupid of me. I *had* been set up after all.

'You're going to need a bloody good lawyer,' Strange said. 'Just tell me where you are and I'll come and pick you up.'

It was more important than ever now that I should stay loose. I had something to do tonight.

'I didn't kill her, Chris. You think I could do that to someone? You know me better than that.'

'Then who did?'

'I don't know for sure. I need a bit of time.'

'There's a call out for you. Every copper in this city has your photo and description. And Armstrong's men are crawling everywhere. He wants you badly.'

'Armstrong? What's this got to do with him?'

'You stupid sod, you don't understand any of this, do you? You know who Angie Maxfield was?'

'She was a model,' I said.

'Not just a model, McLean. She worked for MI5.'

CHAPTER 16

A light was glowing behind the kitchen blind. I listened at the door for a short time. There were sounds of someone cooking inside. I tapped on the glass pane and waited. The blind rattled up and a flood of light dazzled me momentarily. But I caught the flash of surprise on her face as she looked out, then the change to hostility.

'Let me in, Maria. Please.'

She made me wait, not moving.

'I've nowhere else to go,' I said. 'I need your help.'

Maria gazed at me through the glass, then she turned away. I thought she was going to leave me on the step, but she took a key out of a drawer and unlocked the door.

'You've got a nerve coming here, McLean.'

'I know you're angry, I can understand that. You going to let me in?'

She moved aside and I walked past her into the kitchen. I was so cold I could barely bend my limbs to sit down at the table. My joints cracked as if they'd filled up with ice.

'Thank you.' My teeth were chattering, making speech difficult.

Maria switched the kettle on and leaned back on a work-top, her arms folded. She didn't say anything until the kettle had boiled and she'd filled a mug with coffee for me.

'You look awful.'

'I feel worse,' I said, clutching the hot mug in both hands and sipping the coffee gratefully. I looked up at her. 'The other night at the Frog. It wasn't what you thought. I really was working.'

She gave a little shrug, sceptical, or maybe just not interested in my excuses.

'The police were here this morning,' she said. 'Looking for you. They had a warrant, searched the whole house.'

'I'm sorry. I didn't mean to get you involved.'

'There's one of them out at the front right now. In a car.'

'I know. That's why I came through all the gardens and round the back.'

'If they find you here I'm in serious trouble.'

I nodded. 'I'll go when I've finished this.'

'Go where?'

'I don't know. I'll find somewhere.'

She shook her head despairingly. 'You're hopeless, Michael. Maybe you should tell me what's going on.'

'Did the police say anything?'

'Only that they wanted to speak to you. I heard something on the radio too, not much. Something about the murder of a model.'

'They think I did it.'

Maria pursed her lips, not reacting. 'That's preposterous,' she said eventually.

I smiled at her weakly. I was glad that she, at least, had faith in me.

'Unfortunately, the evidence against me is pretty damning.'

I went through the events of the previous night. She flinched at the details. 'Don't tell me any more, I don't want to hear. Poor girl.'

'It was all premeditated too. Someone planned it, then

executed it in cold blood. The police were supposed to find me there, standing over the body. My fingerprints on the knife.'

She jolted upright, unfolding her arms. 'What?'

'Someone got into my flat through the kitchen window yesterday. They took the knife from a drawer.'

'You sure?'

'It's the only way it could have been done.'

'But why? Why frame you for it?'

'To get me out of the way.'

'That's rather bizarre, isn't it? To kill someone just to put you in jail.'

'That was only the secondary motivation. Whoever did it wanted Angie dead. They just thought they could kill two birds with one stone if they got me blamed for it.'

Maria studied me anxiously. 'Is this connected to those other deaths, the two burglars?'

'Yes.'

'I don't like it. There's too much killing. Have you ever thought that you could be next?'

'No one knows where I am.'

'I wish to God you'd go to the police. You can't keep on the run forever.'

'I just need a few more hours. To complete the picture. Then I'll turn myself in.'

I finished my coffee. Already I was feeling better, the warmth seeping slowly into the frozen core of my body, melting the ice away at the edges.

Maria had gone suddenly still, something on her mind.

'Why did you come here?' she asked abruptly.

'For shelter, food, a few hours out of the cold. I've spent the afternoon hiding in a clump of bushes in Whiteley Woods.'

Her gaze was piercing, acutely uncomfortable. I looked away. I was going to have to tell her, but I didn't know if I had the courage.

'These few more hours you say you need. What are you going to do in them?'

'Oh, things,' I said vaguely, my nerve failing me at the critical moment.

'I can smell bullshit, Michael. You've got some other reason for coming here.'

'No, I haven't.'

'Spill it.'

'Honest, I just wanted shelter.'

'You sure?'

'Scout's honour. I had no other reason for coming.'

She seemed to relax. I steeled myself.

'But as I'm here, can I borrow your car for the evening?'

'Is he following us?' I asked.

'Of course he is. What did you expect?' Maria replied. 'Just keep your head down.'

I was lying on the floor in the back of her Mazda, half doubled up between the front and rear seats. It wasn't designed for this kind of thing. Nor was I.

'Do you think we can lose him?' I said.

'I don't know. I've never been tailed before.'

'Give it a try. I'm getting cramp down here.'

She glanced back over her seat. 'You can still change your mind and go to a police station.'

'Maria, you promised.'

She sighed. 'OK. Just checking.'

We had come to an agreement. She had refused to lend me her car again on the grounds that I'd probably smash it up, but had consented to give me a lift to my destination and then wait for me. She'd taken quite a bit of persuading, giving in finally, I suspected, because she was sick of discussing the subject and wanted only to get me out of her house. I have that effect on people. All we had to do now was lose the unmarked police car on our tail.

The Mazda surged forward suddenly, then the whole car slewed sideways. I caught a fleeting glimpse of a double-decker bus towering over us through the rear window before I was thrown violently against the back of the driver's seat. I grunted, then another sharp turn hurled me back the other way. My head banged against the cushion of the back seat and rebounded.

'Christ, what're you doing?' I yelled.

Maria did another ninety-degree turn and accelerated, leaving my head and most of my body behind. Then she braked sharply. My body caught up, slamming hard into the front seats. My knee connected with something solid and a stab of pain shot up my leg.

'You trying to kill me?'

The car slowed to a steady eighty or so, but on a bend so the G-force crumpled me up in a heap against the side panel, my chin pressed tight into my chest. I untangled myself and started breathing again.

'Sorry about that,' Maria said phlegmatically, reducing speed to just about the legal limit. 'But I think I've lost him.'

I struggled into a sitting position on the floor and craned my neck to see out. The unmarked car was nowhere in sight.

'What happened?'

'I overtook a bus and cut in front of it down a side street. The bus blocked the fellow behind. I had to make sure he didn't pick us up again.'

I levered myself on to the rear seat and nursed my bruises.

'And you were worried about *my* driving,' I said.

We parked on the forecourt of a machine tools company about two hundred yards from the Titan Works.

'Give me half an hour,' I said to Maria. 'If I'm not back by then, find a phone and tell the police where I am.'

She swivelled round in her seat to look me full in the face. 'This is foolish, Michael. You can't do it all on your own.'

'There's no one else to turn to. I'm a wanted man, remember. I've got one chance to break this story. I'm not going to blow it now.'

I pushed the front passenger seat forward and stretched to open the door.

'At least explain to me what you're going to do.'

I wriggled out from the back of the car on to the pavement and leaned back in.

'I would, believe me,' I said. 'Only I don't know what I'm going to do.'

Maria opened her mouth to say something, but I'd already closed the door and was turning to cross the forecourt. I didn't look back. When you're stumbling blindly into the unknown it pays to watch your feet.

The Titan Works was a grimy brick building with a windowless frontage on the main road and a goods entrance down a lane to the side. I studied it from a distance, hidden in a patch of dense shadow. There were almost no streetlights here, presumably no one thought them necessary in this seedy enclave of workshops, foundries and metal bashers; a small island of industry that was somehow still holding off the tide of bankruptcy and dereliction that had washed over most of the rest of the East End.

The high mesh gates across the goods entrance were wide open. I walked through them cautiously and passed down the side of the works. As I drew near the back of the building I noticed a dim puddle of light at the end. I slowed down, glancing back to check that no one was following me. Then I approached the corner and cocked an eye round it.

There was a fenced car park running the full width of the site and, beyond it, the hillside and wasteland from which the gunman had fired his shots at James Silvester. Backed up against the rear of the works, its tail hidden through the open doors of a loading bay, was an articulated lorry. A light was on inside the bay, partially shielded by the bulk of the lorry, but with enough seeping out around the edges to illuminate the surrounding area to a radius of maybe twenty yards.

I ran my eye over the lorry. 'Milner Haulage' it said on the side of the trailer. There was nothing to indicate what it might be carrying or where it might be going. It was a right-hand-drive vehicle, British. There was no one in the cab.

I hesitated, reluctant to commit myself. But there was nothing to be gained now by holding back. If I was going in, the timing was never likely to be perfect. I took another look around and scuttled across the intervening stretch of car park, ducking down and rolling underneath the trailer in one fluid movement. I dragged myself along on my belly and looked out from between the rear wheels.

The loading bay was stacked with large wooden cases, each one about twelve feet long and two feet wide. A fork-lift truck was moving one of the boxes towards the lorry. The operator was Pinky Silvester. She was wearing soiled over-alls and a baseball cap to keep her long blonde hair out of the way. My stomach suffered a sudden spasm of nerves. I felt up to tackling almost any obstacle but Pinky Silvester was more than I'd bargained for.

The truck came to a halt at the rear of the trailer and deposited the case inside. I heard footsteps and a scraping noise on the flooring above me. Someone was in there arranging the crates. Pinky reversed, turning the fork-lift back into the loading bay to pick up another crate.

I slipped out under the side of the trailer and checked Pinky's movements. She was at the far end of the bay, her back to me. I risked a peep into the end of the trailer. There was a man inside, facing away from me, but I recognized him without difficulty. It was James Silvester. So the pair of them were getting their hands dirty, doing this themselves.

I edged into the loading bay and dropped down behind the stacks of wooden cases. Stencilled on the side in black ink were various numbers and the words 'Steel Castings'. I crawled deeper into the bay, deeper into the shadows away from the light. Some of the crates were piled four high here so I was completely hidden from sight.

But there was one case standing on its own in the corner. I tried to prise off the lid with my fingers. It was nailed firmly shut. I looked around for something to use as a lever, and froze suddenly.

Jawaad al-Nabil was standing against the wall at the side of the bay, almost invisible in the darkness. He moved fractionally and I saw the automatic pistol in his right hand. A pistol pointing straight at me.

'I'd like to know what's in there too,' he said softly. 'Why don't we find out?'

He stepped forward, gesturing with the gun. He was wearing his black woollen overcoat again, the homburg on his head. He looked as if he was on his way home from a smart dinner party.

I manoeuvred my way through the crates into the centre of the loading bay. Al-Nabil followed, close enough to cover me, not so close that I had any chance of disarming him. Not that I would have tried. He handled the pistol like a pro, and for all his soft-spoken politeness, I could sense he was as dangerous as a viper.

Silvester was just emerging from the interior of the trailer, ready to receive the next crate, as we came into view. He gave a yell and started to jump down when he too noticed al-Nabil's gun. He stopped, half crouched on the tailboard. He stared at the Egyptian, then me.

The fork-lift truck swung round bringing Pinky into the frame. She took in the scene, the shock apparent in her expression. But she recovered fast.

'I wouldn't, Mrs Silvester,' al-Nabil said quickly. 'A bullet travels a lot faster than a fork-lift.' His pistol was aimed directly at her head. 'And at this distance I can hardly miss.'

Pinky glanced at her husband who gave an admonitory shake of the head. She switched off the engine of the fork-lift truck and climbed down.

'Over here, please,' al-Nabil said. Pinky walked towards us meekly, her eyes never leaving al-Nabil's face.

'That's far enough,' he said. 'I've seen what you can do close to. Now, I think it's time we had a little talk.'

'What's *he* doing here?' Silvester said, nodding at me.

'All in good time,' al-Nabil replied smoothly. 'But first, let's see what's in these crates, shall we? It must be something special for the two of you to be loading them at night on your own. Don't you have employees for work like this?'

'We're short-staffed at the moment,' Silvester said. 'There's nothing of interest to you inside.'

'Open them, please.'

Silvester didn't move for a time. Then he shrugged and climbed down off the trailer. He reached back in under a piece of sacking and brought out a crowbar which he took with him to the nearest crate. He forced open the lid and stood back. Inside were two long, shiny, steel cylinders.

I examined them from where I stood. They looked like ordinary pipes to me, nothing more.

Al-Nabil was looking down into the crate. His eyes, suddenly meaner, went from the pipes to Silvester and his wife. 'In the office,' he said peremptorily, his first sign of real emotion.

We walked across to a half-glazed cubicle at one side of the bay. Silvester clicked on the light and we went in. Al-Nabil made us sit down on three chairs round the desk, me nearest the door. The pistol stayed firmly on us throughout.

His first question was directed at me. 'Who are you?'

I told him my name but nothing else.

'He's a reporter,' Pinky said. 'A slimy, interfering freelance hack.'

Al-Nabil looked at me with more interest, something coming back to him suddenly.

'The Grosvenor House Hotel. You were in the lift one evening. And then . . .' He searched his memory. 'Yes, the corridor. Outside my room.'

Pinky leaned closer to me. 'I should have broken your

neck that first day at our house. Saved ourselves a lot of trouble.'

'Ah, regrets,' I said. 'What would life be without them?'

'Why are you here?' al-Nabil said sharply.

'Same reason as you. I wanted a snoop round, that's all.'

'Look, Jawaad,' Silvester said. 'There's an explanation for this if you'll just listen.'

Al-Nabil shook his head. 'I've listened too much already. To your excuses, your lies, your vacillations. I'm tired of your explanations.'

'But I told you. These are your crates, your shipment. I was going to call you as soon as it was on its way.'

'No, I don't think so. You lied about the first load. Why should I believe you now?'

Silvester's voice rose in protest. 'Hey, how many times, there *was* no first load. That's the truth, I swear it.'

'You're lying again.'

'You got proof? Why should I cheat you, Jawaad?'

Al-Nabil seemed to hesitate. Silvester pressed home his momentary advantage. 'I'd have to be crazy to pull a stunt like that.'

'*The Sunndal*,' I said. 'Sailed from Immingham to Bremen on November 15th with a cargo of maraging steel pipes. Does that help you?'

'Why, you little shit!' Silvester threw himself across the desk at me, his hands groping for my throat.

His wife tried to restrain him. 'Shut up, you fool.'

The barrel of al-Nabil's pistol hammered down hard on to one of Silvester's elbows. Silvester gave a yelp of pain and clutched at his arm. Then he turned to find the pistol pointing between his eyes.

'Please,' al-Nabil said mildly, 'sit down.'

Silvester glared at me, then retreated to his chair, rubbing his injured elbow. Pinky shot him a look of reproach, furious with him.

'That's better,' al-Nabil said. 'I don't want to have to shoot either of you, but I will if it proves necessary.'

His remarks were addressed to the Silvesters, I noted
with trepidation. I wondered why I was excluded from his
assurance.

Pinky was watching me intently now, her face glowering
with hatred. Motionless, conserving her anger until it was
guaranteed to achieve something. She wouldn't waste it on
mere gestures like her husband. I looked back at al-Nabil.
He had a gun but he unnerved me less.

'Repeat what you just said,' the Egyptian said to me.

I repeated it.

'*The Sunndal.*' The name seemed to mean something to
him. 'You are sure about that?'

'I've seen the shipping documents,' I said. Give him anything he wants to know, I thought. Anything that will keep
the Silvesters on the spot a while longer, keep his attention
focused on them. Then maybe something I don't already
know will slip out. Or his guard will drop and I'll have a
chance to run for it.

I had a feeling he wouldn't worry too much about keeping me alive once he'd squeezed the information he needed
out of me. Take it gently, McLean, I said to myself. Play
them off against each other, exploit the lack of trust between
them and you might just get out of this mess in one
piece.

'Did Jimmy not tell you?' I said. 'Must have slipped his
memory.'

'Don't believe him,' Silvester said. 'He's making it up.'

'Is it true?' Al-Nabil's attention turned back to me.

'I think Jimmy's reaction just now tells you the answer
to that.'

'How could he know?' Silvester said, trying to brazen his
way out of it. 'Some small-time provincial journalist with
a nose too big for his own good.'

'I've seen the papers, Jimmy. The file from the shipping
agent's office. You remember the file, don't you? The one
Andy Peters used to blackmail you.'

It was a guess, an educated guess, but still a shot in the

dark. And it struck home. Silvester blinked and sat back heavily. He should have learnt to hide his reactions like the inscrutable Pinky.

'That's why you killed him, isn't it?' I said.

He shook his head vehemently. 'Not me. No one's going to pin that on me.'

'And Tony Napier? You want to deny that one too? How's Jason Kinsella, by the way? Looking forward to a big fat bonus when he comes out, no doubt.'

Silvester went white. 'But how—'

Pinky broke in quickly. 'Shut up, James. Say nothing. Can't you see what he's doing?'

'Which only leaves Angie Maxfield. Which one of you did her, or was it a joint effort?'

'You talk too much,' al-Nabil said.

'Yeah, I know. But it's interesting stuff. Jimmy pulled a fast one on you, didn't he? Where did those pipes end up? Not Bremen, that's for sure. The same place, perhaps, that those crates out there are going to end up.'

Pinky Silvester sat forward, her biceps rippling the sleeves of her overalls. There were beads of sweat on her upper lip.

'Listen, Jawaad, we can sort this all out, just the three of us,' she said. 'What's important now is to look after our common interests. Let's deal with McLean first, then resolve our differences. He's the real threat.'

'And the money?'

'We'll come to some agreement on that.'

'Now wait a minute,' Silvester interjected.

'He knows, James,' Pinky said patiently, like a teacher drumming facts into a particularly dense pupil. 'Why try to pretend otherwise?'

She locked eyes with the Egyptian. 'What do you say?'

In reply he simply turned his pistol so it was pointing at me.

'You appear to be outside the circle, Mr McLean. And far too well informed for us to allow you to remain there.'

My blood went suddenly cold, my neck and hands clammy. The talking was over, and al-Nabil was not a man to dwell on his decisions. He was going to shoot me. I gauged the distance between us. Too far for me to have a hope of reaching him before he pulled the trigger.

I braced myself, my fingers curling round the edge of the desk, preparing to hurl my body sideways and tip the desk over at the same time. It might just throw him enough to spoil his aim and in the confusion I could make a break for the door. Desperate tactics, but I was a desperate man.

Al-Nabil smiled ruefully, as if he deeply regretted what he was about to do. He adjusted the barrel of the pistol, a perfectionist to the last. His right forefinger started to bend. I watched it, transfixed, waiting for the moment, praying I didn't get it wrong.

Then something flashed down suddenly from outside the door. There was a dull metallic clank, the sound of bone breaking, and the pistol fell to the floor followed by the handle of a car jack.

Al-Nabil whimpered and doubled up in agony, his shattered hand clutched to his chest. I saw a figure outside in the loading bay. Maria.

'Run!' she yelled.

I didn't need to be told. I was already on my feet, straining for the exit. I battered the Egyptian out of the way with my shoulder and slammed the door behind me to slow down the Silvesters.

Maria was out in the car park, running like a woman possessed, when I caught up with her. We rounded the corner together and started the long sprint down the exit road.

'You cut that bloody fine,' I said breathlessly.

She gave me a look but didn't waste her energy replying. I glanced over my shoulder. Pinky had just come into sight, Silvester right behind her. Maria was faltering on the dark, uneven surface, her breath coming in painful gasps. I knew they'd catch us before we got to the car.

'On the main road,' I panted. 'There's a doorway to the left, the front entrance. Stay in it until I've led them away. Understand?'

Maria nodded once, her pace slowing even more. Just another forty yards, please, I shouted inside my head. Another thirty, twenty. The Silvesters were gaining but we had a chance. Once we hit the front of the works we'd be out of sight just long enough for Maria to hide.

We turned out on to the main road. I pushed Maria deep into the doorway and squeezed her arm.

'Thanks.'

Then I was away across the road, easing off a fraction to make sure the Silvesters saw where I'd gone. I looked back. They were coming through the gateway, pausing for breath. They saw me dart down a side street and came after me without hesitation. I had no idea where I was heading. But that was the least of my worries.

CHAPTER 17

I tilted my head out of the wind and listened. I could hear nothing except the distant hum of traffic. No voices, no footsteps. I leaned back on the wooden fence and tried to relax. The edge of fear was still there, constricting my breathing, but my body sagged willingly. The muscles were too tired to do otherwise.

I was sitting on a bench on Attercliffe Station, alone on the platform in the dark. The trains had stopped running hours ago. Not that many of them actually called at this small outpost on the line to Rotherham. It was not even significant enough to be called a commuter station. No one lived round here to commute. But right now it was shelter, the safest place I could find to hide. If I had to, I would stay here until morning rather than risk venturing out on to the streets again.

I closed my eyes and inhaled slowly, trying to get back some rhythm in my breathing. I was out of condition, and although I was still up to a hard run when my life depended on it, it took my body a long time to recover from the exertion.

I'd lost the Silvesters in the warren of warehouses, tool-works and stockyards that sprawled over this part of the city. By now, I hoped, they'd be giving up the chase, perhaps returning to the Titan Works to finish loading the lorry. I was gone, either hidden away somewhere or so far in front they couldn't hope to catch me before I reached the haven of the city centre, lights, people, protection. It made no sense to keep looking for me. That's how I would have seen it. That's how the Silvesters would see it. I was depending on it.

Something scraped on the wooden steps behind the fence, the steps leading up to the station from the road. I opened my eyes quickly and turned my head. There were no lights on the platform, but the glow in the sky from the lamps in the surrounding area was sufficient to see by. And sufficient to be seen by, I reflected queasily. If anyone came on to the platform, they couldn't miss me sitting there on the bench. And there was nowhere to run except along the railway track.

The sound came again, nearer this time. The scuff of a sole on wood. I had to do something, and fast. It might just be a passer-by, a vagrant or a tramp looking for some-where to kip down, or even a BR employee on some official call, but I didn't think so. It was one o'clock in the morning. It could only be one of two people.

I pushed myself off the bench and flitted across the plat-form, dropping off the edge and lowering myself down quietly on to the strip of gravel at the side of the track. I lay flat out, pressed into the shadow cast by the platform, squeezed between the wall and the ends of the sleepers. Anyone looking straight down would see me, but from a distance I might just blend in enough to be invisible.

The footsteps became clearer, then stopped. Whoever it was had come on to the platform. I couldn't see them, but I could hear laboured breathing. It sounded like a man. A tired man. The footsteps came towards me and a shape appeared indistinctly above. Stocky, a thick neck, short legs. It was Silvester.

I kept very still and stared up at him. I should have turned over to hide the white of my face but it was too late now. The movement was certain to attract his attention. He came to the edge of the platform and looked both ways along the track. I contemplated taking him by surprise, reaching up and grabbing his leg, but I held back. Even with a momentary advantage like that I knew I would lose the subsequent fight. I had more to gain by staying put and doing nothing.

He was listening now. Then I, too, became aware of the sound. A faint humming in the air. Not a human sound, something more metallic. It was stronger in my left ear. I could feel the vibrations on the ground as well as in the air. I realized with a sharp jolt of fear what it was. A train. A train was coming along the track.

Silvester stepped back from the edge of the platform. I lost sight of him. I lifted my head a couple of inches and looked down the steel rails beyond my feet. Their burnished surfaces glistened a dull silver where streaks of faint light cut across them. Then I saw two headlights piercing the blackness beyond, moving steadily closer.

I watched them, transfixed, hardly able to believe it was a train. But the vibrations were buzzing in my ears and the hum was now being submerged by the harsher noise of an engine, the rattle of freight wagons. I wondered which track it was on. The line curved away from me along the viaduct and on the bend, in the dark, the train could have been on either side. Did trains travel on the right or left?

My brain woke up suddenly. Who the hell cared which side they travelled on? It was coming straight for me. I could take a chance and stay where I was, but somehow I didn't have the nerve. I was very close to the track. The thought of lying there as a train hurtled past, hoping that nothing happened to be protruding far enough to skewer me, was more than I could bear. Even Silvester was a better risk than that.

I scrambled to my feet. The train was almost on me, its headlights blinding me. It was on this side. A buffer of air hit me in the face, but I kept my balance and got a leg up on to the platform. I pushed off with the other leg and threw myself over the edge, rolling sideways just as the locomotive screamed past.

Silvester was back along the platform, near the exit from the station. He saw me at once and came running. I barely had time to register his position before he reached me, one foot lunging out to kick me in the head. I twisted over and his shoe scythed through my hair, just grazing my scalp. He kicked out again but I was on my feet by then, backing away in a crouch.

He came for me rapidly, forcing me to defend myself. His right hand caught me in the stomach and my guts shot up through my gullet, choking off the air to my lungs. I brushed aside his left, struggling desperately to breathe and a right hook to my nose sent me tumbling backwards into the fence along the rear of the platform. My back thudded into the wooden planks and something splintered. I hoped it was the wood, not my spine.

Silvester's foot swung up towards my groin but I knocked it off target with my forearm and it hammered straight into the fence. Another plank fractured in two, the rotten wood giving way easily. Silvester grimaced, momentarily off balance, and I took my chance. I grasped his right arm and swung him round in an arc, letting his own weight increase the momentum. Then at the last moment I released him. His body crunched into the fence and seemed to keep going. The planks split open with a crack and Silvester tumbled through and out into space with a piercing scream.

I stumbled over to the gaping hole and looked through.

Silvester was lying on a concrete slab about twenty feet down the embankment, his legs twisted underneath him. He wasn't moving.

I pulled away and wiped the blood from my nose with my sleeve. I didn't dwell on what I'd done. I didn't even pause to regain my breath. I ran out of the exit and down the steps to the road. That scream would have been heard three streets away. I didn't want to be anywhere around when Pinky came to see what had happened.

I knew I was lost. Running blind through dark, oppressive streets that seemed to lead nowhere. My body felt close to collapse. I could hardly lift my feet and my stomach was clenched in a fist of nausea. The temptation to fall down and rest was overpowering, but I resisted it grimly. If I gave in now I knew I'd never get up.

Once or twice I thought I heard footsteps behind me, but when I spun round there was no one there. Just the echo of my own leaden feet in the narrow lanes. I was starting to imagine things in the blackness around me, my senses awry, misleading me. But there was no mistaking the pain in my chest and legs. That was all too real.

I took a side street to the left. It twisted out of sight, ascending so steeply I had to slow my pace to little more than a walk. On the brow of the hill, round a tight bend in the road, I bumped straight into Pinky Silvester.

Fresh, alert, I might possibly have found a turn of speed to escape her outstretched arms. But in my present state I practically fell into them. One hand caught hold of my shoulder, then before I could defend myself a fist like a leg of lamb smashed into my belly. I crumpled to my knees in a wheezing ball.

'That one was for James,' Pinky said unemotionally. 'For what you did to him.'

So she'd found him. I lifted my head, struggling for even a single breath. 'He dead?' I gulped.

'No.'

'Pity.'

It was not the wisest thing to say, but I was past caring. Pinky reached down and pulled me up by my hair until my eyes were just below the level of her chin.

'But everything else is for me.'

'You're beautiful when you're angry,' I said.

That wasn't much wiser. She hooked her fingers between my legs and squeezed. A shaft of fire scorched through me. My eyes watered.

'You won't be needing these where you're going,' Pinky said, squeezing harder.

I clutched at her hand, almost doubled up, a scream halfway to my lips. I could feel her breath on my face, her fingers digging in. My vision blurred over. I flailed around with my arms, hitting her as hard as I could but she just stood there smiling at me, solid and unmoving as a pillar of granite.

Then without warning she suddenly let go. I cupped my groin with my hands gratefully, blinking away tears. But it was only a temporary reprieve for she took hold of me by the neck instead. If she squeezed again I knew I was finished.

'I'd like this to be slow,' she said softly. 'Really slow. But I have to get James to a hospital.'

'Don't bother about me,' I said. 'I'll be fine.'

'So I'll get it over with quickly.'

'Why rush when we're having such fun?'

She probed my windpipe with one of her thumbs. 'You should have known when to stop, McLean. But reptiles like you never learn, do you?'

'Why did you kill Angie?' I asked. 'Jealousy?'

Pinky's lip curled. 'You think I cared about a piece of fluff like her?'

'Jimmy did.'

Her grip tightened. 'He screwed her. That's not the same. He's weak. She took advantage of him. Betrayed him.'

'You really believe that?'

She leaned closer to me, her hands still round my neck. Holding me, but not too tight. There was a manic gleam in her eyes that made me wonder if she was quite sane.

'She betrayed him, you understand. She had to die. Just like the others. But she was worse. A whore, a cheap little slut who flaunted her body, took my husband from me. He trusted her, blabbed to her, then she betrayed him to you. James is a fool, a weak fool. But I am strong. He needs someone like me to look after him.'

'You think killing me will solve anything?'

She laughed harshly, just once like a guttural exclamation.

'No. But it will give me a lot of pleasure.'

I could feel that her fingers had relaxed. I had perhaps a couple of seconds in which to make my move. I brought my fists up and slammed them into the outsides of her elbows, forcing the joints the wrong way. She was strong, but it hurt her just enough for her fingers to lose their grip. I ducked down under her arms and took off across the road, realizing for the first time, from the parapet along the side, that I was on a bridge of some kind.

But Pinky had the speed and reflexes of a stalking panther. I'd gone less than three yards when her arm snaked around my waist and lifted me off the ground. Her other arm encircled my legs, tipping me up into a horizontal position.

'This is what James must have felt,' she whispered in my ear. 'See how you like it.'

Then she launched me forwards and out over the parapet into space.

I hit the water with a jarring thud that knocked the wind out of me and stung my back like a whiplash. A surge of foul-tasting liquid filled my mouth as I sank into the murk. I kicked my way to the surface, coughing and spluttering, and realized I was in the canal. If I didn't drown I'd probably die of poisoning from the effluent in the water.

Up above me, Pinky was leaning over the parapet of the bridge. She looked disappointed. If she'd known the canal was down below to break my fall she probably wouldn't have tossed me over. I didn't intend to hang around to give her a second chance. I struck out hard for the bank and pulled myself out on to the towpath. My dripping clothes stank of something unpleasant I had no desire to identify. In any case, time was short. Pinky had disappeared from the parapet and by now would be searching for a way down.

I shook off as much excess moisture as I could and headed west along the towpath at a clumsy jog. The cold water had revived me a bit but my sodden clothes were an increased burden my legs could well have done without.

I was closer to exhaustion than I'd thought. From the effort it took I felt as if I was moving at a reasonable pace, but when I looked back I saw I'd come only a short distance from the bridge. And Pinky was already down on the towpath, pursuing me with renewed vigour. I should have taken her advice at the beginning and kept my nose out of this whole business. No story was worth this much pain.

I rounded a bend in the path and found myself in the canal basin, a sinister pool of inky water with a boatyard on the far side and a patch of open land in front of me that in daylight was used as a car park.

I didn't know what to do. Pinky had almost caught up with me. If I kept straight on across the car park she would take me easily. I wouldn't escape from her again. This time the execution would be quick, summary. Yet there was nowhere else I could go. Except . . . I looked down at the fetid water in the basin. Few things could have been less inviting. But Pinky was one of them. I screwed up my courage—and my nose—and jumped into the stinking brew.

I floundered across towards the other bank, keeping my mouth well clear of the oily surface. If I could reach the boatyard there would be places to hide, perhaps bits of wood or a scrap of iron I could use as a weapon. The city centre was only half a mile away but I knew I hadn't the strength to run on.

I twisted my neck round to see behind me. Pinky was ploughing awkwardly across the basin in my wake. She swam poorly and the gap between us was starting to widen. My hopes received a small boost, but the odds were still heavily against me.

The wall of the basin appeared suddenly out of the darkness. I reached up and dragged myself out on to the muddy bank. A quick glance back to check on Pinky's progress and then I was away into the boatyard, searching desperately for a refuge.

The bank was cluttered with boats of every size and description. Some half-built, skeletons of timber and iron plate, others awaiting repair, a few just dumped to rot and die, paint flaking off, their fractured hulls warping and cracking under sheets of plastic.

I burrowed into the middle of them, creeping around under the keels until I found a place to hole up. I lay on the earth under a dilapidated cabin cruiser and pulled its tarpaulin cover down to screen my presence. Then I waited, trying to mask the sound of my breathing with a sleeve over my mouth. The cold and my sopping clothes were making me shiver. Or maybe it was fear.

I'd been there only a matter of minutes when I heard a faint squelching sound near by. Feet stepping cautiously through mud. I held my breath and concentrated on the slight gap between the bottom of the tarpaulin and the ground. The toe of a shoe appeared, but before I could take in the details, the tarpaulin was suddenly whipped aside and a shadowy figure looked down at me.

'Perhaps you'd be good enough to come out of there, Mr McLean,' said Jawaad al-Nabil with perfect self-control.

It was the gun in his left hand that persuaded me. The barrel pointing resolutely at my forehead, just as steady as it had been in his right hand which now hung crippled and limp by his side.

I crawled out, ducking my head to avoid the hull of the cabin cruiser. Al-Nabil was standing in open space, his back to the canal basin.

'How did you know?' I said.

'I saw you both on the bridge. It was simple enough to come round the other side of the canal to cut you off. I watched your swim from up there.' He indicated the walled embankment that flanked the boatyard. 'Likewise your hiding place.'

'And Pinky?'

'I will deal with her after you.'

'You've got your priorities wrong,' I said. 'She's more of a threat than I am.'

'Step back a pace.'

'You really trust her? After what she and Jimmy have done.'

'You have no idea what they've done.'

'I can guess.'

I'd raised my voice so it would carry beyond the immediate area. Somewhere in the jumble of boats was Pinky. If I could get her to blunder in I might just create enough of a diversion to get away from al-Nabil and his pistol. Particularly his pistol. But first I had to keep him talking.

'What was it Jimmy did?' I asked. 'That made you fire those shots at him.'

'That is no concern of yours.'

'But I want to know. It was a warning, wasn't it? Your aim's better than that.'

'You ask too many questions.'

'Where did you learn to shoot? In the army?'

'That's enough.'

'I'm interested. You work for yourself or your government?'

Al-Nabil shook his head impatiently and held the pistol out at chest height, readying himself.

I caught a fleeting glimpse of a reflection in the water behind him. A movement. Then a large shape coming out from the bows of a beached narrow boat. I brought my gaze back to al-Nabil.

'You any good with your left hand?' I asked.

The shape rushed forward, a length of timber swinging through the air. Al-Nabil caught the sound and dropped to one knee. I'd never seen anyone react so fast. The timber swished harmlessly over his head. Then in one reflex movement he spun round and fired. I didn't see where the bullet went, but it must have connected for Pinky staggered backwards, the piece of timber dropping from her hand. Her heel hit the raised edge of the basin and she tumbled over into the water and disappeared into the black, unseen depths.

I was so stunned I didn't even think to run. By the time it occurred to me, al-Nabil's pistol was once again trained on me. He appeared entirely unmoved by what had just happened.

'I think that answers your question,' he remarked coolly.

Something inside me was extinguished just then. Some tiny flame of hope, of optimism, of faith. Snuffed out by the realization that this was the end. My last chance had gone. There was nowhere left to run, no one to help me. But before I died I still wanted to know.

'Why?' I said. 'Just tell me why.'

Al-Nabil cocked an ear. In the distance was the harsh, intermittent noise of a police siren.

'You've time,' I said. 'Just tell me. What have you to lose?'

He shook his head. 'Why should you care now?'

'I'd like to know. Curiosity. It's what drives me.'

Al-Nabil frowned, puzzled. He didn't understand. Now, with the sand running out fast, I wondered whether I really understood either. It all seemed such a waste.

'Back at Silvester's factory, what were those steel pipes?'

'Missile casings,' he replied.

'And *The Sunndal?* Where did it end up?'

'Benghazi.'

I nodded. Everything slipped quietly into place. Too late for me to do anything about it. But at least I knew now.

'Anything else?' al-Nabil enquired.

I shook my head wearily. The pistol came up.

'Believe me,' he said, 'I regret having to do this.'

'Not half as much as I regret it,' I said.

He fired once. I heard the explosion. But felt nothing. A hole the size of a penny appeared in the centre of his forehead and he slumped slowly to the ground.

I stood there for a long moment, shaking uncontrollably. Al-Nabil was stretched out in the mud, his head resting in a swelling pool of dark fluid. Then my knees gave way and I collapsed back against the hull of the boat.

I didn't move. I waited, staring out into the night, listening to the water lapping gently in the basin and the sound of my own heartbeat.

CHAPTER 18

'I know I keep saying this,' Maria said. 'But I think you'd better start at the beginning.'

I looked at her over my glass of wine. 'It'll take some time.'

'I'm not going anywhere.'

We were having dinner in the Frog, tucked away at a corner table with a bottle of Châteauneuf-du-Pape and some noisettes of lamb for company. Maria was dressed in pale grey silk, pearl earrings shining in the curls of her dark hair. She looked quite a temptation, but for the moment, as I hadn't eaten in twenty-four hours, the noisettes had the edge.

'Where do you want to begin?' I said, finishing my mouthful.

'How about with James Silvester.'

'OK. The East End boy made bad. A scrap metal dealer on the make. Ambitious, unscrupulous, a couple of previous convictions for violence and some dodgy ideas for making money.

'That's what Jimmy likes more than anything else, making money. If he can do it legitimately, fine. If not, well, he's not the type to worry too much about laws. You've probably met a few like him in the course of your work.'

'My clients are all strictly above board,' Maria said stiffly. 'Men of honour and the utmost integrity. Until they get caught, that is,' she added.

'Exactly. It's getting caught that makes the difference. Now, a few years ago Jimmy did a deal with an Egyptian arms dealer called Jawaad al-Nabil—that's the fellow whose hand you broke.'

Maria winced. 'It was horrible, but there was no other way.'

'I know,' I said sympathetically. 'Sometimes violence is all we have left. Anyway, Silvester did the deal. To supply spare engines for Chieftain tanks to the Iranians. Unfortunately for Jimmy, this happened to be illegal.'

'This was during the Iran–Iraq war, I take it?'

I nodded. 'He got caught of course, but nothing much happened to him.'

'Nothing?'

'It was all hushed up. Some stooge in Whitehall probably slapped his wrist, but that's all. The government has rather a, let's say, equivocal attitude to the arms business, given that they're up to their necks in the slimy trade themselves. If you'll flog anything to anyone for the right price, it's a bit hypocritical to condemn others for doing the same.'

Maria smiled sardonically. 'I haven't noticed ministers ever being over-worried about hypocrisy.'

'But they don't like it to be too obvious. It's bad for their image.'

'How does this all fit in to what happened last night?'

'Nowhere, at least not directly. But it gave Jimmy a taste for questionable arms transactions and introduced him to al-Nabil who was later to approach him with another proposition.'

'When was this?'

'Last year. After Jimmy had bought himself a small steel company called Poseidon Steel. Al-Nabil asked him to produce a load of maraging steel pipes for export.'

'What's maraging steel?' Maria asked. 'And why would an arms dealer want steel pipes?'

'I'll come to that in a bit.' I spiked a new potato on my fork and swallowed it. It tasted of mint and melted butter. 'Excuse me, I'm starving.'

'Didn't they feed you at police headquarters?'

'My wellbeing wasn't uppermost in their minds. I'm lucky I'm not still there.'

I'd spent the day in an interview room being grilled, and more frequently roasted, by Chris Strange and Armstrong. It was not an experience I wished to repeat.

Maria was looking at me curiously. 'How come they let you go?'

'I'm an innocent man, of course.'

'You expect me to believe that?'

'It's the truth.'

'Did the police believe it?'

'No. But you're more trusting than them.'

'Don't bet on it.'

I smiled at her. 'You remember the last time I was here? When you were just leaving with your friend. You believe now I was genuinely working, don't you?'

She sipped her wine slowly. 'Maybe.'

'Angie Maxfield was part of the story. I had to find out more about her.'

'It looked a tough job. You must have found all that overtime hard.'

'Yeah, but you know me. Totally dedicated to the job in hand.'

She almost smiled. But held it back. She wasn't going to be too gentle on me.

'Clearly the police don't still think you killed her then?' she said.

'No. Silvester's made a confession.'

'Admitting the killing?'

'Pinning it on his wife.'

'Such loyalty.'

'She's dead and can't speak up for herself.'

Maria nodded. I'd already told her what had happened in the canal basin, and during the chase beforehand.

'I'm surprised he's up to a confession,' she said. 'After what you did to him.'

'He was trying to kill me, Maria. I was hardly going to stand there and let him. Besides, he got off pretty lightly. A broken leg, fractured wrist and concussion. He's sitting up in hospital eating grapes.'

'Did the police tell you what else he confessed to?'

'They had to. Some of it was directly relevant to the questions they wanted to ask me. And believe me, they asked me a lot of questions. I don't suppose you've ever been interviewed by the plods, have you?'

'Only when they came to search my house in case you were hiding under the bed.'

I looked away guiltily. 'Yes, well, I've apologized for that. Subtlety is not their strong point. When they get you in a room alone they go on and on, asking the same things from different angles to catch you out. But they also give a lot away, they can't help it.'

'Is that how you know about Silvester and al-Nabil?'

'Some of it. The rest I'd already worked out for myself. I might be wrong on a few small points, but most of it's accurate.'

Maria bit off a stalk of broccoli and chewed it thoughtfully.

'Are the police going to charge you with anything?'

'I told you, I'm innocent.'

'That's not what I asked.'

I shrugged lightly. 'They threatened to have me for obstruction and withholding evidence.'

'Neither of which you did, of course.'

'Of course. It's not in my nature. But they won't pursue it. I could be an important prosecution witness. It wouldn't look good if they put me in the dock at the same time.'

She studied me clinically. It was disconcerting. 'You had a whale of a time today, didn't you? Annoying the authorities.'

'I've got to do something with my life.'

She put down her fork and leaned across the table, her face troubled. 'Those people nearly killed you last night, Michael. It's not a game.'

I said soberly: 'I know. But if I thought about it too seriously I'd be a gibbering wreck by now. You see that, don't you?'

Maria watched me for a moment, then sighed resignedly. She leaned back and picked up her glass of wine.

'So al-Nabil asked Silvester for a load of steel pipes. What happened after that?'

'Jimmy did something rather foolish—and he's admitted this too. He took the money from al-Nabil, one hundred thousand pounds, then sold the entire shipment to someone else.'

'That does sound pretty silly. Why?'

'For this you have to understand a bit about Silvester's character, which is basically a mixture of bullyboy and shrewd opportunist. The same ingredients that make up a politician, only without the phoney patina of public concern.

'He made his money to start with in scrap metal, not the most respectable business around. He's not used to operating in orthodox circles, with contracts, lawyers, accountants, paperwork. He does deals on the run, sticks to the terms if it's in his interests to do so and sends round his heavies to sort out anyone who crosses him.

'He moves in a kind of business subculture, some of it patently illegal, nearly all of it dubious in our terms. He was never going to be invited to join the Chamber of Commerce. That's why al-Nabil came to him. British Steel was hardly going to be keen on doing business with an Egyptian middleman with doubtful credentials.'

I paused to wipe up the last traces of sauce from my plate.

'What I'm saying, I suppose, is that Silvester has no sense of honour. A deal to him is not a deal if he can get better terms elsewhere. And someone offered him better terms for the same number of pipes.'

'But surely he must have known al-Nabil wouldn't let him get away with that?' Maria said.

'He was certainly guilty of misjudging al-Nabil. But Jimmy reckoned he could have a bird in the hand and one in the bush as well.'

'I don't follow.'

'He had al-Nabil's money. He thought he could get the same amount off the second buyer for immediate delivery and produce another shipment later to keep al-Nabil happy.'

'So why didn't he?'

'Because by then al-Nabil was getting impatient. And suspicious of Silvester's evasions. He wanted his money back. But Jimmy didn't have it. Being the man he is he'd already spent it. He could have sold something to raise the cash if he'd wanted to, but Jimmy is someone who never willingly parts with his possessions. That's when al-Nabil turned nasty and fired a few warning shots across his bows. Hell hath no fury like an arms dealer deprived of his commission.'

'Al-Nabil did the shooting?'

'He's quite something with a gun. Even with his left hand. It was a doddle for him to put three bullets into a car seat from two hundred yards. No doubt, next time, Silvester knew the bullets wouldn't miss.'

I stopped talking as Ollie Robinson approached the table to clear away our plates.

'Was everyzing all right for madame et monsieur?' he enquired in his wildly exaggerated cod French accent that fooled no one. And he knew it.

'Yes, zank you,' I said.

'You weesh to look at ze sweet trolley?'

'I wish you'd stop talking like that, Ollie. It's like something out of a Feydeau farce.'

He reverted to fluent Wath-upon-Dearne-ese. 'So does tha want any bleedin' pudding or not?'

I caught Maria's eye and she nodded. We made our selection: a strawberry meringue dripping with cream for her, a slice of rich chocolate gâteau for me. There are moments when life seems to have a purpose after all.

Maria enjoyed a lingering mouthful, then looked up at me. 'Did al-Nabil know Silvester had sold the pipes to someone else?'

'No,' I said. 'But he suspected it. That's where the file comes in. Silvester was stalling him, denying that any shipment had actually been made. What al-Nabil needed was absolute proof that Silvester was lying to him, that Silvester had double-crossed him.

'He's a careful man. The gunshots were a calculated risk, to persuade Silvester to give back the money. Before he went further he wanted the full picture. That's why two weeks earlier he'd hired Andy Peters and Tony Napier to steal the relevant file from Silvester's shipping agent in Immingham. I think he knew Andy from the past. That's just a guess, but I know Andy worked in Egypt a few years ago.'

'And the file proved the steel had left Britain?'

'Yes. It also gave the name of the ship, and that's important. A Norwegian vessel called *The Sunndal*. This is where things went out of control, for both al-Nabil and Silvester.

Andy Peters, a small-time criminal with ideas above his station, decided to indulge in a spot of enterprise for himself. He hung on to the file.'

'Why?'

'Because he knew it was valuable. He didn't know exactly why but that didn't matter. He'd knocked around with the low-lives of the East End for a long time. He knew Silvester owned Poseidon Steel and that the file related to one of his business transactions. If al-Nabil wanted it, it had to be incriminating. So Andy put the screws on Silvester. Blackmailed him.

'Silvester panicked and actually paid up, at least once, which indicates something about his agitated state of mind because he is most definitely not the type to give in to blackmail.'

'I don't understand,' Maria said. 'Why should the file worry him so much?'

'Because he knew if it got to al-Nabil he was a dead man.'

She frowned. 'You're missing something out here. It was only a cargo of pipes, wasn't it?'

I shook my head. 'Not any old pipes.' I explained briefly what Sam Fielding had told me about maraging steel. 'That's why al-Nabil came to Sheffield, the special-steels centre of Europe. You can't just knock up a few tons of maraging steel in the back streets of Cairo, it's not that easy.'

'So what were they, the pipes?'

'They were long-range solid-propellant missile casings.'

Maria stared at me, a spoonful of strawberry meringue poised in midair, finally beginning to understand.

'*The Sunndal* left Immingham in November bound for Bremen,' I said. 'But it never went there. It went to Benghazi. The second buyer of the casings was the Libyans.

'Now, what do you think the reaction of the Egyptians would be when they discovered that James Silvester had taken their money and then sold the fruitcakes on their western border the means to make a long-range missile?'

Maria said nothing for a time. Then she murmured: 'Yes, I can see why Silvester wouldn't want the Egyptians to know that. Al-Nabil was acting for his own government, I assume?'

I nodded. 'No private individual would be in the market for missile casings. And that's how he knew *The Sunndal* had gone to Benghazi, and knew what it was carrying. Egyptian Intelligence must have told him. There was no other way. But he didn't know for certain they were Silvester's casings. That's why the file was even more important to him. It linked Silvester with *The Sunndal*.'

'So the Egyptians wanted missile casings too?'

'Everyone wants them. And if it's not missiles, it's some other kind of weapon. It's the one business that never seems to run out of customers or new products to hawk around the world market. Recession isn't a word that features in the arms dealer's vocabulary.'

'And Silvester killed the two burglars because they knew about the file, to protect himself?'

'Not personally. He employs a gorilla called Jeff Kinsella to do unpleasant things like that for him. I thought at one time al-Nabil had killed Andy Peters because I knew he'd been in Andy's flat on the evening of the murder. But then the police found a witness who'd seen a black man coming out of the flats just before I arrived. That confused me for a while.'

'Is this man, Kinsella, black?'

I shook my head. 'Not by race. But he is by habit. He's the dirtiest person I've ever seen. Hardly an inch of his skin is white. He was wearing a balaclava and it was dark so all the witness saw were his blackened cheeks and nose. It was easy to mistake him for a negro.'

'And he killed Andy Peters?'

'Snapped his neck and walked out. It only took a couple of minutes.'

'But he couldn't have done the other one, what's his name?'

'Tony. No, Jeff's brother, Jason, was on remand at Wolds Prison with Tony. He took care of him.'

'That's rather a fortunate coincidence, isn't it?'

I explained what had happened. How Silvester had been worried stiff about the theft of the file, even telling his shipping agent, Hammond, to deny it had been taken in case the police or anyone else started asking inconvenient questions about its contents.

He knew Tony Napier had been involved in the burglary. I'd managed to find that out without difficulty so Silvester certainly could. What he didn't know was that Tony had no part in Andy's blackmail activities. But he still wanted him silenced because he knew about the file. Unfortunately, by the time Silvester decided to take action, Tony was out of reach in prison.

'So one evening,' I continued, 'Jason Kinsella was sent out to have a few drinks, make a senseless attack on two people in a pub and get himself arrested. Silvester knew he'd be sent to Wolds.'

'How?'

'Because there's no alternative. All remand prisoners from Sheffield Magistrates' Court are sent there.'

'And the cyanide?'

'Smuggled in to Jason by a visitor. The cyanide came from Silvester's electroplating works at Tinsley. Cyanide's one of the chemicals they use in electroplating.'

'You've worked all this out, haven't you?' Maria said. 'Guesswork?'

'Partly. But it all fits the facts. And makes sense too.'

'What about the British government?' Maria said. 'Didn't they know what Silvester was making at his foundry?'

'I can't be sure exactly what they knew, or when. But they certainly found out that the casings on board *The Sunndal* had ended up in Libya. That's one of the reasons

MI5 were keen to get their hands on that file. Why they tapped my phone, followed me around, searched my flat in case I'd somehow got it from Andy Peters. They couldn't take the risk of it being made public.'

'Why ever not?'

'Can you imagine the embarrassment at Westminster? A government allowing the export of missile components to Gaddafi. There was no way they wanted that bit of dynamite in a journalist's hands. So our friend Armstrong and his chums in the Security Service were sent in to cover up the tracks.'

'Is that part of their job?'

'MI5 makes up its "job" as it goes along. But yes, they'll do as their political masters tell them. Golden rule of journalism: never underestimate the lengths a government will go to to conceal what they've been doing from the public.'

Maria mused for a moment. 'I'm surprised Silvester wasn't arrested.'

I pursed my lips. 'There was nothing much to gain by doing that. The pipes had already gone by that stage. But there was another reason for leaving Silvester at large.'

'And that was?'

'To keep him under surveillance. They needed proof, something concrete to nail him for. Silvester thought he'd got away with the first load. He even had another consignment ready to go. They wanted to catch him red-handed, and they wanted his Libyan contacts.'

'Did Armstrong tell you that?'

I chuckled. 'Armstrong wouldn't tell a journalist the time. No, I've pieced it together myself, but I'm sure it's correct. That's why Angie Maxfield was recruited. She was already Silvester's mistress, a compliant, rather dim dupe, ideal for MI5's purposes. They used her to keep tabs on Silvester, to coax information out of him. You know, careless pillow talk.'

'And she was killed because Silvester found out?'

'I'm afraid that was partly my fault.'

Maria's eyes opened a fraction. 'Your fault?'

'MI5 tried to be too clever. Angie saw me watching her flat when she came out one evening with Silvester and told Armstrong. She didn't know who I was, of course. She didn't even see me clearly. But she only had to describe my car to Armstrong and he'd have known who it was. He guessed I'd try to approach her so he instructed her to play along with me, find out what exactly I knew. It's the only explanation that makes sense. Why else would she come out to dinner with me?'

Maria gave me a dry look. 'Yes, a girl would have to be pretty desperate to go out with you.'

I pretended I hadn't heard. 'MI5 used her. They carry part of the blame for her death. Not that I suppose they care. To them people like Angie are expendable.'

'And your part in it?'

'Silvester saw me bring Angie home from dinner. He was waiting for her outside her flat. He knew he'd told her things in confidence and assumed she'd blabbed to me. He told Pinky—she didn't know about Angie until then—and she decided to shut Angie's mouth for good, but with the added touch of stealing a knife from my flat and framing me for it. To get me out of their hair at the same time.'

'You know that for sure?'

'Chris Strange told me it was in Silvester's confession. Pinky went round to Angie's flat, forced her to telephone me with a mysterious message and then killed her. She knew I'd show up. What journalist wouldn't?'

Maria shuddered. 'I don't want to think about it. How could she do it?'

'She was evil, completely devoid of feeling. I don't think she cared in the least about anyone other than herself, and Jimmy. She did it to protect him. Perhaps also because Angie was Jimmy's mistress. It must have been a blow to find out about her. I think it gave her pleasure to kill Angie.'

'Please!' Maria said. 'It's horrible. Thank God she's dead.'

I touched Maria's fingers briefly. She didn't seem to mind. 'I saw it with my own eyes. They've been dragging the canal basin for her body.'

'Let's have some coffee. This is all a bit much to take in.'

We talked for a while about other things, inconsequential chat that took the edge off the atmosphere, obliterated for a time the grisly images of death. I felt totally relaxed with her. She was easy company, but not easy to know. Maybe that was one of the things that made her so attractive. The knowledge that there was more underneath. Unknown depths that, in time, she might just reveal.

She waited until her coffee was half finished before saying, 'There's a couple of things I still want to know. Why did Andy Peters call you that night?'

'He wanted to talk. He was scared. I think he finally realized he was out of his depth. He could hardly go to the police and admit to burglary and blackmail, but he wanted to spill the beans. He knew something funny was going on. A reporter was the ideal person to probe deeper, maybe even give Andy a bit of protection. He knew his life was in danger.'

'Why then suddenly?'

'I can't be sure. When I found his body I assumed the murderer had also searched the flat, after he'd killed Andy. I got it wrong. It was searched *before* he was killed. By Jawaad al-Nabil who wanted the file he'd paid for. Andy was out feeding his pigeons. He came back and found the place turned over and I think that unnerved him. Things were getting out of hand. He phoned me, then Jeff Kinsella arrived and broke his neck.'

'A sordid business,' Maria said.

'Murder is.'

So is the arms trade, I thought. Silvester reckoned it was easy money. Andy Peters thought blackmail was easy too. But in the end there's always a price. Three deaths, two more last night. All seemingly so unnecessary. Yet murders are never unnecessary to the people who commit them. They always have a reason, even if that reason appears to us to be flimsy, trivial or deranged.

Maria said: 'So what does it all come down to, greed, money?'

'Fear,' I said. 'Andy Peters, Tony Napier, Angie Maxfield, even Pinky Silvester, were all killed by frightened people. Desperate, frightened people who saw no other way out.'

'They had a choice, Michael. They didn't have to kill.'

'No. But in fear we often make the wrong choice.'

I stirred the last quarter of my coffee, wondering if I too had made the wrong choice. If Angie Maxfield might still be alive if I'd kept out of her life. She was on my conscience, the price that I would pay for making other people's secrets the stuff of newspaper copy. But I should have known. You can't get close to death without being soiled by it.

'What was the second thing you wanted to know?' I said.

'Who shot Jawaad al-Nabil?'

I stopped stirring and looked aside momentarily. The couple at the table next to us were pushing back their chairs, crossing the room to collect their coats from a solicitous waiter. I turned back.

'I don't know,' I said simply. 'A police marksman, maybe someone from MI5. No one's admitting it, but it had to be them.'

'I suppose they had no alternative.'

'Don't shed any tears over al-Nabil, Maria. He was an arms dealer, a merchant of death.'

'But he hadn't killed anyone, had he?'

'That doesn't mean his hands were clean. Who is more morally culpable, the man who goes out and kills one person, or the man who supplies the means to kill a thousand?'

She nodded thoughtfully. 'That marksman saved your life.'

'So did you, if you remember. Thank you for that. It took guts to come in there and do what you did.'

'Not guts. Just a jack handle.'

I smiled. 'You never told me what happened to you afterwards.'

'There's not much to tell. Silvester and his wife ran after you, then I waited for al-Nabil to come out. I didn't dare move until I knew he'd gone. Then I went back to my car.'

'What did you tell the police when you phoned them?'

'I didn't phone them. The silver-haired man did that for me.'

The voices around me in the restaurant seemed to fade suddenly. I was aware of nothing except Maria on the other side of the table.

'Silver-haired man?'

'He pulled in as I ran back to the car. He could see I was distraught. He had a phone in his car. He took care of it all for me. I couldn't have coped without him.'

I said slowly: 'Did he stay with you until the police came?'

'Well, no. I don't know where he went. Why?'

My eyes misted over. For a moment I was lost in my own thoughts.

'Michael? Are you all right?'

I came back with a start. 'Pardon?'

'You were talking to yourself.'

'Was I?'

'Something about marbled Italian draining boards. It didn't make sense.'

'Sorry. I must have been miles away.' I finished the last of my coffee, then said tentatively: 'Why don't we go back to your house? Maybe we could continue there. And this time, I promise, I won't fall asleep.'

Maria smiled, looking at me directly, thinking it over. I waited. She was so beautiful a mere look could choke me. There was a pit in my stomach that filled up suddenly. With anxiety, tension, hope.

'Why not?' she said softly.

We paid our bill and left the restaurant, walking close, almost touching, but not quite. I thought about her, not daring to expect anything, yet at the same time ... Let things take their course, I said to myself. What will be, will be.

We crossed the road to where Maria's Mazda was parked. As we drew nearer a grotesque figure rose suddenly from behind the car. A towering figure clad in dirty blue overalls, with long blonde hair caked in mud shielding the face. A handkerchief stained with blood was tied over one temple.

The figure brushed the lank, matted hair aside with a hand. The streetlight caught her features. I realized with a jolt of horror who it was.

Pinky Silvester.

Not an apparition, not a spectre from the other world. In the flesh, all too real, all too solid. Looking for me, I knew.

I stared at her, unable to move. Taking in the drawn face, the bloody handkerchief. Al-Nabil's bullet must only have creased her scalp. Our eyes met across the street and Pinky smiled. The coldest, most terrifying smile I'd ever seen.

'I've been looking everywhere for you, McLean,' she murmured. 'I saw you leave your flat in this car. Now I've found it. And you.'

She started to walk out from behind the Mazda.

I turned to Maria. 'Don't wait up for me,' I said.